W9-CMF-104

TRAIL OF MURDER

TRAIL OF MURDER

CHRISTINE ANDREAE

ST. MARTIN'S PRESS
NEW YORK

Design by Dawn Niles

Library of Congress Cataloging-in-Publication Data

Andreae, Christine.
  Trail of murder / Christine Andreae.
     p.   cm.
  "A Thomas Dunne book."
  ISBN 0-312-08327-0 (hardcover)
  I. Title.
  PS3551.N4134T7   1992
  813'.54—dc20
                                                    92-26152
                                                    CIP

10 9 8 7 6 5 4 3 2

To my mother,
Mary C. Ewing

I am happily indebted to Robin Pfau, wilderness guide, who helped guide this story. Thanks also to Thelma Elser, wilderness outfitter, and to my agent, Mary Frisque. Special thanks to Andy.

TRAIL OF MURDER

1

I arrived an hour early at the Missoula airport for a plane that was two hours late. It was twelve noon Montana time. Given the delay and the time changes, I wouldn't get back to D.C. until after midnight. I didn't feel particularly frustrated. I felt laid-back and numb. Perhaps it was a side effect of seeing death "up-close and personal," as Jim McKay would say. Or perhaps it was lack of sleep. I'd seen the dawn with an off-duty state homicide investigator.

I wandered into the airport gift shop, examined the turquoise jewelry and gag mugs, and decided to treat myself to a Hershey's bar with almonds and the July issue of *Harper's*. As I leaned over to pick out the magazine, the Missoula paper's headline sucked me in and almost knocked me down:

MILLIONAIRES SUSPECTS IN WILDERNESS MURDER.

Maybe I read it six times.

Millionaires. After listening to them talking poor for a week, it seemed too glamorous a word to describe them—even though each of them was probably worth substantially more than a million dollars. Make that in old money. No doubt they would find the term *millionaire* more offensive than *murder*.

The black type shimmered like tar in the heat. Then the letters dissolved and I was back there with them, stranded in the middle of more than a million acres of pine trees with only snowy peaks on the distant horizon. I felt the sun burning through the thin, blue air. I saw blood-streaked teeth, heard the flies buzzing. In my hand I held a slippery little piece of flesh. It was the end of a tongue. I had picked it out of the red gush of blood thinking to put it on ice, thinking maybe "they" could sew it back on. Then I realized there was no ice, no emergency room, no "they" in green smocks. The shortest way out was a two-day hike. I let the bloody scrap slip off my fingers into the dust.

I stooped and picked up the paper. It wafted a reassuringly civilized scent of printer's ink. Below the headline was a three-column-wide picture of the victims posing in fishing vests and waders. I wondered which one of the party had given—or sold— their film to the paper. Then I saw the smaller photo. It was a snapshot of me. I felt a rush of heat bloom in my face. I squinted at the caption. LADY OUTFITTER PROVIDES CLUES.

They had it wrong, of course. I wasn't the outfitter. And why "Lady" outfitter? I wondered in disgust.

"Excuse me, Miss, are you in line?" asked a large woman in a sleeveless summer dress.

"Oh. Sorry." I folded the paper in half and paid for it. I felt as if I were buying something dirty. Out in the corridor, I put on my shades. I thought a beer might taste good. I looked in at the bar. A balding man wearing a string tie looked up from his glass, interested. Annoyed, I turned away.

The upstairs waiting area was deserted. It was carpeted in warm beige and blue daylight streamed through narrow windows at the end of the room. In a side alcove, a stuffed black bear reared on its hind legs inside a glass display case. Its coat was dull. Its plastic tongue was denture pink. I studied it for a while. It was hard to believe the creature had once been alive.

I took a seat against the far wall and claimed the surrounding area with my slicker, a sweater, and the green nylon day-pack I was using as a purse. Then I took off my sunglasses, put on my half-frames, and carefully unfolded the *Missoulian*.

There was no photo credit under either of the front-page

2

pictures. I studied myself, curbing my impulse toward self-criti-
cism. Forget my hair blown out of its braid. Forget the fan of lines
at the corners of my eyes. I was smiling. It was a good smile, a real
one. I looked happy.

Had I been happy?

Again, I saw the darkening clots of blood in the dust. I had
scraped them up, using my hands like a dustpan and broom. I had
tossed them into the fire along with the uneaten trout. With a
nylon bucket of icy creek water, I had rinsed off the clumps of thin
grass, the trampled sprays of cinquefoil and yarrow.

I gazed at the empty runway out the window and remembered
a great aunt, a scolding woman whose jet-black sealskin fur coat
I liked to stroke. Every Christmas she came to stay. And every
Christmas morning, as my brother and I ripped open our presents,
she snatched away the ribbons and wound them around three
slender fingers of her right hand. We hadn't liked her, my brother
and I.

But there I'd been, sweeping up blood clots, tidying up Montana's high country just like Aunt Clara. It occurred to me that she
too had been trapped—in the domestic wilderness of a family
Christmas. I let my head fall back against the diagonal pine paneling behind my row of seats. Perhaps, I speculated, surviving was
more than a matter of digging in one's fingernails and hanging on.
Perhaps it included the business of sorting out and wrapping up
and folding away. I plucked out a ribbon from the debris of the last
ten days. It was dark blue and crumpled like the surface of a
mountain stream on a golden evening. I began smoothing it out,
winding it around my fingers, one turn at a time.

3

2

It began with a phone call about a phone call.

I was not in great shape. The high point of my days had become the *Washington Post*'s crossword puzzle. That took maybe fifteen minutes. I saved it for evening—a small carrot to get me through the day. After I had cleverly penciled in all the boxes, I felt emptier than when I'd started—like bad sex. I'd had a spell of that too. Successive jugs of Mountain Red in my Sub-Zero seemed to suck themselves dry. The mood was definitely Camus. *"Aujourd'hui, Maman est morte."*

But my mother hadn't died. A friend had died of AIDs, but that's no surprise these days. I'd turned forty in April and that was no surprise either. For a couple of weeks, I postured around trying to mix memory with desire on lined yellow paper, but the recipe was a dud. The resultant poems were fatally tinged with self-pity. A couple of my smooth-faced students were turning out the kind of brave, sweet stuff that I, their "poet-in-residence," had urged them to risk. And for the first time in my teaching life, I felt twinges of jealousy. By the time June dragged around, I was more relieved than sorry to see them go.

Then: one long muggy evening punctuated with the aroma

4

from other people's grills, the phone rang. Carl Jung would have called it synchronicity. The Romans called it *deus-ex-machina:* a god to the rescue.

I was reclining on a poolside chaise like an alienated Madame Récamier. I let it ring five times, then put my vino down on the flagstone and picked up the terrace extension. "Hallerman residence," I answered. Hallerman was the name of the people who owned the Foxhall Road mansion I'd been house-sitting for the last year and a half. They were foreign service, stationed in Nigeria, and independently wealthy—no, make that independently rich. "Wealthy" smacks of gold chains and coconut oil. This was a Harris tweed couple who lent pre-Columbian artifacts to select exhibits at Dumbarton Oaks.

"I knew you were there," said an annoyed male voice. It was Donald Blackburn, long-suffering editor and publisher of a pay-in-copies Washington poetry review to which I contribute (usually) a bimonthly column.

"Hey, I'm only a week past deadline," I protested.

"Try two."

"I've just got to run it through the speller," I lied.

"Lee, I haven't got time for this routine," he snapped. "I'm calling as your messenger boy. Some guy's trying to reach you. I told him we didn't give out phone numbers or addresses, but he insisted it was urgent."

I sat up, interested and contrite. "Donald, thank you. Above and beyond the call of duty. Who was it?"

"Wait a sec." I could hear him fumbling for his glasses. "Pete Bonsecours," he read. He spelled Bonsecours and gave me a number. The area code was 406.

"Where's that?" I asked.

"Search me. I gotta go. Joyce and I were supposed to be somewhere half an hour ago."

"Wait. What did he want? I mean, is he an irate poet or what?"

Donald chuckled. "Never heard of him. Good luck, babe!" He hung up.

Bonsecours. "Good help" in French. Was there such a thing as "bad" help? I found an area-code map in the front of the phone

5

book. Four-o-six belonged to Montana. Montana? I hadn't torn apart any cowboy poets lately. I didn't even know any. A true East Coast provincial, all I knew about Montana was that it belonged somewhere "Out West." I stared at the map. Montana was way up there, sitting squarely on top of Wyoming and shouldering a long border with Alberta (area code 403) and Saskatchewan (306). According to the little clocks across the top of the page, Montana was two hours behind D.C. Which made it just after five there. Irresistibly curious, I dialed the number.

A woman said hello. She had a small, flat voice. "Hi," I said, "My name's Lee Squires. I'm returning a call from Pete Bonsecours. Am I pronouncing it right?"

"Oh," she said. "Yes. Bonsecours." (Bouncy-core, she said.) "Hang on, will you? I'll get him. He's outside somewhere."

I waited. I polished off the wine in my glass and waited some more. Bonsecours came to the phone slightly out of breath. "Sorry," he apologized. "You're Lee?"

"Right."

"Thanks for calling back." He hesitated, then said, "Joey Riley said to give you a call."

"Joey?" A bolt out of the blue. I laughed with pleasure. Joey had that effect on people. If I had to cast *The Tempest* with my friends, I'd draft Joey for Ariel. His wild yellow curls and his slight, acrobatic build made him a natural for the part. "How do you know Joey?" I asked Pete Bonsecours. "Is he in Montana?"

"No, Idaho. He's working for a white-water rafting outfitter. I met him this spring. He was just passing through."

I laughed again. "Figures," I said.

"Oh?"

"Look," I said, "Joey Riley's a total flake—the most enchanting, seductive, infuriating flake that ever mooched off the face of humankind. The guy's addicted to 'passing through.' Mr. Spangles in person."

Pete Bonsecours was silent.

"Don't get me wrong. I love spangles. But the only time you can count on Joey is in an extreme emergency."

"Glad to hear it," he said.

Something in his voice sobered me up. "What's the matter?"

6

"I need a cook." he said grimly.

"What?"

"My wife and I run a wilderness outfit. Started last year. We've got a trip scheduled for next week. And no cook."

"So?"

"Joey said he met you on someone's boat. On a Bermuda race. He was a deck ape. And you were the cook. He said the going got rough. And that you were good."

"That was a while ago."

"My wife and I, we've got a lot riding on this trip."

I suspected the statement was as close to begging as he was going to come. I liked him for it. I wondered how old they were, Pete Bonsecours and his wife.

"Your wife doesn't cook?" I wondered.

"She broke her leg. Yesterday morning in two places."

"Ouch," I said. No wonder it had taken her so long to fetch him to the phone. My head was swimming with questions. "How many people you talking about on this excursion of yours?" I asked.

"Ten. Seven guests, myself, and two wranglers. Eleven counting the cook. We do a fair amount of the food preparation here before we leave. The menus are pretty well worked out."

"You talking about campfire cooking?"

"We do some grilling over an open fire. If the weather's good. But we also use a wood stove."

"I've never cooked on a wood stove."

"Joey said you kept a gimbaled alcohol stove going in twelve-foot seas."

The storm had lasted thirty-six hours. Everyone had taken turns hanging over the leeward rail. I hadn't been able to make it that far. When I wasn't kneeling in the head, I was chewing raspberry-flavored antiemetics. If nothing else, they'd helped with nausea and kept me more or less vertical. "I didn't cook much," I told him. "Chicken soup was about all anyone could keep down."

"My stove doesn't move. And we chop the wood for you." His voice was lighter, almost teasing.

"I'm tempted. What kind of wilderness?"

"The Bob."

7

"Excuse me?"

"The Bob Marshall Wilderness. It's been called the crown jewel of our wilderness system, but it seems to be pretty much an in-state secret. It's never gotten the same kind of hype as the national parks, so you don't get buffalo jams like you do in Yellowstone."

"Buffalo jams?"

"A buffalo crosses the road and the traffic backs up for miles. In the Bob, there aren't any roads. It's part of a million-and-a-half-acre area that's sixty miles wide and about a hundred miles long. The Continental Divide runs right down the middle, like a backbone. You don't get much higher than nine thousand feet, but it's pristine Rocky Mountain back country. Good trout fishing. Bear and elk. Lot of wildflowers. We had a bunch of botanists from the Audubon Society last year. One of the guys was a photographer. His pictures of Bob Marshall's wildflowers were published in their magazine last February. Maybe you saw them?"

"No," I said. "What kind of bear?"

"Black bear. Grizzly at higher altitudes."

"Huh," I said, trying not to sound too interested.

"We go in on horseback for seven days. Our mules take all the gear—tents, sleeping bags, the kitchen."

"Sounds neat." As he spoke, I'd been picturing a technicolor wilderness: dark green forests, waxy white alpine flowers, navy blue streams. But it was the mention of mules that sold me. Suddenly the technicolor became sepia. I saw myself in a battered hat holding up a string of trout in a Karen von Blixen pose. Never mind the fact that I didn't know one end of a fly rod from the other. I was admiring the way my feet looked in a pair of lace-up riding boots borrowed off the set of *Out of Africa*. Then, through my romantic sepia haze, a warning bell dinged. "I find it hard to believe that you can't find a cook out there," I said.

Silence.

"What about Joey?" I asked.

"He's tied up with this Idaho river outfit."

"How long's your trip?"

"A week. After that, my brother-in-law will help out for the rest of the season." He waited. His unspoken question hung on the line between D.C. and Montana. I didn't answer it. "The guy taking the trip is Cyrus Strand," he offered. "He's taking his family on this trip. They also happen to be his board of directors."

"Any relation to Mark Strand?"

After four beats, Pete said, "Who's he?"

"A poet. Our nation's poet laureate, in fact."

"This guy owns Strand Textiles."

The name clicked. "As in Strand sheets?" I'd seen them in a Bloomingdale's catalog for over $400 a set.

"The same. He told me Nancy Reagan bought his sheets for the White House."

"And you were duly impressed," I said sourly. Then I winced. Good for you, Squires. How to blow a free ride into high country.

But Pete Bonsecours didn't get frosty. "I try to get clients to leave their politics behind," he rebuked mildly. "Along with watches, Walkmans, and other props of civilization."

"So if I say I think Howdy Doody could have done a better job than Reagan, you aren't going to retract the offer?"

"You want the job, it's yours," he said.

"On Joey's say-so?"

"You got other references?"

"Absolutely not."

No reassuring chuckle. Just dead air. Clearly he was the strong, silent type.

"I want to sleep on it," I told him. "And I also want Joey's number. But you still haven't told me what the hitch is."

"What do you mean?"

"I mean why you haven't got a dozen people standing in line to cook for your trip."

He gave a small grunt, as if I'd just scored. "I guess you could call it a problem of pay. We want someone with experience. A business like ours depends on word of mouth. We can't afford a bad cook. And I don't mean just the food. Problem is," he paused, then flicked it out like a boomerang: "We can't afford a good one either."

His aim was good. But my ego, when it comes to cooking, just isn't that big a target. "Sounds like you need a wife," I said.

"Tell me about it."

9

"What can you pay?"

"Your airfare. I hope. But tipping the cook is standard and my clients tip big."

"I'll get back to you in the morning."

"We get up early."

"Clean living, huh?"

"A plain living will do," he said wryly.

We hung up. I padded into the kitchen for another refill of Mountain Red, carried it back out to the pool, and looked at it. Then, carefully I set it down on a glass-topped table. I stepped out of my once-fuschia, time-softened Mexican shift and dove into the pool. Somewhere around lap number fifty, I decided to try Montana.

3

I watched the local news before going to bed. Marion Barry's trial had just begun. In addition to the blanket of June humidity that lay over the city, thanks to media coverage, Washington was also saturated with images of its mayor. Every morning, on the front page of the *Post,* we saw the shiny-browed Barry smiling and shaking someone's hand. Every evening, on local and network news, we saw courtroom sketches of him frowning at the defense table, then hasty footage of his grin as he jogged down the courthouse steps. Worse, over and over, in the grainy, gray FBI-sting video, we saw his long, luxuriant inhale of crack cocaine. It had a curious underwater effect, that film, as if the motel room were an aquarium. The players almost seemed to swim around in it, as mindless of the camera as dark finned fish.

Like a toxic electronic fallout, these images rained on the city, dissolving the armor we used to defend ourselves against crack babies, and children armed with beepers and guns, and young men, wearing ties, in their coffins. Against all hope, Marion Barry's addiction was seeping through our thickened skins, exposing our nerve endings to the dark poisons of the inner city.

I turned off the TV. Montana was beginning to look like more than a needed change of scenery. My mind was endowing the Rockies with a redemptive aura of purity. I went to sleep imagining that the cool air from the wall vent was blown from snow-capped peaks.

At four o'clock in the morning, I surfaced through a dream into darkness like a missile shot out of the sea. Scarcely able to tell air from water, I gasped for breath. Then, in a series of soundless explosions, the dream flowered and reflowered into memory: I was down in the metro, waiting on the platform under one of its majestic vaults of coffered concrete, when I caught a movement out of the corner of my eye. At first I thought it was someone's Doberman. But as I turned, I saw it was a bear. There was no mistaking it: a massive black bear, at least four feet high at the hump above its shoulders. In profile, its muzzle sloped like a saucer. As it lumbered through people waiting for the train, I could hear its claws clicking on the platform's earth-red tiles.

I felt no fear, only an overwhelming sense of awe, as if its presence were a gift. "Oh, look!" I wanted to say to the people around me. But either I didn't say it or they didn't hear me. Now the bear was looking at me. It was enormous, but its eyes were small and yellow. They blinked like the platform lights sunk in the tiled floor. I could hear the noise of the approaching train. People began to bunch together. Then the bear attacked. Suddenly it was springing at my chest. I saw its horrible yellow teeth, its pale gums, its dark tongue. In the instant before I awoke, I felt not only a deathly thump of fear, I felt utterly betrayed. I'd been standing there admiring it, but it had not appreciated my admiration. It was going to devour me.

I sat bolt upright in bed, my heart banging as though I'd just run a four-minute mile. I still felt betrayed. I also felt hot and clammy. I wondered if the air conditioning had died in a brown-out. But no, the vent was still spewing chilly, mechanically dried air.

I got out of bed, turned on the light in the bathroom, and squinted at the contents of the cabinet over the sink. Among a collection of lipsticks I'd bought at various times to perk myself up but had never worn out of the bathroom, I spotted a fever thermometer in a black plastic case. I picked it up and turned it over

12

in my hands as though it were an artifact. I hadn't used it since my daughter Rachel died, almost ten years before.

Rachel, my child beyond cockcrow. She died of leukemia eight days after her fourth birthday. She had had her cake at home. She had even drawn a picture of it for me to bake. "This is my birthday cake," she'd instructed. She had drawn a small wedding cake and decorated its tiers with pink loops and a thicket of candles, each one an exact pink crayon line topped with a careful yellow flame. So I copied it for her. I wondered exactly what were we celebrating here. The whole business of the birthday cake struck me as being askew, and it showed in the cake. My pink icing loops sagged (I squeezed them out of a waxed paper cone) and my tiers were lopsided so that the dozens and dozens of candles tilted crazily, and my ex-husband and I burned our fingers getting them all lit. But in some obscure way, it satisfied her.

The glass stem of the thermometer felt cool and oddly comforting under my tongue—as if I were four years old and my mother was in charge. I checked my watch. Then I scanned the medicine cabinet again. Aside from the thermometer, it was bare of help. No aspirin. Only Tums, various jars and tubes of unguents, a collection of vitamins, which, like the lipsticks, I'd bought sporadically for boosts.

I pushed my mind off Rachel and the bear and recalled the phone conversation I'd had earlier that night with my sailing pal Joey. Miraculously, I'd caught him at the number Pete Bonsecours had given me. Joey sounded just the same: slightly distracted, as if he were keeping one eye on an old rerun of "Captain Kangaroo." I asked him about his friend Pete. The conversation went like this:

Joey: "Oh yeah. Indian Pete. What about him?"

Me: "He's an Indian?"

"Half Flathead."

"What kind of Indian is that?"

"A Salish Indian."

"Big help."

"It's a language group," Joey explained. "Traditionally they inhabited the Columbia River plateau. Actually, the inland Montana Flatheads were the only Salish tribe who *didn't* deform the heads of their babies. They were holdouts against fashion. You'll

13

like Pete. He's an interesting guy. And he's got his shit together. But I'm not sure he'll make it."

"Why?

"He's a dirty Injun," Joey said cheerfully.

"Jesus, Joey."

"Lee. Get real. An Indian guide's one thing. All very romantic to the dudes. But running your own outfit takes money and white bankers get uptight when a guy in braids strolls in for a loan. Especially if his credit rating is zip. It's the old song and dance: you can't borrow money if you've never borrowed money."

We talked about other things too, Joey and I. Who was where, mostly. Then he said, "You're going to do it, aren't you?"

"You mean Montana?"

"Do you good, Lee." He sounded solicitous. It made me suspicious.

"Is that why you've told me this poor Indian story—to prime the pump of my liberal sensitivities and make me dash to the rescue?"

"Hey, ease up," he protested.

"Please give me a straight answer, Joey."

"Yeah, well, it'd be nice if you did it. Because I told him I'd do it if he couldn't get anyone else."

"I thought you were running rivers."

"I am."

"Oh," I said, chastened. The admirable, if impracticable, thing about Joey is that his friends always come before his jobs. "Does your Flathead friend really wear braids?" I wondered.

Joey laughed. "No. Pete's not really into the Indian trip." Then he added helpfully, "He's got a degree in finance."

"So that makes him okay."

Joey didn't say anything right away. Then he said, "Sounds like you could use a change of scenery." He sounded as if he cared. I felt like crying.

Yes indeed, not in great shape. But my thermometer read exactly 98.6. Gerard Manley Hopkins's sonorous lines floated through my head:

14

. . . the mind has mountains; cliffs of fall
Frightful, sheer, no-man-fathomed.

A bit overdramatic, perhaps. But the cliffs were real. I knew from experience it was dangerous to step too close to the edge. I also knew it was best not to look down.

So I took a stroll around the dark, air-conditioned mansion, keeping my center of gravity low, feeling the connection between the hardwood of the floors and the bare soles of my feet. I polished the floors once a month. It was hardly necessary: there was no traffic across the spartan expanses of oak flooring. I lived in the maid's wing with a TV (provided), a CD player (borrowed), and my own PC (an antique Apple). But I liked waxing and buffing, the rotating motion of the machine, the fragrance of the wax. So I polished once a month.

The Hallermans used these downstairs rooms for diplomatic entertainments. High-ceilinged and long-windowed, the rooms had the solid feeling of large houses built before World War II. The walnut paneling was an inch thick, the plaster moldings probably weighed over five pounds per linear foot. Befitting the Hallermans' monastic taste, furnishings were sparse, understated, but they were richer to the feel than any monk's furniture. Here a cluster of down-filled, buttery leather armchairs; there a time-polished Italian refectory table; here a Wendel Castel chair sculpted out of satiny fruitwood. Set into the walls on glass shelves were selected *objets* from the Hallermans' pre-Columbian collection: a jade mask, a large terra-cotta vessel, a row of clay whistles shaped like birds. In the dark, the smell of all the wax and Windex I had used over the months was reassuring. Eventually, I padded back to bed and dozed off as the birds woke up in the magnolia outside my window.

I called Pete Bonsecours later that morning and told him yes. He sounded relieved for a monosyllabic second. "Good," he said. Then he gathered up his anxieties and focused them on the expense of full-fare airline tickets. On the next phone call, his wife took over. Her name was Dolores.

Clearly she'd had a lot of practice sorting out arrangements for their clients. By midafternoon, I had a cut-rate round-trip ticket

15

from Dulles to Salt Lake City. This I found in the classified section of the *Post* under "Tickets." The seller was a businessman who had canceled a ten-day trip at the last minute. Our dates jibed. Moreover, the man had a unisex first name—a major plus. His ticket was nonrefundable and nontransferable. A woman traveling under a man's name risked having an airline agent notice the discrepancy and confiscate the ticket. But the businessman's ticket was made out to "Dale." After bargaining, "Dale" came down another fifty. With that kind of luck, I couldn't not go.

Dolores was elated. She went ahead and booked me full-fare for the shorter leg from Salt Lake to Missoula, Montana. She also dictated a list of things to bring: sleeping bag, long underwear, boots, foul-weather gear, sunscreen, gloves, down vest, hat, bathing suit, wool socks. In short, I was to pack no more than thirty pounds of gear for temperatures that could range from below freezing to frying. She also suggested packing everything in assorted plastic bags: Ziplocs for underwear, shirts, and cameras; heavy-duty garbage bags for bedding and jackets and jeans. Just in case it rained the whole time.

"I bet that's fun," I said.

"More than you'd think," she said. "It tends to bring a group together."

Famous last words.

I had a day and a half to get myself together. There was the usual tedious business of leaving. I called the live-in maid next door (on her own private line) and she agreed to take in mail in return for a week of walking her employer's nasty-tempered Jack Russell terrier. I called the police and chatted about the alarm system and night patrols. I called the pool-maintenance people and the lawn contractor. I called my bondsman, Ernie. (People with million-dollar mansions tend to appreciate bonded house-sitters.) I told Ernie I was off to the wild, woolly West for a week or so. He wasn't happy when I couldn't give him a phone number. "What if you don't come back?" he complained.

"Write me off as dead."

"Very funny," he growled.

I was feeling better by the minute.

Most of the gear I needed was stored at my mother's, in her

narrow three-bedroom townhouse in a Northeast D.C. neighborhood that realtors call Capitol Hill, but that's stretching it. Two houses on the block have shiny brass hardware on their front doors. My mother's house isn't one of them.

Two years ago, my widowed mother sold our house in Bethesda. Within a year of moving into her new, ungentrified city house, she had collected three housemates: a former patient at Saint Elizabeth's who now works as a massage therapist; a former priest turned substance-abuse counselor; and a former battered wife turned taxi driver. They eat together at my great grandmother's mahogany table and share my mother's back kitchen and her skinny front parlor whose fireplace was designed for burning coal. The basement apartment, the only renovated part of the house, is reserved as my mother's private office. Dr. Marcella Romann Squires. A semiretired psychotherapist, she still sees a handful of patients. Between house-sitting jobs, I camp down there on her therapeutic couch. I refuse to consider the deeper meaning of this arrangement. Sleeping down there is subterranean enough.

I love my mother. At least I think I do. But by all objective daughterly standards, I have a difficult mom. My brother and I grew up with a large photograph of Carl Jung framed in silver. It sat on the piano, blessing our studio-tinted baby pictures, our Kodachrome gap-toothed grins, our senior smirks for the yearbook. I had no problem with Dr. Jung. His white beard was tidy, his eyes were soft and benign, like a sad saint's. But when my mother's eyes got the same look—well, I don't know. I guess it made me feel transparent. I wanted to bury my head under my pillow or run outside and hide under the bushes. Believe me, it is not easy to grow up with a mother who seems to know the intimate workings of your soul. Try as I might, I could never shock her. The most outrageous, the most scurrilous, the most sacrilegious poem would only make her look wise. If she'd washed my mouth out with soap at puberty, I might have wasted less time on "fucking" poems.

Bringing my sleeping bag and other gear down from the attic, I bumped into Tommy, Mom's holistic masseur. Despite his reliance on healing crystals and healthy herbs, he has a soft, pasty look. For some reason, he reminds me of a Good Humor man. All he needs is a white cap on his receding, mousy brown hair. He might be thirty. Or sixty. Like many adults who have been institutionalized for mental illness, he is without obvious signs of age. Perhaps it's the drugs he was prescribed. Or perhaps when you're locked up and never have to decide what to buy for dinner, your face shows no ordinary wear and tear.

"Going camping?" Tommy inquired as we passed each other on the stairs.

"Out west for a week."

His brown eyes searched mine. "It's good to sleep on the ground," he declared.

"I don't know, Tommy," I bantered. "I'll probably need your services when I get back."

He nodded solemnly. I trotted on downstairs. As usual in my mother's house, I had the feeling that I'd missed something in the banal little exchange. It was as if Tommy and my mother, and the others, all knew the secret of why it was "good" to sleep on the ground. They seemed to share an unspoken subtext that was inaccessible to outsiders. No doubt my mother would say that all families have a private, silent language.

We had tea together down in her office. She brewed a strong pot of Darjeeling and poured it into a pair of shallow, Sèvres teacups, light as eggshells. The ladylike mouthfuls of tea cooled quickly. We sat at her worktable in gray tweed ergonomic chairs with the teapot between us. Through the shuttered windows behind my head, late afternoon light bounced off the sidewalk and filtered down in soft bars across her papers and books.

The delicate web of lines on her oval face seemed less sharply etched than the last time I'd seen her. And the crimson of her knit top, the silver of her earrings, set off her short cropped hair. Except for maybe five gray threads, my mother's hair was still dark at sixty-six—an unfair, but natural phenomenon. "You're looking good," I told her. She did not return the compliment.

I told her about Joey and my conversation with Pete Bonsecours. She was interested, supportive. I felt I wasn't getting through to her. There she was, sitting over a teapot like a Gypsy bird, my mother who had borne and bathed and battled with me, and there was no contact.

18

"I was attacked by a bear in the metro last night," I said, trying for a rise.

She cocked her head. "Oh?"

I told her the dream.

"Is that all?" she inquired.

"For God's sake, Mom, what do you want? I've got this bear flying at me, it's about to eat my heart out . . ."

She didn't laugh. She was alert, cautious, trilling with interest. "What sort of bear?"

"A big black one. I don't remember." For a microsecond, the power of it flashed back to me. "It was kind of frosted along its back." I suppressed a shiver and refilled our teacups from the pot.

My mother examined the amber liquid in her featherweight china cup. Then she looked up at me. "Be careful," she warned.

I stared at her.

"I mean it, Lee."

I felt engulfed by a wave of exasperation. "Stop it!" I burst out. "You sound like a goddamn soothsayer!"

She put her teacup down carefully. I waited. She said nothing. The game was called How Comfortable Are You with Silence? I didn't feel like playing.

"Well?" I demanded. "Are you going to clue me in? Or is that against your principles? Maybe you'd rather watch me sink or swim in the Great Collective Unconscious? You could do a paper on it."

Bull's-eye. Her chiseled features were set. Her eyes were too shiny. Terrific. "I'm sorry," I said, embarrassed.

She nodded and smiled, still not speaking. We sipped our cooling tea, bitter and astringent on the tongue. The phone rang. Saved by the bell.

She didn't pick it up. "My machine's on," she said humbly. She leaned back in her chair, rocking slightly against its springy back, as if still reeling from my anger. But her voice was back in its teacherish gear. "Do you know what the medicine wheel is?" she inquired.

"No," I said.

"The Native Americans saw life as a circle, a circle we move around, often many times, as we grow from birth to death to

19

rebirth. The medicine wheel is a ritual representation of life's circle. You enter it from the east, with the rising sun, and move clockwise around the compass. Each direction has its totems, which are symbolic of types of energies in our lives. It's a very sophisticated system. I've been working with it recently and find it—" she hesitated. "I find it deeply moving," she admitted, her voice almost husky.

Her emotion made the hairs on the back of my neck prickle. She added, "As well as useful." She smiled wryly, as if conceding a point to me.

I wanted to hug her. To tell her it was okay. That I wasn't deprived because I had grown up with a psychologist mom. Instead, I sat still, my tongue in a Gordian knot.

She went on, giving in to her enthusiasm. "Now you come and tell me you're going west. Well, in the medicine wheel, the spirit guardian of the West is Mudjekeewis." She looked at me expectantly.

I shook my head.

"A black grizzly," she said.

I felt my brain bouncing off the inner curve of my skull, *bong, bong-a-bong.*

Satisfied, she went on: "Black is the color of night, of hibernation, of looking within. The bear knows its own heart. The bear is one with its heart."

I took a sip of lukewarm tea. "Sounds like a heavy-duty totem," I said.

"Just your ticket," she said crisply. Then she said worriedly, "Remember to breathe."

"Right."

We smiled. A family subtext. Ever since the doctor smacked our newborn backs on the delivery table, she'd been telling her children to breathe.

I cabbed it home with my old L. L. Bean down sleeping bag, a set of expedition-weight polypro underwear, my foul-weather overalls, an old cast-iron Dutch oven I'd bought years ago at a flea market on the Eastern Shore, and a felt hat of my father's reeking of mothballs—a gift from my mother. Tommy gave me a small polished lump of carnelian, dark as a blood clot. My mother nodded approvingly. "The heart of the bear," she said to no one in particular. I ignored it, as if she had let out a small fart. I slipped the stone in the back pocket of my jeans and kissed her good-bye.

In the cab, I took out Tommy's carnelian as we crept down Constitution Avenue. The lights changed and we moved two car lengths. Evening rush hour. Normally, I would have been twitching, one eye on the meter, one eye on the bumper ahead of us. But fingering the warm pebble of red-brown stone was oddly soothing. I gazed out the taxi's window at the Capitol's manicured grounds. It occurred to me that in another time, another place, my mother could easily have been burned as a witch.

4

The 7:32 A.M. Delta flight from Dulles to Salt Lake was not crowded. I had a window seat. The aisle seat in my row was taken by a man in a pale blue polyester short-sleeved shirt. He had furry forearms—wheat-colored fur—and wore a large, black diving watch. Since I didn't want to encourage conversation, I avoided taking a peek at his face. The middle seat between us was empty. He took up half of it turning the pages of *USA Today*. I claimed the other half with my day pack.

I bought a three-dollar Bloody Mary with breakfast. The furry-armed diver retracted further inside his newspaper tent, as if a hit of vodka in the morning might turn me into a shark. It turned me sleepy. I dozed, was woken by a flight attendant with two packs of peanuts I didn't want, and I dozed some more.

Waking as we descended, my first glimpse of the Great Salt Lake was disorienting, almost hallucinatory: the water below the wing of the plane was the exact blue-green color of shallow Caribbean waters. There were even brown patches that might have been underwater reefs. But there was no lush tangle of growth on the mountains that ringed the lake and the flat spread of city. The taupe-colored mountains were desert-bare, every wrinkle and crease exposed to the air, which was white and heavy with industrial-looking smudges. Why did the pollution surprise me so? Did I really expect the West to be as pure and simple as an old Lone Ranger episode?

For the first five minutes, the Salt Lake City airport was indistinguishable from, say, Logan in Boston or Chicago's O'Hare. They all sold five-dollar hot dogs. They all had mile-long corridors diffused with blue-gray light. Then I noticed that along these corridors in Salt Lake, there were no alcoves filled with beer-drinkers watching TV. Perhaps Mormon architects had hidden a bar somewhere behind the janitor's closet, but booze was nowhere obvious. Moreover, Salt Lake passengers seemed to walk differently. I realized that every other man, girl, and granny was wearing high-heeled cowboy boots. (Moms and kids seemed to favor running shoes.)

On my connecting hop, flying northward over the Rockies, the air became bluer, the mountains' peaks were snow-covered, their lower flanks black with dense pine. There were small green lakes hidden in the high hollows and tortuous alpine streams flashing silver. I felt an anticipatory thrill. There was nothing pastoral about these rivulets. From the air, they might have been varicose veins, pulsing, twisting, surfacing crookedly through the muscle and sinew of the wilderness.

The Missoula airport was folksy. Like travelers in a fifties newsreel, we disembarked down a flight of aluminum steps open to the dry, shimmering air of a western June afternoon. Single-file, we crossed the tarmac and entered the brown-and-yellow spaces of Missoula's air terminal. The decor was rec room: travel posters and glass-eyed deer heads hung on varnished pine walls.

Pete Bonsecours found me at the baggage-claim area. I didn't ask how he recognized me. If Joey had given him a description, I didn't want to hear it. Or maybe I was the only one there who wasn't being hugged. "Lee," he said. I turned and there he was, an Indian all right, brown skin, black eyes, straight black hair clipped short. His square face was pitted with acne scars and a greasy black stripe slanted across one cheekbone. It looked like battle paint.

"Hello," I said. He made no move to shake hands. He was

one big Indian. He was only an inch or so taller than I—maybe he was five ten, eleven in his cowboy boots, which were worn down a good half inch on the outside of the heels. He was slightly bowlegged, as though his legs had given way a bit under the mass of his torso. He must have weighed at least two-twenty. His denim shirt puckered across his chest between the buttons, but there was no sag of belly over his belt. If he was shaped like a barrel, it was an oak cask with tight hoops.

"Sorry I'm late," he apologized. "My truck's acting up. My mules are more reliable, I promise you." He smiled and was suddenly less formidable, almost boyish. I noticed that his hands were also smeared black. It was engine grease, not war paint, on his face.

I decided not to make a crack about it. Instead, I said, "It's okay. They haven't even unloaded the baggage yet."

He nodded and went off to wash up.

I had checked two pieces of luggage: a canvas duffle packed with my sleeping bag and an agonized-over selection of under-, outer-, and overwear plus a duct-tape-reinforced cardboard carton. It contained my Dutch oven packed with my father's hat, a whetstone, a pair of carbon-steel knives, a liter flask of bourbon whiskey, and an antique plastic *Star Wars* vacuum bottle that contained my sourdough starter. The starter was a valued leftover from my marriage: Clint's grandmother had given it to me and claimed that it had been passed down in the family for over a hundred years. For good measure, I had tossed in a plastic bag filled with dried herbs that looked suspiciously recreational but were in fact culinary. I retrieved my box and bag from the conveyor belt and met Pete by the door. He took my duffle and seemed surprised.

"About seven pounds light," he said approvingly. "Most people overpack."

"Well," I said, wincing, "I'm over when you add this in." I hefted my box. "I brought a Dutch oven along."

"We've got Dutch ovens," he said.

"I wanted my own."

He retracted almost imperceptibly. I didn't need a mind reader to translate: Had Joey sent him a prima donna?

24

Pete Bonsecour's truck was a matte-finish, pale green pickup whose rounded fenders were speckled like the eggs of shorebirds with rust. Inside, it smelled of dust, grease, and burned coffee. He drove to a supermarket called Tidyman's in a shopping plaza that could have been anywhere USA, except that half the vehicles in the lot were pickups. Pete handed me half of a two-page daisy-wheel printout. It was a grocery list. I had Produce, beginning with forty-four apples, and Miscellaneous, ending with eight rolls of toilet paper. He took Dry Goods, Cans, and Dairy. A good while later, we met at the check-out aisle.

I stared at his cart. He had topped off his mountain of groceries with thirteen cartons of eggs. As we waited in line, I recounted them to be sure and started calculating. The math took me a while, especially since I found it hard to believe the results and kept redoing the figures in my head. One hundred and fifty-six eggs divided by eleven eaters equaled fourteen eggs per person. That was over two eggs a day per person, a generous month's supply sucked up in one week. The mere thought of it was enough to make little cholesterol buds start blooming on the walls of my arteries. Good thing Tommy had given me a magic crystal. "Carnelian works for the heart," he had said.

Meanwhile, Pete was eyeballing my selections. I prided myself on having kept to the letter of his list:

Cabbage, 1 green, 1 red
6 cucumber
4 bunch carrot
1 doz. peppers . . .

"You got red and yellow peppers?" he asked. I looked. Yep, there they were, chugging along the conveyor belt toward the register. Pete didn't sound happy about them.

"You wanted only green?" I wondered. "I was thinking about roasting them. A little color helps the presentation."

He said nothing.

"What's the matter?" I demanded, irritated more by his silence than his taste in peppers. "Too yuppy for you?"

"If *yuppy* means three times the price, yeah, they're too yuppy."

"What, you want me to put them back?"

The cashier stopped ringing up and looked at us. She was wearing a green smock. Her dark hair was shaved on one side of her head, giving her a gray five-o'clock shadow around her ear. Three little silver stars pierced the curled rim of her ear. In the lobe, she wore what looked like a microchip.

"Look," I said to Pete. "I'll put them back. No big deal." I had not spoken loudly, but everyone in the check-out aisles seemed to be listening.

The cashier snapped her gum impatiently.

"Ring them up," Pete told her.

"You sure?" she said sarcastically. She made a show of looking from Pete to me and back again, as if she were following a tennis ball.

I gave Pete a second or two. His jaw didn't open.

"We're quite sure, thank you," I told her. "And your name is?"

She shut up. I let it drop. Pete pulled out a check from his wallet and filled it in. He folded the receipt tape into a thick packet and tucked it into his shirt pocket. Then we loaded the bags into the back of the pickup and covered them with a blue plastic tarp.

"Seems like an awful lot of food," I remarked stupidly. I was trying to get past the acrid taste the cashier left in my mouth.

Pete seemed cheerful. "Wait till you add what we've got in the freezer. It'll come to about four hundred pounds. Two and a half mules' worth."

He pulled out of the parking lot and got the truck up to a noisy fifty on the highway. A dry wind whipped through the open windows. Pete put on a pair of aviator shades he pulled off a strap on the visor. I wrapped my head in a scarf to keep my hair out of my eyes. Ten minutes later the low-rise slurbs of Missoula dissolved into the kind of western landscape I'd hoped for. A newly improved road followed the bed of the Blackfoot River, a shallow, dark-winding stream etched with white lines made by riffles hidden in the shadows of the mountains on either side. Then we would

26

round a curve and see the water sunlit and bubbling like soda over a bottom of rounded rocks.

The road left the Blackfoot and plunged straight across a green valley floor, fenced and farmed, and sheltered by distant hills. The sun was pleasantly hot through the windshield and the wind-buffeted silence in the front seat was comfortable. But I was too hopped-up and curious to ride with it. "Tell me about your client," I asked over the noise of the truck.

Pete nodded, as if I'd said something intelligent. "I took him hunting a couple seasons. I was working as a guide for this couple. Same ones that sold me the business last year. I worked a long time for them, almost ten years. I started back when I was still in high school. I guess you could say they kind of became surrogate parents for me. After I finished college, they gave me this deal working for a share of the business instead of pay. They were one of the smaller outfitters licensed in the Bob, but top-notch. It was almost a word-of-mouth club. I'll bet over the years half the men we took hunting were Fortune Five Hundred CEOs."

He stopped. I opened my mouth to jump in with another question, but he wasn't finished. "She had a stroke, the wife. So they decided to sell. We figured I already owned half the business. Which meant I had to come up with a hundred thousand for the other half. It was a little high. But they needed the money. Her stroke had eaten up all their savings."

He shook his head. "A lot of the equipment is old, needs replacing. One tent, two years ago, this fella got sick in, and you can't get the stink out of it. You're talking five hundred dollars here, one thousand dollars there. The banks wouldn't buy it."

Again he paused. This time I waited. His deliberateness disconcerted me. He didn't run on. He seemed to speak in full-blown paragraphs—with triple spaces in between.

"So I got in touch with a number of clients I'd taken out. Cyrus Strand liked the idea of getting involved with an outfit. His company's in North Carolina, but he's got a place down in Cody and has been coming out there for years. It's where he wants to retire. Of course, he'll get the Wyoming tax advantage, but if that's all he was after, he could have bought a condo in Florida. The Old West turns him on. He's something of a history buff and he likes to hunt. He's a big supporter of the National Wildlife Federation."

"What kind of tax advantage?"

"There's no state income-tax in Wyoming. And no estate taxes. Same in Florida."

Studying his face as we rumbled along, it occurred to me that Pete was a good-looking man despite his pocked skin and his disapproving expression. His face was as square as his body, but strong-boned with hollow cheeks and a jutting chin. His disapproving look, I decided, was an accident of his mouth, which was the exact shape of an unstrung bow. A narrow, unrelenting curve, it slashed across the lower half of his face, ending in naturally downturned corners. When he wasn't talking or smiling, he seemed formidable. He glanced at me from behind his shades.

"Go on," I said.

"So the guy loaned me the money. As security, I took out a life-insurance policy for the same amount, payable to Cyrus Strand Three. He's into his roman numerals. He puts three slashes after his signature and the slashes are bigger than his name."

"Huh," I said. "The family looms larger than the individual? An Old World concept."

"You could say New World, too," Pete pointed out. "The tribe comes first." His face was deadpan. "So Cyrus Strand Three and I, we worked out a payment schedule, signed on the dotted line, and I'm in business." There was a bitter edge to his voice.

I let a mile roll by. "How far behind are you?" I asked him.

He accelerated on a long curve. We were beginning to climb. "Three months," he said flatly.

"He paying you for this trip?"

"We agreed on expenses. The market's gone sluggish on textiles and he's crying poor. But his company's gross sales are stable, they've got no liabilities, and the old man controls around thirty percent of company stock. Which means he's worth twenty-five million in stock alone. Give or take a few points on the Dow Jones. And he says he can't afford full rates to take his family into the Bob."

"To paraphrase old F. Scott, 'The rich ain't like the rest of us.' So what happens? You pull off this trip and Pops says, 'Stay cool, as a token of my appreciation, I'm not gonna foreclose'?"

Pete raised his eyebrows maybe a millimeter over the gold-tone wire rims of his sunglasses. "You sound like my wife," he said. "She doesn't believe in fairy tales either."

"I guess you're what's called the dreamer type?"

"Call it a longshot. Us Injuns have a thing about gambling."

"I thought it was drinking."

"That too."

We rode along with the wind between us. Suddenly I felt tired. But my curiosity still nagged at me. "Pete?" I asked, trying out his name for the first time.

"Yeah."

"How come you aren't doing something financial? Joey said you had a degree."

"You mean, like be a bank teller?"

I ignored the sarcasm. "Whatever."

After a moment, his face softened. He grinned mischievously. "Maybe you'll figure out the answer to that one when I get you up into the Bob."

Pete and Dolores Bonsecours lived in a trailer at the end of a dirt road that ran past Upsata Lake. They owned ten acres of pasture-land roughly fenced with bark-covered pine poles—"jack leg" fencing, Pete called it. His corrals, he explained with some pride, were less than five miles away from the forest station at Monture Creek, a convenient entrance into the wilderness. Which meant he could wrangle his stock to the trailhead, thereby saving the expense of hauling his mules and horses by truck.

There were no trees around the trailer, which sat on cinder blocks beside a dilapidated fleet of cars and trucks. Among the rusting heaps, a passenger van, a two-ton truck, and an old Honda Civic looked serviceable. The trailer was questionable. Its weather-streaked, pinky-beige siding buckled in places. The color reminded me of the "flesh" crayons I'd once used on princesses, whose hair I'd always made yellow. The trailer was at least as old as the crayons. It had not been designed to sit in a mobile-home park. It had been built for the road: its streamlined corners were rounded, giving it the look of a long, homemade loaf of bread. Along the front side, Pete had added a porch. It was roofed with corrugated

29

fiber glass that sheltered a freezer on one side of the front door, and on the other, a kitchen table surrounded by webbed aluminum chairs. On the table, an exuberant bouquet of wild daisies sprouted from a blue-glazed crock.

Dolores rose unsteadily from behind the daisies as I followed Pete up the steps onto the porch. She was wearing an oversized plaid shirt that almost hid her cutoffs and an enormous, white walking cast on her left leg. Aside from the cast, there were other things immediately striking about her: she looked about fifteen years old, about ten months pregnant, and she glowed with a lazy, late-pregnancy kind of beauty. Her shoulder-length hair was a glossy Asian black. Her skin was somewhere between honey and vanilla, and her features had a delicate oriental cast. As interesting as it would have been to know the particular pool of her genes, I've always considered the question, What are you? as obnoxious as, Who are you? So I settled for a tactless "My God, when are you due?"

They both laughed. "Not till next month," Dolores answered. There was nothing child-bride about her voice. It had authority in it. Later I learned that she taught elementary school in the nearest town, which was called Ovando, and that she was twenty-seven, not fifteen. (Pete was thirty-two, she told me. They'd been married five years.) As for the cast, she said her leg "got in the way of" a gate while she was working with a new colt.

"A month away from your due date and you were going off into the wilderness? What if the baby decided to come?" I asked.

"Oh," she said airily, "I'd just drive a couple stakes in the ground and hang on." She glanced at Pete. "The old-timey way," she teased.

He wasn't amused.

The provisions we'd bought took up all the built-in dinette and half the "pecan"-paneled living area. We ate an early supper out on their porch. The distant hills seemed to draw closer as the afternoon shadows lengthened. Golden puffs of dust rose from the corals as the mules and horses regrouped themselves. The clang of the bells hung around the lead mares' necks carried pleasantly on the dry, cooling air. There were no gnats, no mosquitos.

I sat with Dolores, her cast elevated on a chair, while Pete

30

cooked a hash, well peppered, richly meaty, and with an absolutely perfect brown crust. He served it up with ketchup, pickled beets, and caramelized sweet rolls that Dolores's mother had dropped off that morning. The wood of the tabletop had warped, its three broad planks curving slightly like the open palms of three hands, and Dolores's stoneware plates rocked as we ate off them. The motion, the crammed space, made me feel as if we were eating in a cockpit on a secure anchorage. Dolores and I split a beer in jelly glasses. Feeling like a lush, I accepted a second one. Pete drank only coffee.

The meal took me by surprise. Its down-home textures and its sharp, sweet-sour contrasts were at once exotic and familiar. My notion of a colorful pepper salad suddenly seemed effete. "Great hash," I told Pete. "What'd you put in it?"

"Elk mostly," he said, watching my reaction.

"Really good. It didn't taste gamey at all."

He seemed pleased. "It's good, clean meat. That's what we're taking in with us. Normally, we pack in only U.S.-inspected beef and chicken. There's a state law that prevents outfitters from serving game unless they also serve domesticated meat at the same meal. Not very many outfitters want to go to the trouble, even if they can afford it."

"Wait a minute," I interrupted. "I don't get it."

"Our legislators think they're conserving Montana wildlife. They don't want outfitters poaching to feed the tourists," Pete said sourly. "But there's no law against feeding hunters their own kill. What we're taking in is Cyrus's elk. He shot it last fall, had it butchered in Missoula, and left it in our freezer to feed this trip he had in mind. The venison he took back with him."

"I've never cooked elk before," I worried.

Dolores shrugged. "I'll bet the dudes haven't eaten it before. Except the old man." She frowned. "By the way," she warned, "you better not call them dudes to their faces. 'Guests' is safest."

"What do I call Pops? Mr. Strand?"

Pete suggested, "If you ruin his elk steaks, call him 'Duke' and he'll eat 'em out of your hand. He's big on John Wayne."

"Thanks for the tip," I said.

*　　*　　*

After supper, Pete introduced me to the wood cookstove I'd be using on the trip. It was shoe-box-shaped, welded out of steel, and sat on four legs just low enough to send you hobbling to a chiropractor for your back. My back, that is. Pete admitted he'd designed it for a shorter cook—namely Dolores. The thing also had a six-foot-tall exhaust pipe. To pack the stove, you collapsed its legs, which folded up under the firebox. Then you knocked the pipe down into segments, fitted them one inside the other, and stowed it inside the stove box along with picket stakes and shoeing equipment for the horses. I took the contraption apart and put it back together three times. Then I unrolled my sleeping bag on the daybed that served as a sofa in their living area. I slept lightly, but not badly. I could feel the floor heave as they moved from bathroom to bedroom. Half waking in the dark, I could feel the plywood wall at my back pressing, releasing like a bulkhead at sea. Maybe I was dreaming. Maybe it was wind. Against the opposite wall, above the bags of groceries, the screen of their TV caught the starlight from a window cut into the wall over my head. I remember wondering, How do they manage in winter?

I spent all Friday, the next day, with Dolores, who gave me a short course in packing a camp kitchen. The big Don't on the syllabus was: Don't let anything rattle in the pack or you'll spook the mules. Her refrain was, "Don't worry, Pete will be there if you get stuck."

Typically, as it turned out, I didn't see Pete all day.

At five on Saturday morning, Dolores and I started wrapping frozen elk chilies, elk meatballs, and elk steaks in layer after layer of newspaper. We packed them, last meal first, in plastic crates, along with butter and daily packets of sliced luncheon meat and cheese.

At seven, Pete's two wranglers showed up: a sullen girl named Cory who had packed with Pete for several years before he bought the business, and a new, chatty kid named Brett who said he ski-bummed at Aspen in the winter and was eight credits short of a degree in sports science from the University of Denver. By eight o'clock, we'd loaded nearly two thousand pounds of saddles, tents, tools, and food into the two-ton. The wranglers saddled up and yipped the small herd of horses and mules through the north pasture toward Monture Creek. Pete took the passenger van to Missoula to pick up his party at the Holiday Inn. I was to take the loaded truck and meet the horses at the trailhead. I got behind the wheel and managed to grind what sounded like a good sixteenth of an inch off first gear as I jolted the thing out of their yard. I glimpsed Dolores's face in the mirror. Through a veil of dust, she looked pained.

5

Cyrus Strand looked more like a general going fishing than an exec with a passion for the Old West. His only concession to horseback travel was a pair of dark, new jeans. He wore well-oiled engineer's boots, a time-bleached khaki shirt with shoulder tabs, and a khaki canvas field hat. He was a tall man with an unyielding posture that gave a slight jerkiness to his movements. Cyrus Strand III carried his chin a notch higher than most and seemed to blink less, like a bird of prey presiding over his nest.

The nestlings, on the other hand, had gone all out and collectively spent a small fortune feathering themselves with magnificent unblemished Stetsons, untarnished silver set with monumental lumps of turquoise, and unscuffed lizard-skin cowboy boots, probably hand-sewn on the Via Veneto. What wasn't Ralph Lauren was Banana Republic. I thought of Thoreau's admonition: "Beware of enterprises that require new clothes."

I was too busy unloading their duffles from Pete's van to sort them out immediately, but there was, underneath the expensive trappings, a certain physical familyness to them. They were generally tall and vaguely Irish-looking: fair skin here (the old man's ruddy and weather-ruined), fine, long noses there, a scattering of blue eyes and pale lashes. They all seemed to flash good teeth and tease one another in confident voices that carried across the corral. An attractive bunch, at first sight.

Instead of posts, the fencing at the Monture Creek corral was nailed to a circle of tree trunks, which gave the place the secret, self-built feeling of a child's hidden fort. Sun slanted through the pine tops overhead. The horses, saddled and bridled, stood sleeping, as reliable as stuffed animals. The mules looked smarter, their straight backs tense, their long ears moving like antennae tracking unknown objects.

Outside the corral, on the grassy forest floor, Pete and his wranglers distributed piles of gear on squares of white canvas. The tarps, Cyrus announced, were called "manties," from the Spanish *manta*, meaning cover.

None of his family was interested.

Then, belatedly, an elegant older woman cocked her frosted-blond head. "Ah," she said, her vowel bright and foreign sounding. "Like the señorita's mantilla—a *little* cover, no?"

Cyrus smiled approvingly.

Kneeling and folding the canvas around the guests' gear, Cory and Brett and Pete tugged and tied the manties into tidy rectangular bundles. They worked as quickly and deftly as nurses making beds. Then, one after the other, they hefted the canvas packs onto the mules' saddles, looping rope over and under, pushing and shoving each pair of packs into balance. Cory, who was my height but slim as a tube in men's jeans, appeared at no disadvantage. She swung the 100-pound packs from her knee up to the mule's back with the practiced economy of a professional ditchdigger.

Cameras clicked.

Cyrus, wearing his khaki hat, posed arm-in-arm with a pot-bellied man with luxuriant, wavy white hair. Together they squinted into the sun for the European woman's Pentax. I wondered which of the two men was hers. She fussed possessively at both of them, but managed to sound charming, flirtatious even, as she bossed them into smiling for posterity. Her riding outfit was French-flavored. Like a cowboy from La Camargue, she wore slim-legged jeans tucked into knee-high black boots, a cotton checked shirt that bloused artfully over her trim waist, and a wide-brimmed black hat angled over her eye with an air of *chic sportif*. She, it turned out, was Cyrus's wife number three, Lucia Strand, pronounced Luchee-a. "Like the song," she said, helpfully humming a few bars of "Santa Lucia" for Pete. The corners of his mouth remained turned down.

She was a native of Milan, she told us, a fabric designer by profession, and she had brought along her paint box as well as a macrolens for her Pentax. Cyrus had promised her wildflowers. She tried out a smile on Brett. It seemed to work just fine. How old was she? I wondered sourly. Fifty something? Or sixty, lifted and tucked? Then I wondered: Was I jealous? Or just insecure?

The white-haired man Lucia Strand had photographed with her husband was Nathaniel Rosenfeld, Cyrus's lawyer, old friend, and the one outside director of his company. Nat, as he told us to call him, was wearing a skintight pair of leather chaps. He had borrowed them from a polo-playing friend, he confided several times. "I'm hoping they'll convince my mount," he joked nervously. The chaps made his legs look like a pair of suede sticks. His soft stomach hung over them in a rather endearing fashion. I found myself wanting to pat it, the way people are drawn to patting pregnant bellies.

After the mules were loaded, Pete, by some unspoken command, gathered his party around the back of the truck to issue water bottles and the sandwiches Dolores and I had made at six A.M. It was now just past eleven. Pete made a one-way introduction: "This is Lee, your cook," he announced. "And behind you, Cory and Brett."

Brett doffed his hat. Cory, her arms folded across her chest, gave an awkward nod.

A collective murmur of greeting arose from the group.

Cyrus looked me over. "A lady pan-slinger," he observed. He turned to Pete. "We've got a token woman this time out," he joked.

I smiled weakly.

Thus encouraged, Cyrus shook his head in mock distress. "I don't know, Pete," he elaborated. "If you really want to keep ERA off our backs, we need two of them."

"Cory's female," Pete said laconically.

36

Cyrus stared at Cory. She doffed her hat as Brett had done, but managed to make the gesture ironical, defiant, even. The sun glanced off her soft brown hair.

Cyrus was clearly surprised. Someone in the group made a *sotto voce* comment. Someone else let out a small snort of disgust.

"Well," Cyrus exclaimed heartily, "a crew of two women and an Indian oughta keep those Affirmative Action people happy. All we need is a handicapped!" He turned to Brett. "You handicapped, son?"

Brett grinned agreeably. "Not physically," he quipped.

"Atta boy," Cyrus barked happily.

"Lunches," I sang out, waving one of the bags like a checkered flag at the finish line. Just call me big Ms. Peacemaker.

The other woman in the party, a buxom brunette laden with silver jewelry, had the same idea. She cornered Cory. "Hi," she said. "I'm Adrienne. You'll have to forgive my father. He seems to need new glasses," she apologized.

"That's not all he needs," Cory observed.

Pete wheeled around. The arc of his mouth was drawn tight. Cory's gray eyes challenged.

Adrienne peered at her. "You got it, honey," she said dryly.

Pete relaxed. "How many of you are experienced riders?" he asked. He acknowledged Cyrus and Lucia and a slickly handsome, younger man with curly black hair who was called Henry. No one else volunteered.

Nat, the family lawyer, said pompously, "We were given to understand that experience was not a requirement for this excursion."

Pete smiled. "The only requirement is that you enjoy yourselves." He gave a little speech about how not to worry, every one of his horses was surefooted and mountain-wise. "Listen to what your horse tells you," he instructed. "If he balks on the trail, check it out before you give him a kick. If you're carrying a raincoat behind your saddle, be careful putting it on. Flapping raincoats probably cause more wrecks in the mountains than anything else." He surveyed the faces of his guests. A sparkle flickered in his black eyes. "Cheer up," he coaxed. "We haven't lost a guest yet. Just remember what the old-timers used to say: If you come to the end of your rope, tie a knot in it and hang on!"

And on that upbeat note, the group drifted into the corral, where Pete assigned them horses. "Okay, everyone, mount up," he said. "Cory will lead out with her mules. Just fall in after her."

The woman called Adrienne approached the rump of a large, black gelding.

"Nice horsey," she said, stroking its tail. "I'm listening to you, sweetheart. Now tell me, how the hell do I get on?"

"Adrienne, darlin'," called a lazy male voice, "if I were you, I'd steer clear of the ass end of that pony."

She took a quick step back and bumped into me. "God Almighty," she swore nervously.

"Come up along side of him," I suggested. "No, other side. Here." I untied the halter from the railing and held the horse while she hastily stuffed her water bottle and lunch in the saddlebag. The animal stretched its neck, leisurely curling its lip up to reveal its large, yellow teeth. "My God, Billy," she worried, "this one's dangerous at both ends."

Billy strolled over in his new boots, brandishing an Instamatic. "Hi," he said pleasantly. "Billy Caton."

"Lee," I said.

"Yes, one of our two tokens of femininity," he teased as we shook hands. His grip was dry and firm. His accent was southern in the extreme.

"You note," Adrienne said acidly, "that Daddy did not count me in his ERA tally."

"He never counts you, darlin'. That's why you married me." He turned to me, holding out the camera. "Could I trouble you to take a picture of me and my fearless wife? She's the only wife with enough balls to come along."

"The others weren't invited," Adrienne reminded sharply.

"Nonetheless, I feel we should document our sartorial splendor. A 'before' photo, as it were. Who knows what we'll look like after."

"For heaven's sake, Billy, do shut up," Adrienne snapped.

He didn't. "The real reason she decided to come along was

38

the opportunity it gave her to explore the western look. Annie Oakley suits are big out at the country club this year."

Her eyes opened wide. "*Who* spent five hundred dollars on a pair of boots?" she inquired, her voice dangerously sweet.

"You guys want to smile at the birdie?" I suggested.

They stood on either side of the horse's nose, Billy holding the halter rope, Adrienne with a tentative hand on the neck. They might have been posing for a Christmas card with a problem teenager between them. Their smiles were wary, their clothes as bright as tinsel. Adrienne wore sandcast silver cuffs on each of her capable-looking wrists (a tennis-player's wrists, I was willing to bet), silver and turquoise in her ears, and a silver-studded denim jacket. Billy was fringed: his suede jacket swung with long, fettucinilike fringes; the fringes on his yellow gauntlets jiggled like spaghetti. *Sergio Leone*, I thought as I peered through the viewfinder, *Where are you now?*

Adrienne had less trouble getting on than one might expect, given her apprehension. Despite her fulsome figure, she was limber and managed to swing up into the saddle rather deftly.

"Well, look at you." Billy sounded both impressed and annoyed.

"*Brava*," I congratulated. I hoped I could do as well. I hadn't been on a horse in a very, very long time.

She beamed down at us. "I'm not sure I can get off," she disclaimed modestly. But she sat well on the big, black horse, her back straight, her shoulders comfortable.

"You never rode as a kid?" I asked.

"I was four years old when Daddy moved the mill from Massachusetts down to High Point. You know High Point? It's a real old-money, old-family sort of place, and if you think they're snooty now about Yankee interlopers, they were even worse back in the nineteen fifties. Mother never did get me into the pony club."

If she'd been born a Massachusetts Yankee, there was no hint of it now in her voice. Both Adrienne's intonation and her slightly flirtatious delivery suggested Scarlett O'Hara—a Scarlett gone maternally plump, but no less fierce under the soft cushion of middle age. She surveyed the corral, twisting in her saddle like a cowboy counting cattle. Cyrus and Lucia were the only other ones up in their saddles. "Come on, Billy," she urged, as if their team was about to edge ahead by a point.

Billy had more difficulty than his wife. His flapping fringes unsettled his horse, a sturdy, butterscotch-colored mare who sidestepped as he tried to get a leg up. On the third try, he made it halfway on. His rear end hovered precariously in midair. I reached up and gave the seat of his pants a firm shove in the right direction. He plopped down on the mare's broad back and let out a hoot. "Lee, honey, we are going to have to do that again! It just felt so gooood, I mean, I am putty in your hands!"

"Your tail sure is," commented Adrienne.

He laughed. "My dear lady wife, I wouldn't talk too loud about fat behinds, if I were you."

Nat Rosenfeld had found a stump outside the corral and used it to get on his horse with dignity. Henry the Handsome (I kept feeling I'd seen him in an ad for something expensive) mounted easily, but the other Strand man, whose name was Gene, required assistance from both Pete and Brett. His legs were as unyielding and awkward as a pair of broomsticks joined by a rubber band. His new hat fell off and the horse stepped on it. The man's eyes watered. He sneezed repeatedly, the horse flinched, Pete kept a firm hold on its head. Brett encouraged, a bit too cheerfully, "There's a first time for everything."

Cyrus watched, then turned away in disgust.

My own horse was a wide, undistinguished-looking bay with the serviceable name of Joan. I managed to get on my first try. The saddle felt fine—they always do for the first ten minutes—but one stirrup was a notch longer than the other. I hopped off and began the tedious business of unlacing and relacing the shorter stirrup strap. The group, all mounted now, gathered under the trees. Pete came over to give me a hand. "I'm going to ride up front with Cyrus—he likes to be in the lead," Pete said, taking the laces from me and whipping them through the holes with the blind speed of a knitter. "You stay toward the back. Brett will bring up the rear with his string. We'll see how it goes. When we stop for lunch, if everyone's comfortable, you and Brett and Cory can go on ahead to set up camp."

I guessed that meant eating my PB & J in the saddle. Still,

riding with the mules instead of the clients would be ample compensation. Talk about old-timey! Brown and black and white-speckled, the mules looked as if they'd walked right out of an old John Huston movie. Their packs might have held prospecting pans instead of Orvis fishing rods. To hell with Isak Dinesen's aristocratic boots: my father's old brown felt hat fit right in with the Gabby Hayes halos radiating from those mules.

Cory led her string of four mules over to her horse and mounted up, lead rope in one hand, reins in the other. Her horse, a mare with Arab lines, was remarkable looking: a creamy white, except for a brown head. The animal might have been wearing a medieval jousting hood. One white ear poked up through the brown mask. Her mane and tail sprouted dark. Cory, perhaps in a festive impulse, perhaps bored with waiting, had braided a red ribbon in her mane. The mare's name was Joker.

Cory nudged Joker forward through the pines. The mules fell into step. Lucia, pleased by the sight, cocked her glamorous black hat up out of her eyes, fished her camera out of her saddlebag, and snapped away. Cory was turned backward, inspecting the way the packs rode on the mules, when Joker suddenly swerved, smashing Cory's right knee against the trunk of a trailside pine.

Cory shot up as if about to fly out of the saddle, then curled over the pommel. I could hear the pain-shot intake of air through her teeth. She rocked for a second or two before she straightened up a bit shakily. To a concerned chorus of "Are you okay?" she rode back to Pete and me.

Without a word, she handed over the mules. Then, with a fierce kick, she loped Joker directly at the offending tree. Joker stopped short, nose inches away from the bark. Cory kicked the animal's ribs, whipped her rump with the reins. The mare balked, and balked again. "Goddamn bitch," Cory swore between clenched teeth. She leaned forward, one hand short-reining the horse's head around the tree, one heel punishing its inside flank. Joker trotted a tight circle around the tree, jerking her head in protest.

The party watched in solemn silence. Cory exhaled words like a stream of bullets: "No. Don't you do that. Bitch. Don't you do that again." She walloped Joker into a miserably tight lope around

41

the tree, then repeated the exercise in the other direction. I don't know how many times she muscled Joker's nuzzle around the tree trunk, this way or that. It seemed to take forever.

Pete showed no impatience. He handed me the lead mule's rope to hold and finished lacing up my stirrup. The Strands watched, their faces slightly shocked. All except Pops. When Cory was done with it, and rode out past him with her mules, Cyrus boomed approvingly, "Gotta show her who's boss."

A short, nasty laugh came from the rear. I turned to see who it was, but all the faces were bland under the lineup of new hats. Pete and I mounted up. We were off to see the wilderness.

6

For the first mile or so, the trail into the forest was a level road carpeted with pine needles. The air was cool and scented with resin. Rays of sunlight streamed through the canopy of ponderosa as if just off to our left, or ahead there on the right, we might stumble across a saint transfixed in heaven-sent light. Despite the width of the road, we clopped along nose-to-tail in a long line. Brett and his mules brought up the rear behind me. In front of me rode Gene of the watery eyes and the broomstick legs. He kept pulling a red bandanna out of his pocket and blowing his nose. I wondered if he had some kind of allergy problem. In front of Gene rode the man called Henry, apparently a family member, but without Cyrus's fair, Irish look. Henry was dark and almost beautiful, his eyes heavily lashed, his mouth sensuous. His work shirt was exactly the same shade of light blue as his evenly faded designer jeans. Only the large, greenish turquoise in his belt buckle saved him from total matchdom. I couldn't help hearing Carly Simon's lilting complaint: "You're so vain. . . ." Perhaps it was the way he held his shoulders, a bit too far back, as if he were about to strut.

In front of Henry rode Lucia Strand in her black gaucho hat.

They chatted back and forth, Lucia bubbling like a happy child, and Henry allotting her suavely mature smiles, like a superior young soccer player indulging an older woman's enthusiasm for the game. Only nonsensical snatches of their conversation floated back to me, but the sexual tension between them was loud and clear. Were we packing a real-life Oedipus complex into the wilderness?

Gene, in front of me on a wide chestnut gelding, turned back in his saddle and caught me staring at them.

"You all seem to have the same hat," I said, sidestepping. And in fact, five of them, Gene and handsome Henry, Nat the lawyer, Adrienne and her fringed husband, Billy, wore large, fawn-colored Stetsons.

"We hit this western store in a Missoula mall," Gene admitted cheerfully. "Lucia already had a black hat. So the rest of us decided we had to be the good guys."

"Cyrus is your father?" I asked.

"Right. I'm Gene Strand. Adrienne is my sister. And Henry up there in front of you is our adopted brother."

Perhaps there was something chilly about the way he said "adopted." Or perhaps Henry was supersensitive to the word itself. In any case, both Lucia and Henry twisted back in their saddles. "What's that?" Henry inquired.

"I was telling Lee about our shopping expedition, how you're hoping for rain."

Henry shrugged.

"Oh no," Lucia objected prettily. "No rain, please!"

"Henry bought himself the most magnificent riding slicker," Gene explained. "Oh, damn." His face contracted. He fished out his bandanna and sneezed violently into it.

Sturdy old Joan woke up and twitched her ears. I patted her neck.

"Sorry," Gene sniffed.

"Hay fever?"

"Actually, I'm allergic to horses."

My jaw landed on my first shirt button and bounced back. "You're allergic to *what?*"

"Horse dander," he said, satisfied by my reaction. "And dog

hair," he enumerated. "I'm also allergic to cats and hamsters. Goldfish are okay. Needless to say, I'm a disappointment to my children."

"Why did you come?" I asked, fascinated.

He smiled gently. "Call it a command performance."

Gene Strand had a nice face. He had his father's sharp nose and high forehead and the same angular body. But they inhabited their bodies differently. If Cyrus came across with the force of a raptor, Gene Strand at thirty-nine had the awkward vulnerability of a fledgling. "You work for your father?"

"No, I'm just on the company's board. I'm a psychologist."

"Huh," I said. "So's my mom."

He smiled. "It doesn't sound like your favorite profession."

His listening skills were sharp enough. But I'd had a lot of practice thwarting this particular kind of expertise. "She's semiretired now. Does Pete know about your allergy? I mean, you should be riding up front. Back here you're downwind of all the horses."

"It's okay, I'm on antihistamines. I'll be fine as soon as the pills kick in."

Well, I thought skeptically, he's a grown-up. The trail narrowed as we began to climb. Now and again, I caught glimpses of Monture Creek rushing far below us at the bottom of the wooded ravine on our left. On the right, I could reach out and touch boulders and tree trunks. Joan began to huff and puff like an out-of-shape matron. I felt sympathetic. The trail steepened. Gene and Henry and Lucia were no longer ahead of me, but above me. Behind me, Brett and his mules had fallen back out of sight. Twice Joan's outside hind leg slipped on the edge of the track. As I recovered from the blasts of my own adrenaline, I wondered exactly how "surefooted and mountain-wise" Pete's fat nags really were. Others in the party must have had similar doubts. Conversations trailed off. Pretty soon there was only Lucia excitedly calling out the names of wildflowers as if she were greeting old friends.

"Oh look at the lupine! And here's paintbrush! Indian paintbrush!" She pointed to a stand of brilliantly red flowers beside the trail. "And oh, Henry, what is this one? I forget the name. Look how lovely! Gene, Lee, do you know these, the white ones? The

45

name, it is gone completely out of my head. I am senile!" (Sea-NILE, she pronounced it, with a luxuriant *l*.)

My horse wheezed onward and upward. I let her rest for a moment and peered at the creamy flowers scattered thickly along the high, shady bank on our right. The whorls of green leaves looked familiar. I nudged Joan on. "It reminds me of dogwood," I said to Gene's back.

"Is it some kind of dogwood, Lucia?" he called, passing my guess forward.

"Ah!" she bubbled. "That is exactly it! *Cornus.* And the English name is bunchberry! The deer like to eat it."

The trail became rocky. Among the gray boulders along the bank, breaths of tiny pink flowers floated above a creeping carpet of small, shiny leaves. Twinflower, Lucia called it. In the next breath, she burst out, "An orchid!" She twisted back to Henry behind her. "Back there, did you see it?"

"An orchid?" he asked. "Where?"

"Oh, stop!" she called back to us. She reined her horse to a halt. In a chain reaction, the horses behind her stopped in a bunched-up line. "Just behind you, Henry, by that big rock. You see it, Gene?"

"What are we looking at?" he inquired.

"A mountain lady-slipper! It is very rare."

"Oh, I see." He pointed to a patch of shade. I still didn't see it.

Neither did Henry. He shortened his inside rein, turning his horse sideways on the trail for a better view. The horse, a rusty-colored animal speckled with white like a coarse tweed, took a step forward up onto the bank. Then suddenly his hind legs were frantically scrambling on the edge of the drop-off. In the next instant, horse and rider were somersaulting backwards down the gorge. It happened so fast that all I saw were sickening flashes of pale belly and all four hooves simultaneously thrashing in air. The horse crashed through the trees, tumbling head over heels all the way to the creek bed, a 100-foot drop below. Then I spotted Henry a third of the way down. He lay curled against a large rotting log. He wasn't moving.

At this point, everything went into slo-mo. It seemed to take me a very long time to decide which side of Joan to dismount from. There was no room on the correct side, only the steep drop off the trail. But would she allow me to get off on the uphill side? Exactly how mountain-wise was she? Wise enough, as it turned out. She stood still as a stone while I got off. Gene and Lucia were frozen, mouths open, in their saddles. I told them to get Pete. (Later they told me I was screaming for him.) I slid on my heels down the ravine to the log where Henry was now stirring. Miraculously, he sat up. Then some gear shifted in my brain and things began to gain speed.

"Are you all right?" I demanded.

"I think so." He brushed a rotten leaf off his shoulder. His face was blurred with shock.

His horse, its eyes rolling white, its saddle askew, came plunging back up through the brush. It veered away from us, regaining the trail behind my horse just as Brett appeared with his string of mules. Brett calmly dismounted and gathered up the fallen horse's reins.

I found Henry's new hat in the leaves and picked it up. Henry took it, smoothed back his black curls, and settled it on his head as carefully as a man who's had a few too many. Unsteadily, he pushed himself up against the log onto his feet. He took a couple steps uphill.

"Maybe you should wait a moment," I suggested.

"I'm okay," he said. As if to prove it, he began to scramble up the ravine. I kept close behind him, trying not to huff and puff too loudly, but wondering why we were *running* uphill. The back of Henry's shirt was torn below the shoulder blade, but I saw no blood. As we stumbled up onto the trail, Cyrus and Pete were making their way to the rear of the line.

"What happened?" Pete asked. His dark eyes were intense, but his voice was in neutral.

Henry caught his breath. "Goddamn horse fell off the trail. With me on it." He made it sound like Pete's fault.

"It is my fault," Lucia wailed. "I wanted Henry to see the lady-slipper. Oh, Henry, I am so sorry!"

"Shut up, Lucia!" Cyrus snapped. He turned to Henry and looked him up and down. "You hurt?" he demanded.

47

"No," Henry retorted sourly. "I'm just fine and dandy." He took his hat off, smoothed back his hair, and put his hat on again. He turned to Pete. "If you think I'm getting back on that animal, you've got another thought coming."

Pete considered the statement. "There's no room here to switch anyone."

From up ahead Adrienne called back, "What's happened?"

Pete went on, "We can stop a couple hundred yards ahead and take a break for lunch."

Cyrus approved. He moved up the line, squeezing past horses and riders to give the order to Cory.

"Daddy, what's happening?" I heard Adrienne insist.

I didn't hear Cyrus's answer.

Pete moved back to inspect Henry's horse. Henry followed him. His handsome face was flushed, his eyes at once ashamed and angry, as if he had just been demoted to the back of the class.

Brett had straightened the animal's saddle and sorted out the tangle of reins and halter rope. There were sticks in the horse's mane, but the only visible injury was a gash about six inches long on the rust-speckled right rump. A line of dark blood had threaded its way down the leg. The horse was surprisingly tranquil. With casual flicks of the tail, it swished away flies buzzing around the wound.

I glanced up at Gene sitting rigidly on his horse. His face was grayish.

Pete stroked the wounded horse's neck with a slightly cupped hand. "Can you walk him a short ways?" he asked Henry.

"Yes," Henry said curtly.

Pete secured the horse's reins around the saddle horn and handed Henry the halter rope.

Since I wasn't sure I wanted to attempt to mount Joan with the ravine yawning six inches from my stirrup, it was more out of lack of nerve than kindness towards Henry that I decided to keep him company and lead Joan along on foot. This didn't work out as easily as I had expected. Even in the hiking boots I was wearing (I hadn't wanted to spring for a pair of cowboy boots), the path was demanding: uphill, studded with slippery rocks and droppings from the horses in front. Joan, despite her dramatic wheezing on the way up, was, in fact, a faster walker than I was. This meant she kept her nose on my hat. When she wasn't nudging my head along in front of her, she was trying to scratch her forehead on my shoulder blades. Jabs to her face with my elbow worked for about half a minute at a time. I glanced behind me at Henry. He seemed to be having no such trouble. Even in his dress cowboy boots, he didn't stumble as I did. His wounded horse followed politely, a good arm's length behind him. He was clearly still angry, but he seemed to be spinning a hero-sized cloak out of the accident. With each step, his shoulders became more noble, his jaw became more manly. He might have been a matador about to step into the ring. I imagined Lucia flinging a wild rose at him.

Instead, she threw herself at him. After about ten minutes, the trail leveled out and widened into a small mountainside clearing. Lucia slid quickly off her horse, tied it on a slender aspen, and rushed over to Henry. "*Caro, mi dispiaci! O bello,* I am so sorry!" she apologized. She embraced him for a moment too long, then clasped his head in two hands and drew it down towards her breast. It was an operatic gesture, but both his height and his resistance made it ungainly and embarrassing. She lost her footing, released his head, grabbed his arm for balance.

"Lucia," he warned.

"My God, I have almost killed you!" Still clutching his biceps, she examined the back of his chambray shirt. "Look," she wailed softly. "Your nice new shirt is torn."

Henry looked annoyed. "My shirt's torn?" He peered over his shoulder, then pulled his shirt out of his jeans and over his head like a jersey. "Shit," he muttered crossly as he fingered the rent.

His naked upper body was square, with slightly over-developed pectorals and biceps. A column of curling black hair climbed upward from his turquoise belt buckle and fanned out between his nipples. His olive-gold tan was perfectly even: his neck and belly matched his shoulders. You wouldn't lose money betting that he belonged to a health club with free weights and an electric beach.

"I will buy you a new one, *bambino,*" Lucia apologized. "It is my fault."

"Let him buy his own shirts, Lucia," Cyrus ordered as he

strolled over. "Let's have a look at this fella." He walked right on past Henry to the horse.

"My God," said Adrienne, still on her horse and noticing the horse's wound for the first time. "Lee? How do you get off?"

"Just a sec," I told her. Gene was swaying in his saddle, his eyes unfocused, all traces of color drained from his face. "Pete," I said, as he walked by me towards the wounded horse. I indicated Gene. We strolled over to him.

"How you doing?" Pete asked.

Gene didn't seem to hear. Pete untied the halter rope from the saddle horn and handed it to me. He touched Gene's leg. "Take your other leg out of the stirrup," he instructed. "Okay, now put your hand on my shoulder and swing down."

Gene managed it well enough, but on landing, his knees crumpled. Pete and I steadied him, one on each side. "Get your head down," I said.

He bent over. His hat fell off. His hair was fine and gingery, thinning around a bald spot as gray as his face. He swallowed a small groan.

"What the hell's wrong with him?"

It was Cyrus. His voice was as sharp as ammonia. Gene jerked himself upright. He was still the color of dishwater, but his voice was steady. "Nothing. It's just my allergies," he said.

Adrienne and the others managed to dismount and tie up their horses. They clustered around.

Cyrus stared at his son. "Jesus Christ, look at you," he scolded in disgust. "You'd think you were the one who'd taken a spill." He stalked off.

Adrienne, bustling with maternal competence, took over. "Do you have your medicine?" she asked Gene. "Come on, get your head down. You still look like death warmed over."

Pete and I moved to across the clearing, where Cyrus was supervising Cory's examination of the injured horse. She had taken off the saddle and given Cyrus the reins to hold.

"What do you think?" Cyrus asked Pete.

Pete ignored him, eyes on Cory as her long fingers tested the flesh around the wound. Off to our left, in a grove of small aspen

50

where we'd tied our horses, Brett moved among them, checking and retying inept knots, loosening cinches.

"Pete?" Cyrus demanded.

"Cory's the doc," he answered.

"She's a vet?"

Pete shrugged. "As close as we've got."

Cory said, "It's not at all deep. I think we can handle it with a few stitches. We'll need the kit. Who's got it? Harley?"

"Smokey," Pete said.

I wasn't very swift. It took a minute for me to figure out they were not talking about forest rangers bearing sutures. They were talking mules.

"Cyrus," Pete assigned, "would you mind walking Rex here while we unpack the mule? Just so's he don't stiffen up."

"No problem," Cyrus accepted heartily. "C'mon fella." He gave Rex a brisk pat and led him up the trail.

Pete turned to me. Lowering his voice, he said, "I'm going to give Henry your horse and put your saddle on Rex after we sew him up." He looked at Cory. She nodded approval.

"He's got a tender spot under the blanket," she submitted. "It wasn't there this morning."

"An open sore?" Pete asked.

"Not yet," Cory said.

They looked at me expectantly.

"Clue me in, folks. I'm just a dudely cook."

Pete smiled. "Let's just say Henry's not one with his horse."

"That's putting it kindly," Cory observed sarcastically.

"What makes you think I can do any better than Henry?"

"You can do better than Henry," Cory answered. "Believe it."

"Anything else I can do for you guys?"

Pete took the offer seriously. "Go eat lunch with the guests," he instructed.

My cute mouth. I felt as if he'd told me to go eat my lunch in a beehive. Suddenly I wasn't hungry.

They were lined up in a long, loose row in the dappled sunlight on an apron of grass at the edge of the ravine. Below, the rush of whitewater sent up a muffled roar. They were sitting, curiously

51

enough, in almost the same order as we had ridden. Nat Rosenfeld, the lawyer, sat upstream along with Cyrus's daughter Adrienne and her fringed husband Billy. Lucia and her adopted stepson, Henry, sat together in the middle. Gene, the allergic son, was downstream. I gravitated toward Gene. "May I?" I asked.

"My pleasure," he said.

I sat down with my water bottle and lunch bag and unwrapped a PB & J.

"Hey Lee," Adrienne called down the row. "I just want you to know that this is the first time since second grade that some one has made me a peanut-butter-and-jelly sandwich!"

"Just call me mom," I told her.

"Mom," she said, "I really *hate* peanut butter!"

Everyone laughed.

"Just for that, you pack your own lunch from now on. I'll put your name on the Velveeta. Any other complaints?"

"Don't you worry, Lee," Billy drawled. "Adrienne's not going to go hungry. She brought along enough candy bars to feed an entire cavalry."

"They're not candy bars!" Adrienne objected. "I bought them at the health-food store."

"Hey, Billy," Gene called up the row to his brother-in-law. "I hear they had to bring an extra mule along to carry all your booze."

"Don't come begging to me when you run out," Billy retorted. With a comic flourish, he pulled a small pewter flask out from a fringed pocket and took a "so-there" pull.

In good humor, the group turned back to their sandwiches and the discussion of Henry's accident.

"You're looking better," I said to Gene.

"I don't know what happened to me." He sounded discouraged.

"You had a ringside seat."

"The horse went right over backwards on top of him. I thought he was dead," Gene said grimly.

I took a long drink of water. "Me too."

Up the row, Adrienne laughed loudly. Then glancing over her shoulder, she hushed as her father paraded Rex past the picnic site.

"Cyrus," Billy Caton called to him. "Don't you want your lunch? Here, let us take a turn." Billy started to rise, but Cyrus affected not to hear. As if ignoring hecklers, he marched briskly on with the scraped-up gelding.

Lucia clucked her wifely annoyance. "He is impossible. It is the same with my little parties. I can never get him to sit down and be nice. Always he must be *doing* something."

I took another pull on my water bottle and looked at my sandwich. Half of it had gotten squished around the water bottle. It was as thin as a Communion wafer. I took a bite. The peanut butter and blackberry jam tasted surprisingly delicious.

"My father's never forgiven me for surviving my older brother," Gene said.

I looked at him.

"He was killed in Vietnam in 'seventy-two. Second Lieutenant Cyrus Strand IV. Varsity soccer and lacrosse at Chapel Hill, top of his class at OCS. He was perfect. 'King' we called him. That was his nickname. King Strand."

"I'm sorry."

"Yeah," he acknowledged with a yawn. "Poor King, he got even more perfect after he died." Gene lay back in the grass and shut his eyes.

While the picnickers dozed or discreetly wandered off to find a bush, I joined Cyrus to watch Cory and Pete doctor Rex. It was an extraordinary performance. The horse twitched and shied as Cory sprayed the slash with disinfectant. I was wondering how on earth she was going to keep him still enough for her needle when Pete hugged the animal's neck with both arms and pulled its head down against his massive chest. "Atta way, atta way," he soothed. "You ready?" he asked Cory.

"Go ahead," she said.

Whereupon Pete opened his mouth wide, took a large bite of Rex's ear, and clamped down with his teeth. Rex shivered and stirred uncomfortably, but his eyelids drooped slightly and he stood still enough for a dozen stitches. When Cory had tied the last knot, Pete released Rex's ear, then hacked and spat.

"Old Indian trick?" asked Cyrus.

Pete shrugged. "An old trick, anyway. It seems to take their minds off the problem. The nasty part is all the hairs in your mouth!" He wiped his tongue with his fingers and spat again.

Cyrus chuckled a dirty-joke chuckle, then glanced at Cory and me and thought better of it. He and Pete grinned at each other. Cory hunkered down over the first-aid kit. The brim of her hat obscured her face, but despite the festive gingham of her shirt, her shoulders looked hostile.

It was 2:30 before we moved out again. Henry complained about Joan and after I'd gotten up on Rex, I could see why. Rex's full name was Rex Harrison (on account of his tweed coat, Cory said). He not only felt perkier than Joan the Barrel, he was a good foot narrower—a circumstance that promised the rider diminished pelvic pain, if not complete comfort.

What I found surprising was Cyrus's offer to ride Joan and give Henry his own horse, a large, dark gelding that he had ridden before on his hunting trips with Pete. This move was vetoed by a loud chorus of objections from his family and his lawyer, Nat Rosenfeld. Henry hesitated then joined ranks and refused Cyrus's offer.

"Listen up," Pete called out. "If you need to turn your horse on these trails, turn him *downhill,* not uphill. That way, he can see where he's putting his feet. Any questions?"

No questions.

We made camp that evening at Burnt Cabin, a small clearing bounded by a high wall of gray scree and an icy black creek. We were still in the Lolo National Forest. Pete had planned to spend the first night in the Bob Marshall at a site some eight miles or so up the trail, but no one complained. It had clouded over in the afternoon and we set up the green two-man tents in a cold drizzle. Somehow the stock was secured, the water drawn and filtered, the latrine dug, the wood gathered and chopped, the stove lit. Pete set up a fly over the cooking area. As I heated up Dolores's elk meatballs in sour cream, the Strand family gathered round with their flasks and breathed whiskey down my neck while they warmed their hands over my (note the possessive) pots. Somehow I managed: (A) Not to burn the elk balls; (B) Not to clear myself cooking space with one lightning-fast, all-encompassing karate chop; (C) To serve the noodles perfectly *al dente.*

We ate perched on damp logs Brett had dragged under the fly. There were brownies for dessert and more bourbon and instant decaf in scalding tin cups. Only Cyrus and Pete drank the real stuff I'd boiled up in a battered, gray enamel pot. No one complained about the food. Billy Caton's jokes earned a few groans, but in general, fatigue and bodily aches made the group docile. They retired to their various tents by the time I'd finished washing up—all except Nat Rosenfeld, who had volunteered as dish drier.

"Well," he remarked as he polished the last plastic plate with his terry-cloth towel, "two down. I hope that doesn't mean one to go." His voice was plummy and oratorical. It was easy to imagine him in pinstripes dispensing advice across a boardroom table.

"Two down?"

"Accidents. They say things come in threes."

"But it was just Henry," I objected.

"You're forgetting that trouble Cory had with Joker. Did you see her limping?"

"You mean the mare?"

"No, I meant—" He realized I was teasing. "Cory's a tough young woman," he agreed. "Adrienne says she works for a horse trainer when she's not out with Pete."

"Figures," I said.

He nodded. His belly and his thick white hair suggested Santa Claus, but his eyes weren't merry.

"If you want three casualties," I offered, "you could count Gene. He was still a bit gray at supper. Rex's dive seems to have affected him more than Henry."

Nat took a handful of flatware from the rinse basin. One by one, he dried the forks and laid them in a foam-cushioned drawer in Pete's kitchen box. After a moment, he reflected, "Gene was always sickly as a child. We thought he'd outgrow it."

"He said there was an older brother who was killed in Vietnam."

"King." Carefully, he slid the flatware drawer shut. "Cyrus doesn't speak of him." It was half statement, half warning.

There were only a couple of pots left. "Thanks," I said. "I'll get these." But he would not be dismissed. "How long ago was Henry adopted?" I asked.

Nat gave me a piercing look. "That's another sad story."

I waited. Just when I'd decided he wasn't going to tell it, he began slowly, "Henry Flores was nine. His father, Tony, was Cyrus's right-hand man up in Massachusetts." He paused, then picked up his pace. "Everyone liked Tony Flores. Portuguese fellow. He started out at the mill sweeping floors when he was eleven and by the time Cyrus took over from old man Strand, Tony Flores was virtually running the place. He knew every nut and bolt in that mill.

"When Cyrus moved the business down to North Carolina in fifty-seven, he wanted Tony to manage the new plant. So Tony moved on down. The wife had died the year before. Cancer, I believe it was. There were no other children, just Henry.

"You must understand that in these old New England mill towns, management and labor weren't segregated. I don't mean they entertained each other socially. But old man Strand used to go duck shooting with his workers. The kids all went to the same school, ran around together. Cyrus and Tony Flores had grown up together. So when Tony's wife died, Cyrus more or less took Henry in along with his children. Henry was just a year older than King.

"About two months after the move, the old mill was destroyed by fire. Tony Flores happened to be in the mill that night and was killed along with the night watchman. He'd gone back up to Massachusetts to settle on his house. And apparently, the night of the fire, he'd been out drinking with some of his friends and decided to have a last look at the mill. By all accounts, he was pretty tanked up. Perhaps he and the night watchman had a few more together. The coroner said they'd passed out and died of smoke inhalation.

"Not a bad way to go, when you think about it," Nat reflected. "Cyrus and Tony had been very close. Cyrus felt responsible for Henry. After the funeral, Cyrus came to me and we arranged the adoption. So you see," he concluded, his voice becoming more southern and ironical, "Henry was never intended as a replacement for King. If that's what you were thinking."

I met his gaze. Now there was nothing comfortable about the man. In the drizzly gray light, his face was as judgmental as an Old

Testament patriarch's. I felt embarrassed, as if he'd caught me peeking in a forbidden window.

I folded up the dish towels. "You're not from Massachusetts," I said.

"No," he agreed. "I hooked up with Cyrus when he came down to High Point."

It was 9:30 and still light when I zipped myself into my sleeping bag. I had the tent to myself. Despite the misting rain, Cory had elected to sleep out near the horses. This meant there was ample room to snake my bag around between leaks. The faded green nylon created a luminous, watery twilight, as if I were floating below the surface of a pond. The faces of the Strand family drifted by like reflections broken by wildflowers. Paintbrush, bunchberry—the names escaped me but the colors seemed to glow on the backs of my retinas: crimsons so intense they seemed to vibrate, purple-blues deep enough to dive into, salmon and cream as absorbent as velvet, reflective buttercup yellow, translucent shell pink. Then it occurred to me that in all the excitement of the moment, I never did get to see the rare little lady-slipper that had pitched Henry off the trail.

7

I only knew I had slept because my alarm woke me at six. The walls of the tent were still twilight green and still dripping, no longer from rain, it appeared, but from the condensation of my body heat. My bag felt soggy and cold and I felt stiff and cold. I pulled on a couple of sweaters and jeans over my damp polypros and crawled outside. It was foggy. There was a thin layer of ice over the tent. I found it hard to straighten up. The foam pad Pete had issued me was about as cushy as concrete.

The guests' tents were quiet. The pile of split stovewood under the cook fly was dry enough to catch easily. I got the stove going and the coffee started, then after a visit to the latrine, jogged up the trail a mile or so to work out the kinks in my back. Scattered under the skinny pines on either side of the trail were the most extraordinary flowers: white plumes at the end of three-foot stalks. Bear grass, Cyrus had called it yesterday, and the name had startled me. For a fleeting moment, I saw again the black bear lumbering through the metro station of my dream. But the flower itself was so commanding that, like Cyrano's heroic white feather, it banished the enemy in the dark. It was composed of minute creamy stars, opening from the stem up, so that many of the rounded racemes sported a tight nipple of buds. "Angel tits," Cyrus joked. Not listed as such in any field guide, but the nickname was certainly descriptive, even if angels are traditionally portrayed as male: Michael, and Gabriel, Raphael, Uziel. I stopped and stuck my nose in a clump of them and pulled back. Even in the cold morning fog, their scent cloyed. The sweet muskiness seemed more animal than vegetable.

By the time I got back to camp I felt pretty decent. Pete and Cory and Brett were standing around the stove drinking my coffee. Their duffles were neatly piled under a nearby tree. "Morning," I said. "Do I have time for a cup before I kick you out of here?"

"Help yourself," Pete said.

"I was communicating with the bear grass. Or the splendor therein." I poured myself a cup. Perhaps the only *al fresco* taste-treat as pleasurable as the first sip of hot coffee on a cold morning is the first swallow of a cold beer on a hot afternoon.

"If you want bear grass," Brett said, "wait till later this morning when we get up on Hahn Pass."

"How's your knee?" I asked Cory.

"Knee?"

"The one Joker smashed."

She looked surprised that I remembered. "It's okay. A bit sore," she admitted gruffly. She ducked her head to blow on her coffee. After a moment she volunteered, "I was telling Pete, Joker did okay last night. She's a new mare and she can be real tricky at times, but she's a natural leader. We've been training her on the picket at home, and last night I put her out with a couple other bell mares. No problem."

"What's a picket?" I asked.

"It's a way to tie up a horse," Brett explained cheerfully. (He was clearly a morning person.) "We strap one foot to a length of chain and stake the chain out in the middle of a meadow. If you picket the leaders, the other horses will stay with them. The mules too. They'll follow a mare like Joker to the ends of the earth!"

"And how's Rex?" I asked them.

"Lookin' good," Cory said. "No sign of infection."

"That was a nasty spill."

59

"We were lucky," Pete observed with such sincerity that for the first time I realized that the accident had shaken him.

There was an elephantine groan from the nearest tent, followed by a muffled noise of scolding.

Brett raised an eyebrow. "Sounds like the Catons are awake."

Cory smiled, but a door slid shut over Pete's face. He checked his watch. "Six-thirty. Breakfast at seven-thirty?" he asked me. "I'd like to be underway around nine." He took a last sip of coffee. "You'll want to put a pot of water on. Cyrus drinks tea. And some of the men may want to shave."

I took out my first carton of eggs, used a couple to mix up a corn-bread batter for my Dutch oven, and with a quick prayer to whichever angel presides over camp cuisine, set it to bake on the back of the stove as my contribution to lunch. Breakfast was as western as you can get: bacon, fried eggs, and a mountain of pancakes. There was even Dolores's homemade chokecherry syrup: wine red and tart-sweet, you could almost taste the sun on the wild fruit. It was a delicacy that deserved cut crystal, not a yellow-capped plastic jar.

But Cyrus seemed to be only one in the party who enjoyed the food. Beneath the jokes about tentmates' snores and aching body parts, the family was uncomfortable and edgy. Lucia, who ate standing up in her black cigarette jeans, complained sharply that she didn't see why Pete couldn't have brought along at least folding chairs—when she'd gone on safari in Kenya, the outfit had brought along chairs *and* tables. There had even been white linen tablecloths. (And probably a laundry crew to wash and iron them.) Nat Rosenfeld took one look at my pan of fried eggs and asked if we'd brought any oatmeal. We hadn't. Adrienne was passing out Advil. I thought about getting back on Rex and took one. Henry, the only one to shave, showed up too late for an egg. Brett, thinking himself the tail of the line, had scooped up the last five.

Henry looked immaculate and impervious to the cold. His black hair was slicked back with water, his skin ruddy. While the others huddled over their plates in down vests and designer jackets, Henry displayed himself in nothing heavier than a navy-and-teal plaid flannel shirt open at the neck. The teal in his shirt matched the big turquoise in his belt buckle.

Gene looked up from his plate. His eyes were red and he still looked pale. "Ah," he announced, "our brother has arrived for breakfast." The word *brother* came out almost with disgust, as if he were holding it away from himself with his fingertips.

"Henry," said Billy Caton, picking up the ball, "you look absolutely perfect. Have you ever considered a career as a male model?"

"Why?" Henry demanded suspiciously.

"You know," Billy persisted, "we could feature you in our next ad campaign. Yes, I can see it: the unshaven Euro-male lounging in Lucia's bath sheets, that smoky, come-hither look—"

"Jealous, Billy Boy?" Henry smiled as if Billy's images pleased him.

"I like it, I like it. Just think, Henrico, a painless way to boost the family fortune. We might finally have found the way for you to make your mark."

"*Billy.*" Cyrus sounded weary.

"Cyrus, the great outdoors certainly is inspirational." Billy Caton made a sweeping gesture with his fork.

"You just got egg on your sleeve," Adrienne said dryly.

Her husband examined his leather fringe. "So I have. Well, as long as it's not on my face, right Henry?"

Henry's jaw tightened. Nat Rosenfeld shifted on his log. A night on the ground seemed to have loosened the skin on his face. A patch of stubble on his jaw glinted white. "Pete," he asked, pushing the conversation onto neutral turf, "what do you do after hunting season?"

Suddenly, everyone seemed to be waiting for his answer. "I log," Pete said. "For a gypo logger over in Seeley Lake. We usually start logging in December. But this year, I'm kinda hoping to start work on our house. We've got a log house in mind. I've cut all the wood. I just need the time to put it together."

The nods were encouraging, as if Pete's ambition were somehow a relief. If only life were so simple. No doubt they owned at least a couple houses each. Big, complicated houses. The kind that needed security systems. The kind that kept me in the house-sitting business. Thanks to people like Cyrus and Lucia Strand of Cody,

61

Wyoming, and High Point, North Carolina, and maybe some-where in Italy, I'd been living rent-free since my divorce.

"And what about you, Lee?" Gene asked, as if he could read my mind. "What do you do when you aren't cooking for Pete?"

"I'm an English teacher," I said.

All of a sudden, I became invisible. I could have said, "I'm a poet" or "I'm a house-sitter" and everyone's ears would have perked up. But a teacher? Tune-out time.

"What do you teach?" Gene inquired dutifully.

"Creative writing." A lie. What I do is read. What I do is tell my students how I, at a particular moment in time, read what they've written. How can anything "creative" be *taught*? What lesson plan can dish up a Muse of Fire?

"What about you?" I asked Gene. "What kind of psychology?"

"I work with disturbed children."

Cyrus stood up, impatiently rattling his fork against his plate. "Let's get a move on," he commanded. "Adrienne, why don't you give Cookie here a hand with the dishes." He winked at me.

"Sorry, Daddy," his daughter said as sweetly as Miss Scarlett herself. "But I'm going to help Cory saddle up the horses. She said she'd show me how." There was a slight question in her voice. She turned to Cory.

If Cory was surprised, she kept a poker face. "Sure," she said.

"Keep her away from my horse," Henry ordered disdainfully.

Adrienne ignored him. "Daddy, I'm sure Lucia would be glad to give Lee a hand."

Lucia snorted. "Don't be ridiculous! Lee is being *paid* for the dishes!" She turned to Cyrus. "If it amuses you to help, you know very well how to wash the dishes. I am going to take myself for a little walk." She gave me a gracious smile and handed me her plate, as if it were a tip. "Lovely pancakes," she said. "So light!"

She'd eaten one. Yes, I'd counted.

"Looks like I'm left holding the dishrag," Cyrus said good-humoredly. He clapped Pete on the shoulder. "They don't make squaws the way they used to!"

Pete smiled.

Yes, Massa, I thought.

"In the old days," Cyrus elaborated for my benefit, "the chief used to ride into camp and sit down on the ground and his women would set up his tepee around him. Right?" he asked Pete.

"You're the historian, Cyrus," Pete sucked up.

Where were my Tums when I needed them?

Around 9:30, while Cory helped the guests mount up, Brett and Pete finally loaded my kitchen on Harley, an enormous black mule. To my annoyance, I was the one who kept everyone waiting. Despite Cyrus's help with the dishes, it took longer than I thought to do the lunches and pack up. Then Pete returned one of the boxes for repacking. It had rattled when he'd gone to lift it onto Harley's high, straight back. "Harley don't care much for rattles," he said. "He hears something clinking on his back, he's liable to spook. And on this trail . . ."

I saw Rex crashing on his back, hooves flailing in the air. "Say no more," I told him. I knelt down, took the first layer out of the box, and shook it. *Clink-clink.* I unpacked some more, rearranged pans, cans, knives, while Brett and Pete stood over me watching. I shook the crate again. *Clunk-a-ping.* Brett and Pete didn't move. Not an eyelash. Maybe it was part of the code of the Old West: Don't give greenhorns any help. Angrily, I pulled off one of my sweaters, punched it down into the cracks around the pots, kicked the box, and *ecce,* no light metal for Harley to dance to.

The trail became increasingly precipitous. Monture Creek had been named after one George Monture, a half-breed killed by Indians—this tidbit was related by Cyrus, who unfortunately didn't know the whys and wherefores. Nonetheless, in a gorge some four hundred feet below us, the victim's creek tore vengefully over boulders in its bed. When we reached Monture Falls, I found I could manage only quick glances at the plunging white water below. The drop-off beside Rex's feet made me nauseous. I kept my eyes carefully glued to roots and rocks embedded in the opposite bank.

But at Hahn Pass, the vistas opened up, and as Brett had predicted, the bear grass was so thick on the sides of the mountains that from a distance it could easily be mistaken for snow. We were at about 6,500 feet and there was, in fact, still snow on the trail.

The horses clomped through drifts a foot or more deep, then splashed through shining mud to the next patch. Small, yellow lilies had sprung up through the crusty edges and in places the snow was streaked with pink algae. Watermelon snow, Pete called it. The dudes were delighted. The sun came out and warmed our shoulder blades, loosened the tendons in our necks. By the time we stopped for lunch in an alpine meadow, I felt as if I'd ridden into Dante's redemptive vision of Beatrice: after thirty long-suffering cantos of the *Purgatario,* she finally appears to him in a cloud of flowers rising and falling around her as if they were breathing. It seems unlikely that the profusion of flowers in that high meadow were all white, but that is how I remember them: a miraculous, soft-breathing sea of white drifting against a field of Renaissance green. And above and around this vast lea, so evocative of Old World poetic idylls, there rose the sheltering, sharp-edged mountains of the New World with their dark marches of pines, raw patches of red stone, glinting silver threads of runoff. In such a place, it seemed crass to munch ham and corn bread (a bit underdone on top); and positively sacrilegious to wander off and squat and pee in lilies and asphodel.

Looking back, I see this noontime as the trip's zenith. The warmth of the sun, the dreamlike masses of flowers, together with the respite from the saddle, inspired a celebratory mood. Everyone was kind and funny. Lucia gaily picked bouquets and wove wreathes for our hats. Henry spotted mountain goats, three white specks high up on a red ledge. Cyrus passed around his binoculars as if he were passing out cigars. Adrienne collected the cores of everyone's lunch apples and fed them to the horses. Then the group all pulled cameras out of their saddlebags and began photographing each other, posing and snapping and wisecracking. It's going to work out, I thought with a surge of relief. Pete seemed to think so too. He sent Cory and Brett and me ahead with mules.

It was a long eight miles to camp. One of the advantages of riding with the guests was the regular rest stops. Cory and Brett kept their strings moving smartly along. Three and a half hours in the saddle didn't faze them. There wasn't much chat on the way. Brett showed me bear scat on the trail, and some scratch marks on a lodgepole pine that he said had been made by porcupines. Cory silently pointed to a white-tailed doe in the forest below us. I replotted the dinner menu: since the sky was clear, steaks grilled over a campfire. Dolores's elk chili could wait. I contemplated a Dutch-oven dessert. Save the fresh pineapple. A cobbler with canned peaches, I decided. When the pain in my knees and pelvis began creeping up my spine, I chanted newly learned names of wildflowers, over and over, like a rosary of mantras. Just as I was starting to numb out into Bliss, we arrived. When I slid down off Rex, I had to hold on to his saddle for a moment before my legs remembered how to support me.

The campsite was spectacular: a grassy bank beside a navy blue creek that promised the fishermen in the party native cut-throat trout. On the other side of the creek rose a sheer wall of rock, some fifty feet high and golden-colored in the late afternoon sun. Near the top of the wall, swallows darted in and out of a wide, black cave. With Brett and Cory's help, by the time Cyrus and company arrived, I had the stove going and tea ready: wheat bread, huckleberry jam, oatmeal cookies.

I had an odd sense of having dismounted into a time warp. Perhaps it was crossing Hahn Pass and the peculiar sensation of riding through early spring during what was high summer back home. Perhaps the thin air was doing peculiar things to my brain. In any case, as I unpacked the food, the shape of the day felt strangely familiar. I had done this before. Great Earth Mother cooks again. And again. And again. As if food were an endless, circular liturgy that, if only observed correctly, could soothe away all pain, cure every ill. When my daughter was sick, I had virtually force-fed her double consommés brewed from organic chickens. I had screamed at her over spoonfuls of strawberry tofu milkshakes. And at the end, my heart had soared with joy every time she asked for a sip of Coca-Cola, as if next she might sit up and demand a burger and fries. How could I not have learned my lesson? Why, deep down, did I still hope that a nursery tea of bread and jam laid out on a blue plastic crate had the secret power to bring peace on earth?

Well, it didn't. They picked and jabbed at each other while they ate. I unwrapped the steaks for supper. They were still frozen hard. "Dinner's going to be late," I announced. Some authority in my voice shut them up. They nodded meekly. Wilderness survival lesson number one: don't piss off the cook.

They decided to go fishing while the meat defrosted. Pete and Brett would show them the holes. They went on bickering as they geared up, so I hiked out of camp to the long meadow where Cory had picketed Joker and two other mares. One looked like Pete's horse, but without Pete on it, I couldn't be sure. The three picket horses grazed alone. The rest of the stock had wandered to the far side of the field. I lay down in a grassy depression at the edge of the meadow. The sun was still warm on my face. I closed my eyes and tried to let my anger dissolve. A fly buzzed. Perhaps I dozed off.

Voices pulled me back. I opened my eyes and blurrily through the grass saw Cyrus standing not far away. He was wearing his fishing vest, but carried no pole. Hands on hips, he blocked the path of Gene, who was coming from the stand of pines where we had unsaddled. Then I saw it wasn't Gene. Wrong hat, wrong height, wrong sex even. It was Cory. In her boys' jeans, she looked as angular as Gene, but she moved like an athlete, comfortably loose at knee and hip, casual at the shoulder.

"I'll be glad to get whatever it is you want," Cory insisted.

"My saddlebags are my business, young lady," Cyrus snapped. He took a step forward.

She held her ground. "Everything's secured for the night."

"You think I don't know how to secure a tarp?"

Cory said nothing.

Cyrus's chin went up. He stepped around her and strode toward a green plastic mound in the pines.

She followed him. He wheeled around. "Look," he said angrily. "Maybe Pete hasn't told you this, but *I'm* in charge here. What I say, goes, on this trip. And what I don't need is a smart-ass dyke telling me what I can do and what I can't do."

Cory's mouth opened. She let out a high, incredulous sound, like a crow's caw.

Cyrus gave a worldly chuckle. "Tell me you can't keep your eyes off Adrienne. I've watched you. Well, good luck. She could use a little fun. That husband of hers, he's had his dick pickled in Kentucky sour mash for the last ten years."

Cory stepped out of his way, keeping her eyes on him until she was clear, then she turned her back and walked off across the open meadow.

Cyrus strolled over to the pile of saddles under the trees. I heard the scrape of plastic as he wrestled with the tarp. *None of your business,* I told myself. *None of your business.* Then I saw him walking back toward camp. He was carrying a holster bundled up in its wide belt. The holster wasn't empty. I couldn't see what kind of gun he was carrying, but I could see the satisfaction of it in his step.

My timing was a bit off on the steaks and the thinner ends got overdone, so I decided to guild the lily and dished the carved slices up with hunks of butter into which I'd mashed rosemary and thyme. On the side, I did a hot puree of canned navy beans (mashed through a grater and beaten with a spoon) and a sweet-sour red cabbage slaw, spiked with horseradish from a jar. It worked pretty well, I thought, with the lean, wild meat, unless you were compulsive about putting something green on every plate.

The cocktail hour had been too long, *mea culpa,* and it was dark by the time we finished eating. The mood of the party was still abrasive and the verbal sparring around the campfire was at once funny and painfully sharp. I found myself alternately wincing and smiling at Gene and Billy's more savage thrusts.

Pete turned down all offers of scotch, bourbon, and vodka. ("No firewater, ha-ha-ha?"), Cory and Brett politely accepted. I decided to wait for a nice, big, solitary hit from my own flask after everyone went to bed. Cyrus was the only one of the dudes not drinking. He produced a stainless steel Thermos and instructed me to keep it filled with tea. "I'm a teetotaler," he said. "Literally." I didn't know whether to respond with condolences or congratulations. But I felt a hair easier about his packing a pistol.

Brett had joined right in. He was sitting next to Lucia, hatless, his blond curls catching the firelight, his good-natured face clearly impressed as he listened to Lucia dropping names as charmingly as lace handkerchiefs: an Italian film director; an actor whom she said was gay; a notorious American tennis player she'd met at some cocktail party.

Cory sat back from the circle slightly behind Adrienne and Nat, nursing her tin cup, listening with uncertain eyes to Gene and Billy's parries. Of course they noticed. They began playing to her, Gene the clinical straightman, Billy the fringed clown, daring her to giggle, to laugh, and when she finally did, they whooped in triumph and splashed more whiskey into her cup. Her reserve softened. She was not exactly pretty, even in the firelight, but her face was young and smooth. The word *comely* occurred to me. It had an old-fashioned ring that suited her narrow nose, the almost prim arcs of her eyebrows, the shy twist of her mouth. She raised her cup slightly to the two of them and said something I couldn't hear.

Billy Caton's head jerked in surprise. He turned to Gene. "Do mine ears deceive me? Or is the child a Tarheel?"

Cory smiled, but said nothing.

"Speak to me, Babydoll," Billy demanded.

Cory lifted her chin, as if accepting a dare. "I was born in Missoula," she stated. But both the cadence of her words and the shape of her vowels were stunningly southern.

"Tarheel," Gene pronounced solemnly.

"Darlin', 'fess up," Billy said to Cory. "You are North Carolina born."

Cory shook her head. "I was born here in Montana," she insisted in her usual voice. "But my grandparents were from North Carolina. I used to spend summers with them."

Adrienne, who had tuned in, asked, "Where in North Carolina?"

"Bakerville," Cory said guardedly.

"But that's right outside High Point!" Adrienne exclaimed.

Cory nodded.

"What was your granddaddy's name?" Billy inquired.

"Johnson."

"Lot of Johnsons in Bakerville."

"That's amazing!" Adrienne said, awed by the coincidence. "Henry!" she called.

Henry, who was sitting across the fire with Cyrus and Pete, looked up.

"Henry, Cory's grandparents lived in Bakerville."

"Oh?" Henry said. His tone was polite. But it managed to locate Bakerville on the wrong side of the country club.

"You any kin to Cleatus Johnson?" Billy asked.

"I don't think so," Cory said.

"Johnson," he persisted. "That your daddy's name?"

Cory's face closed. "They were my mother's folks."

Billy lost interest.

When, at Cyrus's command, the party broke up, I tugged at Pete's elbow. "Can we talk?"

He nodded. We walked away from the row of tents, past the kitchen into the darkness under the trees.

"You got rattlesnakes up here?"

"No. There's no poisonous snakes in the Bob. Why?"

I couldn't see his face. "Your friend Cyrus is packing a sidearm," I said.

Nothing.

I said, "Did you know?"

"Yeah, I knew. I asked him not to wear it on this trip. When I take him out hunting, he won't take it off. Makes him feel good, maybe. What, you want me to take it away from him?"

I heard Billy Caton cackling over by the tents. Pete shifted impatiently in the dark. Fear brushed me like the edge of a dry leaf. In the thin, night air, I sensed or imagined a black hump of something solid. Overhead, stars winked, as indifferent as diamonds. "There's something wrong here—with your group," I blurted. "It scares me."

"You?" Pete sounded amused.

I didn't say anything.

"Hey, it's okay," he said. He put out his arm and drew me into a hug. It felt warm and full of wisdom. His body was as solid as a pillar holding up a corner of the earth. I hugged him back hard, and laughed a near-tears laugh. "It's okay," he repeated, as if he was beginning to believe it himself. We moved back toward the dying fire.

8

I half woke around five to what sounded like a party of drunken rafters whooping and yelping as they floated down the creek. Their cries bounced off the stone cliffs above us in long, laughing echoes, but oddly enough, instead of getting louder as the current drew them toward our camp, the racket eventually retreated upstream. At breakfast Pete asked, "Did you hear the coyotes this morning?"

The morning of Day Three (it felt like Day Six) was again icy, but clear. Our filtered drinking water was so cold it made my teeth hurt. I cooked in a woolen watch cap and the dudes ate wearing gloves. Afterward there was no shortage of volunteers willing to get their hands in hot water along with the dishes. Nat and Gene made lunch sandwiches with the leftover steak and Cyrus helped me knock down the stove. Thanks to family teamwork, it looked as if we'd get off before nine. Pete and Brett were baling up our tents and duffles in the manties when Cory strode up to them, followed by Adrienne, who was slightly out of breath. Cory announced angrily, "We're not going anywhere just yet."

"Oh?" Pete said.

"Some animal's gotten at the tack. Looks like a goddamn

porcupine. The quarter straps on two of the Deckers are gone and the breeching's all chewed up. Likewise a couple bridles. And a cinch on one of the saddles."

"Mine, to be exact," Adrienne stated.

The family gathered around.

"What's a Decker?" said Gene.

"A pack saddle," Adrienne said, pleased to be able to explain. "It's what they use on the mules."

"A porcupine?" Nat asked. "What do they usually eat? Why would a porcupine eat a saddle?"

"For the salt," Adrienne told him. "The leather gets sweaty and tastes salty." Despite the crisis, Adrienne had a radiance about her. She shone with the enthusiasm of a young girl in love with Black Beauty or Misty of Chincoteague. I supposed her brother Gene could spout a theory about the psychology of "horse-crazy" women, but I wasn't sure I wanted to hear it.

Pete asked Cory, "How'd it happen?"

"Don't ask *me*," she spat out.

Pete's big, square face hardened. "It's your responsibility."

"I left everything secure."

They faced each other like a pair of boulders.

"Whatever it was didn't chew through the tarp," Adrienne put in helpfully. "It must have pulled it loose somehow."

Cory ignored her. "I left everything secure," she repeated, her eyes fixed on Pete's.

I glanced at Cyrus, waiting for him to own up. His face was expressionless. Lucia stood next to him, solemn-faced and willowy as a model beneath her puffy down vest. Absently, he put an arm around her shoulders.

Finally Pete exhaled. His breath formed a cloud like the speech balloons in comic books. "Let's have a look at the damage," he said. He and Brett and Cory walked off toward the picket area. Adrienne bustled after them.

"Where do you think you're going?" Cyrus demanded.

Adrienne turned, surprised at the question. She ran a hand through her wilted dark curls. Her silver bracelets caught the pale morning sunlight. "I just thought I'd see if I could help."

He sneered. "How did you get so expert all of sudden?"

71

She looked confused. "What do you mean?" The poise and snap she projected as a well-established, competent adult woman dissolved. She suddenly seemed as vulnerable as an overweight thirteen-year-old.

"Stay out of their way," Cyrus said abruptly. He reset his khaki hat with a sharp, final tug and walked away.

"I only wanted to see—" She broke off and shoved her hands into the pockets of her denim jacket. "I thought this was supposed to be a learning experience, Daddy," she drawled sarcastically.

Cyrus turned. "I said, stay out of their way."

Adrienne stared at him. A look of disgust came over her face. "Oh, fuck," she said wearily.

There was an almost inaudible snicker. It might have been one of the mules in the distance. In the next instant, Cyrus wheeled around. In two angry strides, he was nose to nose with his daughter. There was a discernible hesitation, like the second or two a baseball arcing through the air appears to hover between rising and falling. Then Cyrus hauled off and hit his daughter with the full force of his open hand.

Adrienne reeled backward, clutched at Nat, pulling him down with her as she fell onto one of the mantied packs. Disentangling herself from the lawyer, she shot back onto her feet, gasping for breath, blinking away involuntary tears. "That's cute, Daddy," she said. You could see the white marks of his fingers against the side of her face.

Cyrus's lean face was flushed scarlet. A blue vein bulged through the crinkled skin at his temple. "I don't have to put up with filth like that from the mouth of my own daughter!" he raged. "Goddamn you! Goddamn you to hell!"

Lucia was tugging at his shoulder. "Stop it," she cried. "Cyrus, stop it this moment!"

"Really cute," Adrienne continued, more in control of her voice. "I know I don't count. You've never given a shit about me. But you know something? If you hadn't smacked King around so much, he wouldn't have had to run off to Vietnam. You know that, Daddy? You know that?"

There was a horrified silence. Cyrus broke it. "That's not true."

72

"That's what he told me!" she shouted. "He told me that before he left."

"Hey, babe. You okay?" Billy took his wife's arm. Subdued by a hangover, he was unshaven like the "Euro-male" he'd conjured up for Henry.

Nat and Lucia huddled around Cyrus. Henry came back from the creek with a wet silk handkerchief and pressed it against Adrienne's cheek.

"Oh God," Adrienne said grimly. "Now I've done it."

"He'll get over it," Henry said.

"The voice of experience," Billy teased.

"You know it, pal."

Adrienne groaned. "I'm sorry," she told them. She pulled a half-eaten granola bar out of her jean jacket and took a bite. "Mouth still works," she said ironically.

No one commented.

"I blew it," she said with her mouth full. "It's my fault. Gene? Do something," she pleaded.

He looked at her. "No," he said. "I'm on vacation." Then he added clinically, "Our father is not your fault. Let's go fishing," he suggested to Billy.

I moved away. What had she "blown"? I wondered. Simply her temper? Or had she violated a family taboo? Was she apologizing for evoking her dead brother? *Cyrus never speaks of him,* Nat had warned me on our first night out.

Pete came trotting back, light and quick on his feet despite his heavy boots and massive torso. "You ever play football?" I asked.

"It got me through college. On scholarship." He took in Adrienne sitting on a kitchen crate, Henry and Billy buzzing anxiously around her like bees at a disturbed hive. Gene, at the fringes, might have been standing guard. "What's happening there?" Pete asked, looking around for the right mantied pack.

"There was a fight. No fatalities. A couple of walking wounded," I reported.

Pete shook his head, untied two of the packs, and coiled up the ropes. Then he unsheathed the knife he wore at the back of his belt, made a cut at the edge of canvas, and ripped off a long, wide strip. He bundled it up along with the rope. "Bring along that

73

sewing kit." He indicated an old cigar box held shut with rubber bands. An antique dealer would have salivated over it.

It took Pete and Cory and Brett most of the morning to repair the damages. They untwisted the two ropes and from the strands made three skinny ropes. They passed leather strings and awls back and forth and sewed and spliced together chewed-up leather, canvas, and rope, even incorporating Pete's tooled belt, which had the virtue of being considerably the longest. Cory's belt, a plain brown strap, lay curled at his feet like an offering. As the sun heated up, they took off their jackets and turned back their sleeves. The air began to smell thinly of pine, of damp earth. No one said much. Whatever the frustrations of the setback, the nature of the work, the piecing, making do, fixing up, appeared to be satisfying.

Cyrus drifted over with Lucia to inspect. Her demeanor was formal, like an upper-level manager invading the workers' lounge. Cyrus, on the other hand, was relaxed, his mood genial. He shone with the sort of generosity men exude right after their football team has won a particularly agonizing game. "That's what I like to see," he complimented. "Native American ingenuity at work— no pun intended!"

"Damn porcupines," Pete growled, flattening the end of a waxed thread with his teeth.

"Makes you wonder why the Good Lord invented them," Cyrus mused, his voice man-to-man and uncharacteristically folksy. "Sure ain't worth eating. Anything we can do?"

"A couple more stitches and you can hold a mule for me while I see if this rig is going to work." He turned to Cory. "I think we're about ready for Columbine." He held up his handiwork.

"Lookin' good," Brett said.

Cory flipped a hank of hair out her eyes, unfolded her long legs, and, in a quick, birdlike scurry, was on her feet.

Pete picked up her belt off the ground and held it out to her. "Here," he said.

Brett became intent on his sewing.

She hesitated a moment, then took it with a quick nod and, stepping past Cyrus without a glance, moved off to fetch the mule for its fitting.

*   *   *

74

We rode off with Cory's belt around her waist and Pete's belt under a mule's tail. Brett, who had sacrificed his bridle for parts, rode with a rope hackamore elaborately knotted under his horse's chin. The family was subdued but civil on the surface. Their smiles and responses were just a hair off tempo, as if they'd come together for a morning-after brunch and all needed sunglasses.

The trail took us north, high above Youngs Creek through more mossy forests of pine, then descended to the junction of the Danaher which, together with Youngs Creek, formed the South Fork of the Flathead River. We were still on the western side of the Continental Divide: the entire network of blue creek lines on Pete's green topographic map fed the Pacific Ocean. Molecules of the Danaher would eventually waft past Hawaii. But another day's ride over the mountains, and all water moved toward Ireland. This fact of geology seemed significant, but like a Zen koan, the more I played with it, the more elusive its "significance" became.

We stopped for lunch at a clearing on the banks of the Danaher. Lucia took two bites of her steak sandwich and wandered off with her field guide to Rocky Mountain wildflowers. Just as everyone was balling up their plastic sandwich bags, she came back with two samples for us to inspect: both large, flat, lacy blooms composed of small, white flowers with a greenish cast.

"What are they?" I asked.

"Ah-ha!" she exclaimed, her enthusiasm resurrected. "This is the question. If you make a mistake on these ones, you will have a regret!"

"Cow parsley?" hazarded Brett.

"Yes, the parsley family. This one is the water parsnip. And this, the water hemlock. The two of them, they are poison. But this one will kill you for sure."

"Which?" Adrienne asked.

"The water hemlock." She held it up. "It is relative to the hemlock which Socrates was made to drink. Look here, the veins of the leaves? You see how they end in the notches, not the points?"

"Pretty," Adrienne commented. Gene picked the flower up, examined it, and passed it on to Henry.

He took a sniff. "You going to put them on your sheets,

Lucia?" He was poking fun, but his condescending tone irked me. Gone was the kindness with which he had pressed his cold, wet square of silk to Adrienne's jaw.

Lucia laughed. "Now this I did not think of! Maybe I should add some nightshade to my pretty bouquet. And also the death camas!"

"Poisonous percales!" said Billy. "Henry, I think you've got something. 'Sleep like the dead.' I like it. We can package it in black satin ribbons."

Henry tossed the sagging flower to his brother-in-law. "All yours."

Pete's arm reached out and intercepted the pass. He studied the plant's soft, curling leaves with interest. "I think my grandmother used to call this cowbane," he said. He gave it back to Lucia. "Let's keep it away from the stock," he said. "Where did you find it?"

"Where a little stream arrives into the creek." She nodded downstream toward a stand of white pine. "It is away from the horses," she reassured him.

Clouds banking in from the west turned the afternoon cool. Around five, the horses began to perk up and step more lively, as if they knew camp was not far off. The trail widened, descended. The forest floor became more open, the trunks of its trees thickened. Huge, crusty-red ponderosas listed like ancient columns on decaying bases. Pete pointed out a two-foot-high, oval scar in the bark of one giant. The explanation passed back to our end of the line was that the Indians used to eat bark. "In the springtime," Henry, who was riding in front of me, relayed. "The cambium layer. A delicacy, Pop says."

His disrespect was wry. It was hard not to smile, to show sympathy. When his vanity slipped, Henry seemed the ragged underdog of the pack. It was his determination that rescued him from prettiness, which gave him a physical intensity that was hard to shake off, even riding a proper length behind him. Pushing forward, vying for a place, he trailed an aura of pheromones, an exhaust of sexual molecules. Obviously Lucia was infected. And now I was picking it up.

I tried to sound like an interested grandmother. "You have a

76

wife at home, Henry?" I asked him. (*You asshole,* I told myself.)

"Not for the past two months," he said with spritely bitterness.

I decided not to ask about children.

He turned his dark head back. "And you?"

"No," I sighed. "No wife." He didn't get it. "A bad joke," I apologized. "I'm divorced." Change the subject: "You work for Cyrus?"

The self-importance came back into his voice. "I'm a vice-president at Strand."

"And Billy?"

"He's supposed to be in charge of sales."

I let the *supposed to be* go by. "So Gene has no part in the company?"

Henry shrugged. "Well, we're all directors. But no, Gene's not on salary. He just counts his dividends."

"And you don't?" Adrienne's sardonic voice called from behind. "What are you going to pay dear Linda off with? You think you're going to get off any easier than Gene? He not only had to fork over half his stake in the company. He's got college tuition for the twins. You know what Yale costs these days?" she taunted.

Henry's back stiffened. Maybe his kids hadn't gotten in.

Gene, the subject of conversation, was riding up front, a reluctant concession to his allergy. He had a bandanna tied bandit-style around his nose and now and again his head jerked, as if his pills were putting him to sleep.

"Gene's divorced too?" I asked.

"Honey," Adrienne answered from behind me, "this family's Dee-vorce City. I'm the last holdout. And that's only because you can't divorce your father." She dropped her voice a notch. "Not if you want to hold on to your money, anyway. My grandfather used money to keep my father in line and now look at us. Here we are literally in line. You think any of us would have come along on this trip if Daddy hadn't dangled his great big golden carrot in front of us?"

Henry turned back, his face an awkward, angry puzzle. For a second, it was as if one could see spaces between the pieces. Then his voice, urbane and dry, pulled it back together. "That sounds fairly obscene, Adrienne," he observed.

"Damn right," she retorted.

"You're off base." He directed the words around me back to her. "Old Mr. Strand, your grandfather, he refused to move the mill down South. And Cyrus went ahead and moved it. That's not exactly under the old man's thumb."

"Yeah, but it was over his dead body. Or almost dead body. By the time Daddy finally got around to it, my grandfather was out of it. Daddy waited so long the company almost went bankrupt in the move. All my grandfather's machinery was worthless, the buildings had already been depreciated down to zero, and you had all that old, oil-soaked wood flooring just waiting to go up in flames—as you know very well. If Daddy had stood up to his father and moved Strand out of Massachusetts sooner, he might have had enough capital to keep some of his old workers, to bring them down to High Point along with your father." She paused, then added thoughtfully, "That was the main reason my grandfather was so adamant. He saw his competitors moving away, leaving their workers in the lurch, and he didn't want any part of it. Mother said he didn't seem to care that if he stayed, the company would go down the tubes and Daddy would be out of luck along with all the workers. She said she brought it up one time with grandfather—he was in the nursing home by then—and he blew up. He ranted on and on about how Daddy could make it on his own, the way he had. Finally the nurse came and gave him a shot."

Henry didn't respond. He took a leg out of the stirrup and stretched it sideways. Old Kate turned her head to glance at his shiny boot wiggling in air. Henry inserted his boot back in the stirrup and massaged his knee. My own knees didn't feel so bad. But my sit-bones hurt like a pair of cavities. I was thinking a shot of Novocain right between the legs might be nice when we finally turned off the trail. We crossed a shallow creek rippling over a white stone bottom, then a network of black mud ditches winding through aspen, then rode up into a vast meadow where, according to a forest service sign, the Blackfeet and the Flathead indians had fought a couple centuries ago. After the cramped viewlines from the dense forest trail, the battleground's openness seemed to wash away tension and fatigue. A steady breeze blew from the west, turning up the pale green backsides of leaves on the bushes at the edge of the field. Above the distant mountains in the west, Cecil B. de Mille shafts of sunlight pierced a purplish bank of clouds. There was a slight greenish cast to the light and an exciting, prestorm freshness on the wind. The horses' ears moved like antennae, their backs became alert, wide muscles twitched.

We pulled up, everyone suddenly lighter in their saddles. Cory and Brett kept moving, leading their mules across the meadow toward the campsite. "Photo-op," Billy sang out. And postcard perfect it was: Cory and Brett riding with hats slanted down, backs in an easy slouch, the two lines of mules with their roped canvas packs kicking up small puffs of golden dust, the mountains lavender-blue under the heavy clouds. *Dear Mom, Having a wonderful time.*

Adrienne and Lucia and Gene fumbled in their saddlebags for their cameras.

"Watch your horses," Pete instructed. He indicated a stand of lodgepoles on the far side of the battleground. "We'll unsaddle over there." Henry nudged Kate and she broke into lumbering trot. "Walk your horses, please," Pete ordered sharply. Henry trotted on.

"You ready with that camera, darlin'?" Billy demanded. He took off his hat and gave Adrienne a "Heigh-ho, Silver" salute. "Wait," she laughed. "Do it again!"

"Whoa," Billy told his horse, but with one jerk of its head, the animal trotted off after Henry's.

"Pull on your reins," Adrienne called after him. Elbows and knees akimbo, his seat slapped leather in a heavy staccato. I could almost feel the pain of it running up my own spine, but Billy, excited by sensation of speed, whooped with pleasure. His horse broke into a lope, dashing past Henry, who was posting along toward the pines. Billy heaved and flopped precariously in the saddle. "Whoopee!" he yelled delightedly as he hung on with both hands. We all laughed.

"Shit," Pete said. I could almost see the tenents of his insurance policy unscrolling behind his eyes: Thou shalt not let thy dudes out of a walk. "Hold your horses!" he commanded the rest of us, and he took off after Cowboy Billy Caton.

Cyrus, evidently believing that his investment in the outfit exempted him from any insurance company's commandment, took off after Pete.

Easier said than done, this "hold your horses" bit, especially when half the flock has already flown. Rex was tossing his head up and down in protest and doing something offbeat with his feet and the others weren't much happier, so I led out across the field, concentrating on keeping Rex and the others behind me in a rolling walk instead of a rollicking gallop, and I didn't see Cyrus's fall. All I saw was a grouse skimming over the cinquefoil like a fighter jet flying low under radar and Cyrus sliding easily to the ground. The horse stood there stolidly, the gentle dip of its back outlined in liquid gold light. Then I realized its saddle was on the ground with Cyrus.

The astonishment on Cyrus's face erased every wrinkle. Opened-mouthed, he looked as innocent as a nine-year-old stooge. The kid-who-stepped-on-the-banana-peel. His expression sparked another chorus of laughter, Nat providing the bass note, Lucia a silvery descant. The two of them, however, had the wisdom to cut it short. Gene and Adrienne kept going, forcing sheer comic joy into a meaner, gloating kind of laughter.

Gene, catching his breath, called, "Way to go, Dad!"

"Are you all right?" Lucia inquired, trying to suppress the smile in her voice.

"I've got it on film!" Adrienne chimed triumphantly. "How the mighty shall fall!"

I reached Cyrus as he disentangled his foot from the stirrup. "Need a hand?" I asked. I caught him under the arm. He latched on to my forearm and staggered up to his feet, straightening up slowly. Suddenly he seemed not nine, but ninety. A film of dust covered his wrinkles, his blue eyes watered, wondered who I was, then remembered. "Goddamn horse spooked on me," he explained. His voice was steadier than his legs. "Maybe you ought to sit a moment," I suggested.

"Cyrus," Nat worried from his horse, "are you all right?"

"Of course I'm all right," he said crankily. "Don't be such an old woman. I just took a little tumble."

I pulled the saddle blanket out from under the saddle. It was warm and sticky and surprisingly heavy. I slipped it over the sweat-darkened back of his horse. Then I began to try to sort out his saddle. "Was your cinch loose?" I asked.

"Not that I noticed."

"Look." I showed him the end of a strap. It had teeth marks in it. "What's this piece?"

"A latigo. It holds the cinch on. Looks like that damn porcupine again." He snorted his contempt. "All the time Pete took this morning fixing those Deckers, you'd have thought he'd have bothered to check out our saddles as well."

I studied the broken strap. Then I handed Rex over to Cyrus. "Why don't you get the others to camp? My stirrups will be a little short for you, but—"

"I'll manage," he said rudely.

Prince Charming. I held Rex for him as he climbed on. Off they clopped across the battlefield, his engineer's boots dangling below my stirrups, his family in tow. As they passed, they gave me embarrassed nods. Nat was the only one who would meet my eyes. "Thanks," he said.

I raised an eyebrow at him. "Don't mention it."

I managed to swing the saddle back up on Cyrus's horse without spooking him again, then started hiking. Pete walked out to meet me. I showed him the strap. It was on the opposite side of the cinch ring. No one could be blamed for missing it during a routine cinch check. And clearly something had nibbled at the strap. But the teeth marks were scattered, as if the animal had been merely taste-testing. Moreover, where the strap had snapped apart, the leather hadn't been chewed. The severed edges were clean. "Looks like a knife," I said to Pete. "Or a razor. Someone cut it."

He stared at the break, then fingered the leather. "Who?" His black eyes were intense.

My first thought was Cory. I wondered if it was his too. I doubted he knew what Cory had against Cyrus. (I couldn't see her confiding: "Hey, boss, Pops was the one who let in the porcupine.

And guess what? He thinks I'm hitting on his daughter".) Nonetheless, it had been obvious from the beginning that Cyrus rubbed her the wrong way. Of course, he rubbed the entire group the wrong the way. I said to Pete, "Everyone was milling around the horses during lunch, getting stuff in and out of saddlebags. It could have been anybody."

"Take a guess."

I shook my head. "No."

Pete took Cyrus's horse. We walked back, each of us wrapped in a silence as heavy as a wet horse blanket.

Dear Mom, Wish you were here.

9

What did I do for supper that night? A chicken-and-dumplings thing, I think, as a change from red meat. Yes, in my Dutch oven in the campfire that Pete and I debated, the weather looking so iffy. There wasn't enough room in the pot for my dumplings, so I steamed them in gravy on the stove in one stainless steel washbasin. The other I used for a wilted spinach salad with red onion and bacon. Then after I'd cleaned everything up, I mixed up a marinade for the next night's elk stew. No red wine, too bad, but wine vinegar at least, and a good dose of the herb mix *de Provence* I'd brought along and oil and a couple carrots chopped up for sweetness, then a measure of gin begged from Billy and lots of black pepper and lots of squished garlic. I made travel packs, Ziplocing the still half-frozen elk and my marinade into plastic bags. All very Girl Scout. Only I was running short on vinegar and had to resort to a bottle of Crayola-orange, candy-sweet "french" for my next salad. Not that anyone cared what they ate by that time. But I'm ahead of things.

By the time supper was ready, the air felt crackly. The sky darkened early and an erratic wind blew in damply from the west. Violent gusts grabbed the tops of the pines and shook them like terriers breaking spines. The thunder was still too far away to hear over the noises of the wind and trees, but sheet lightning flashed behind the livid clouds, outlining their mass and weight as they shouldered their way up over the mountains, across the ancient battlefield where Cyrus had fallen (the horses were now picketed there) and over the stand of pines that sheltered our camp. The group mood was fairly leaden as we sat around the fire with plates of fricasseed chicken dusted with blown cinders. My dumplings, thank you Great Mother, were blessedly buoyant—bantamweight, if not featherweight. Things were heavy enough without heavy dough. I kept wondering how Pete was planning to handle the business of the cut girth. Had he already talked to Cory and Brett? I got up to make coffee. Cory and Brett excused themselves to check the horses.

"Wait," Pete said. "I want everyone here."

I hunkered back down. Cory and Brett stood at the edge of the circle. "Cyrus," Pete said. "I think you should know this." Heads turned, interested. "It wasn't porcupines that took a bite out of your latigo. Someone made a cut."

Several incredulous voices said, "What?"

Cyrus stopped chewing. He frowned, then swallowed his mouthful. "You sure?"

"That's what it looks like."

"Oh, no," Lucia protested. "Who would do that?" She searched the faces around the fire. "No one here would do such a thing!" she scolded Pete.

"No one's here to do it except us chickens, Lucia," Gene said dryly.

"I'm surprised the darn thing didn't give when you mounted up," Pete said. "There wasn't much more than a thread holding it together. We were lucky it didn't happen on the trail. It could have been nasty."

"Oh, for heaven's sake," Adrienne said, "look at what happened to Henry and he's okay. I mean, Daddy, you could have fallen off when that bird flew up even if the whatsyamacallit hadn't been cut."

"What are you saying?" Billy asked Pete. "That Cyrus ought to watch his back?" The idea seemed to amuse him.

84

"I'm saying someone cut his latigo."

"Somebody's idea of a joke," Henry said.

"Maybe we all ought to watch our backs," Nat put in. "Or at least take responsibility for our own saddles."

"Oh, *good idea,* Nat." It was Gene.

Cory cleared her throat. "Speaking of jokers," she said, "we've got one picketed out there that don't care much for this kind of air. . . ." She looked to Pete for permission. He nodded and she and Brett walked off.

Wind fanned the fire. Sparks sprayed inside billows of resinous smoke. Adrienne and Gene sputtered, waved their hats, moved out of the way.

Cyrus raised his head. "Do you know it wasn't one of yours?" he asked Pete.

"Oh, darling, really," Lucia objected.

"No," Pete answered. "I can't say that."

Cyrus's face was thoughtful. Absently, he turned the wedding band on his finger. He might have been sitting in an executive's high-backed leather chair instead of on a log. He appeared attentive, dispassionate, sensible—as if problem solving was his true element. I could imagine him coming up with logical, creative solutions that minimized loss and maximized gain. I could imagine his workers trusting him. He glanced around the fire at the middle-aged members of family, then allowed himself a small, grim smile. "I can't speak for mine, either," he said to Pete.

"Jesus," Billy muttered into his tin cup.

Right on cue, his cup suddenly radiated an electric halo of tiny sparkles. Fringes flapping, Billy hopped off his log, dropping the glowing cup with a yelp. "My God!" Adrienne cried, "look at the knives and forks!" It was as if in a split second, Tinkerbell had swooped down to sprinkle an electric Disney dust over our implements. Then in the next blink of an eye, it was all back to normal. "What the hell was *that?*" Henry demanded.

"You ever seen that before?" Nat asked Pete.

"No, sir." He grinned. "I've heard of rifles sparking before a storm, but never knives and forks!"

"Damn," Billy said. "Went and spilled my whiskey!"

"Maybe there's a message there," Cyrus drawled.

"You think it's safe to pick it up now?" Billy wondered. "Lee, honey, would you mind handing me that cup there on the ground? Right over there by my brother-in-law's left bootie."

"Don't touch it, Lee!" Gene warned. Clowning, he dangled said left boot over the cup, then jerked away as if the tin had seared his toes.

I pulled back my sleeve like a magician about to perform a feat. "You say you want fried fingers for dessert?" I asked Billy.

"Caton, why don't you do your own dirty work for a change?" Henry demanded.

"Oh Henry, shut up," Adrienne said.

Henry scratched his handsome chin. "It's a bird," he intoned. "It's a plane. No, it's Supermatron in a hot flash."

Adrienne's eyes widened, then narrowed. "At least my hormones produced, Henry. How about it? You think maybe you can make a baby with that new bimbo of yours?"

"Adrienne," Lucia clucked. "This is not nice."

Adrienne opened her mouth, then shut it. She glanced around the group for support. No one would meet her eyes. She considered the knife on the plate by her feet. She reached out and touched it, then picked it up. "It's not even warm," she said to Pete.

He stood up. "We've got a long ride tomorrow over the Divide," he announced. "You might want to hit the sack before this storm breaks."

The group scattered. The first fat drops of rain fell. There was a flicker of lightning above the tree line on the hill behind us. One hippopotamus, two hippopotamus. I counted ten. Thunder rumbled. Ten miles away, supposedly. I stoked up the stove under the fly and prayed that the thunderbird would ignore the stovepipe while I heated up the dishwater. The trees overhead creaked and groaned. The plastic fly billowed and cracked like a sail luffing in a gale. Gene, in a yellow slicker, ducked in and helped me tighten the guy ropes. It began to pour. I dumped the flatware into the basin of hot, soapy water. Gene hovered like a bored child. "What's the matter?" I asked.

"Nothing. I just don't feel like crawling into a tent with Henry, yet. You aren't looking for a well-mannered, nonsnoring roomie, by any chance?"

"Sorry." I handed him a dishrag. "I'm booked."

"You are?"

I smiled at his surprise. "Cory. At least she put her bag in my tent. I don't think she'll be sleeping out tonight like she did the last couple nights." I reached out with a soapy hand for my mug and took a swallow of bourbon and creek water. "You want a drink?" I offered. He hesitated. It was too dark to see his face. "I'll make coffee, if you'd rather."

"I'd love a drink. It's just I tend to do better around Dad if I'm sober. Things stay clearer. I see where he's coming from, the dynamics. It makes it easier."

I shrugged. "He's gone to bed."

Gene laughed. "Well, thanks for the permission. I accept."

Feeling generous, I poured him a stiff one. I set a small battery lantern on one of the food crates and in the shadowy light we worked through the dishes, not talking much. Rain hammered on the fly and blew under the edges, but it was companionable around the stove and I stopped worrying so much about getting skewered by lightning on its way down the stovepipe.

"What do *you* think about all this?" Gene asked with genuine interest.

"What, you mean your father's latigo getting cut?"

"Well, that too, but the whole business, this trip?" He waved a Gore-Tex arm to include the tents scattered at discreet distances from each other in the darkness.

I thought about it. Finally I said, "I never imagined such wildflowers."

"Tactful." He took a swallow of whiskey. "And?" he persisted.

I handed him a pot to rinse.

"I'm not going to let you off with wildflowers," he said. He was flirting.

I said crossly, "You want to know what I think? I think that after you pass ten years old, the best part of any family trip is looking back at it and saying, 'Well, we survived, it wasn't all that bad, actually, it was pretty neat. Hey, remember all that bear grass?' "

Gene folded his dish towel.

"I think that's all your father wants," I told him.

The silence sounded forlorn—O Keatsian word! I switched into pep-talk gear. "Hang on in there. Tomorrow you're over the hump. Literally. We cross the Continental Divide and its downhill, wee, wee, weeee, all the way home."

"Interesting," Gene muttered. "You think he's after a bonding experience."

"Call it the dream of a happy family." I felt a wave of sorrow. Okay, Squires. Time to cork up the flask before you start weeping for your own father.

Gene was not swayed by my poetic turn of phrase. He persisted in his analytic mode: "No, I think his goal is more didactic than that. Dad's fantasy is to have Mother Nature teach us a lesson, turn us into *real men*. None of us could ever measure up to Henry's father. He ran the plant for Dad, you know."

Adrienne a "real man"? I kept my mouth shut.

"I've always wondered about Dad and Tony Flores," Gene mused a little drunkenly. "What their relationship really was. Anyway, Tony was a self-made man. Able 'to stand on his own two feet,' as Dad is so fond of saying. The irony of it is he can't bear any one of us standing up to him. Look at what happened with Adrienne this morning. He's got a real problem with control issues."

"Whoever cut his latigo also has a problem with what used to be called self-control."

"Someone was angry." His voice was authoritative.

"You got an idea who?"

"No. Of course not. It could have been any of us. *Cookie*," he teased, pointedly.

"You don't sound very concerned."

"I'm not. You forget I work with disturbed children. I see and hear unbelievable stuff. When it comes to malice, this saddle business is just a stray drop in the bucket. Trust me."

Trust me. What is it about men who say "Trust me?" Maybe they aren't lying through their teeth. Maybe they actually know something and are simply too lazy to bother laying it out for inspection. But Gene might as well have snapped a red flag in my face. I was saved from charging by Billy, who ducked in under the

88

fly, dripping wet and monkish-looking in a hooded, long black raincoat.

"Let's keep it down a bit over here, shall we?" Billy's tone was severe. "You two can be heard up and down the whole line of tents." He sounded like a dorm master patrolling the halls.

Gene blinked. The lantern light bleached his long-boned face. Rain hammered on the fly overhead.

"Gotcha!" Billy burst out with a happy cackle.

The corner of Gene's mouth turned up and for a second he might have been Cyrus, the resemblance was so strong. They both had the same narrow nose, the same almost invisible, gingery eyebrows over deeply set eye sockets. Their features had a thirteenth-century asceticism, as if they were crusaders carved for a gothic portal. I wondered what the dead brother had looked like. "I was just trying to remember what I'd been saying," Gene admitted with relief.

Billy pulled a flask out of his slicker. "It's Howdy Doody time, boys and girls."

"Okay, Clarabelle." Gene thrust his cup out. "Where's Adrienne? It's barely ten o'clock."

"She's out like a light. How come you're up? You usually fade before she does," Billy observed.

Gene took a swallow from his cup, then gasped. "Gin?"

"I'm rationing my whiskey."

"Gin without ice?"

"Pretend you're British. Do it for the Empire."

I fooled around with the marinade (pouring in a generous lashing of Billy's gin as an inspired sub for juniper berries—yes, it really worked) while they bantered and talked, mostly about colleges—inept admissions interviewers and the torment of application essays, who might or might not get into to Yale or Chapel Hill, or Duke, the family's various alma maters. Billy sounded jovial, but Gene's words were beginning to slur. Then somehow Henry's name came up. It seemed to hang between them like a balloon neither wanted to claim.

Gene shook his head. "The guy drives me up the wall. I almost forgot. I haven't seen him in four years and guess what? He still drives me up the wall." He laughed without humor.

Finally Billy said, "You know, a lot of people at the plant think he's okay."

"The boss's right-hand man. Vice-president in charge of sucking up to Cyrus. What the hell *does* he do there anyway?"

Billy waved the question away. "Seriously. People like him. He's got friends. If you and Adrienne could get off his case for a minute . . ."

Gene thought about it. "The kid was a natural victim." He thought about it some more. "King was the worst," he said slowly. "King couldn't stand him."

Lightning momentarily tore away the night. I blinked. After images of tree trunks floated on the insides of my eyelids. One hippopotamus, two hippopotamus. At five, thunder hit. Billy and I jumped. Gene seemed oblivious. "My father spoiled him rotten," he said. A gust of rain hit the plastic tarp like a handful of pebbles.

Billy perked up. "Who, King?"

"No. Not King. Dad was shitty to King. Henry. When Henry came to live with us, it was always, 'Henry do you want this, Henry do you want that?' Dad always, *always,* took Henry's part. It didn't matter what he'd done. Dad would go into his bit: 'Well, you have to make allowances.' The poor little orphan. Orphan Fannie, King used to call him. But you know what? I don't think Dad even liked Henry. It was all for Tony Flores. It was Tony Flores he loved."

We stood around the stove listening to the rain streaming off the edges of the fly. "Oh God," Gene sighed. "I miss King." Then, to our astonishment, he pressed the heels of his hands into his forehead and let out a great sob.

At that moment, Pete and Brett ducked under the fly. They'd snapped plastic covers over their hats and wore long rain ponchos. They stared at Gene, head bowed with grief, his back shaking.

"Ah, the Irish," Billy said cheerfully. "A bunch of soulful slobs. Eugene, m'boy," he said in a bad imitation of a priestly Bing Crosby, "the parrty's over."

Gene raised his head. His face was pale, his long cheeks wet and shiny in the lantern light. He smiled sweetly. " 'Evening, gentlemen." Then he staggered out into the dark rain.

"You think he can find his tent?" I wondered.

Billy shrugged. "He only had one drink."

"That can do it at this altitude," Pete said.

"I gave him one too," I confessed.

"He's a big boy," Billy said. "Besides, last night I discovered the sole advantage of sleeping on the ground. You can't fall out of bed when you get the whirlies."

"Yeah, but in this weather, he might drown sleeping on the ground," I objected.

"Yes, Mom," Brett teased.

"Alas poor Lycidas," Billy declaimed grandiosely. "He must not float upon his watery bier unwept." I don't know which astonished me more: Milton coming out of Billy's mouth or the leisurely, distinctly southern way he massaged the poet's vowels.

"We'll just holler if we trip over a body," Brett said.

"Without the meed of some melodious tear," Billy persisted. He flung his arms around me. The scent of suede surfaced from beneath the crackle of his raincoat. His body didn't feel as soft as it looked. "The bard of Avon!" he crowed triumphantly. I didn't correct him. His breath was a bracing blast of warm, sweetish gin. I undid myself from his arms, steadying him as he teetered a step backward. Pete and Brett looked amused. "Aren't you impressed?" Billy demanded, peering into my face.

"Very," I said.

"Compliments of my eighth-grade English teacher. Miss Becker. Let me tell you, she had a pair of knockers! Not that yours aren't magnificent, sweetheart," he said kindly to me. In the lantern light, his round face was as red as a polished apple. "But Miss Becker . . ." He shook his head in wonderment.

" 'Bout time to secure the kitchen," Pete said. "There's another front moving in behind this one."

I was soaked by the time I figured out that the zipper on my tent went down instead of up. Dripping wet, I crawled into blackness. The dark had a presence. It was Cory, breathing quietly in her bag. I kicked her once while wrestling my wet boots off, then managed to knee some bony part of her as I burrowed waist-deep into my duffle looking for my flashlight (at the bottom, of course). But she lay still through all my "shit"s and "sorry"s. Not until I was zipped into my bag and my groans had warmed it up a bit (is there any fabric icier than damp nylon?) did she offer a meek " 'Night."

I swore again. There was a needle-like rock under my left buttock. Cory giggled. "Where did you sleep last night?" I asked grumpily.

"By the trail we came in on." In the dark, she sounded very young. "Pete and Brett each camped by outgoing trails. Just in case the stock decided to do a little midnight sightseeing. It's our first trip out this year," she explained. "You can't get out much earlier. The snow's too deep in the passes. And when the horses and mules are fresh, you have to watch 'em a bit more. But we've been checking the pickets since this storm started and they're doin' okay. Even Joker," Cory said with some pride. "She can handle it."

Thunder rumbled. A cold drip hit the left side of my forehead. I slid my head to the right. "So where's Pete tonight?"

"He and Brett set up their tent next to Cyrus's." There was an odd tone in her voice.

"Pete's worried about Cyrus?" I said casually.

She didn't answer.

"On account of this cinch business?" I pressed.

"More like Pete's worried the old man'll nail someone with his antique forty-five. Someone gets up to take a leak, and bam."

We listened to the rain.

"No one's out to kill the guy," Cory said softly. Her words were apologetic, as if she were talking to a priest in the dark of a confessional.

I let out a small grunt of absolution.

I was almost asleep when she asked, "Your father alive?"

"No," I said. "He died a couple years ago."

"Oh," she said. Then she asked. "What was he like?"

"He was okay. Look, Cory, can we have this conversation in the morning?"

She said nothing.

I suppressed a pang of annoyance. I did not want to conjure up my relationship with my father in a cold, leaky tent in the middle of the night in the middle of the wilderness. "What about yours?" I asked by way of diversion.

"I never really knew my father. He was killed in Vietnam."

"Did your mom remarry?"

"When I was five."

I waited for her to go on.

Instead she said, "Goodnight."

She slept soundly through the storm that kept waking me up. (Or was it the fault of the rock I had to keep worming around?) Thunder seemed to stir the ground. Violent cracks of lightning silvered the sides of the tent like a home-movie screen. I remembered making shadow dogs, rabbit ears, a swan in the white light of 35-mm projector after birthday-party cartoons. I remembered raising the shadow of my third finger, the way my brother had taught me, and getting sent to my room without any of my chocolate-iced angel-food cake. Nineteen fifty-four. I was four years old. Then bingo, in the space of a blink, I was forty, skin losing its hold on elbow and knee, my brother already gone gray.

10

"Cory." Pete's voice, sharp as a blade, ripped through the thin, dripping nylon of our tent. The light was dark gray and it was still raining. The sweater I'd balled up for a pillow had vanished and my neck felt like one of the mules had stepped on it. After a moment of cautious experimentation, I discovered I was not, after all, paralyzed. I wormed my arm out of my bag, stretched it over my head, and squinted at the faintly luminous numbers on my "lady"-sized Timex. A fuzzy 5:56. Pretty soon I was going to need either gentleman-sized numbers or a pair of specs.

"Cory!" A second, urgent jab from Pete.

I shook her bag. From the depth of it, she made a small noise. "What's the matter?" I said to Pete through the tent.

His voice was quiet and intense. "Get out here. Both of you."

Fear tugged at my stomach. "Cory," I hissed.

Ten minutes later, without rebraiding my hair, or even a detour to the latrine, Cory and I stood in our cheap, rubberized rain gear under the dripping pines staring at Joker's picket. At that moment, of course, I didn't know what it was, this metal spike and eight-foot length of chain that Pete threw down at Cory's boots like a gauntlet. Specks of mud splashed our faces. The vehemence of his gesture startled me, made me take a step between them. Perhaps sleeping in the same tent with Cory—or the childishness of her voice in the dark—made me protective of her. But Cory stooped and picked up the chain, running it through her chafed, capable fingers, and stared at the last, empty link.

She scowled. "Where's the strap?"

"She broke it clean off," Pete said.

"You mean, she's gone?" Cory's voice rose on an incredulous note.

Brett shushed her, gesturing to the sleeping tents.

"I checked it!" Cory exclaimed in a hoarse whisper. "There was nothing wrong with the strap. She was acting snorty but she wasn't going anywhere. I checked her three, four times. *You* checked her!"

"It's all old leather, those picket straps," Pete said flatly. Under his plastic-sheathed hat, his large, pockmarked face seemed to have shrunk slightly, like cement hardening. There was something at once noble and exasperating about his stoicism.

Brett said, "She's taken them all, Cory. Mules, horses, they're all gone. All but the other two pickets. Joker, she must have just gone wild in that storm." There was admiration on his sleep-thickened face. Dampness had darkened the blond curls under his dripping hat, and there were smudges on his upper lip and chin of boyish beard, definitely sprouted but not yet spread. He had the tanned, radiantly healthy, but unformed looks of a champion Frisbee tosser or a world-class mogul skier. Add twenty years and a fistful of wrinkles and he might make handsome.

And Cory? Twenty more years, laugh lines and crow's-feet—would my beauty recipe work for her? Would wrinkles soften the pinched look of her prim, oval face? She dropped Joker's picket and took a breath. "Let's go have a look, then," she said to Pete.

"Right."

"You want me to stay here?" Brett didn't sound happy.

"For now."

"You guys don't want breakfast?" I asked.

"We'll be back for it," Pete said. "There's no rush about it, anyway. Might as well let the dudes sleep in."

They strode off through the pines toward the meadow where

95

the last two horses stood calmly in the rain. Brett and I headed for the cook fly. "What's going to happen?" I asked.

"They'll track 'em down and bring 'em back. Sooner or later."

"You wanted to go."

"He's worked with Cory longer." Brett held no grudge.

"But hasn't all this rain washed away the tracks?"

"If it hasn't washed away the trail with them," he agreed. He mulled over the problem, rubbing the back of his neck, then raising his head and observing, "There'll be road apples."

"Road apples?"

"The droppings," he said, delicately.

"Oh. Wait a sec. You mean real live cowpokes don't say 'horseshit'?"

"No, ma'am. Not to ladies."

"How sweet."

He shot me a sly look. "Nor muleshit, neither."

I laughed. "Okay, Cinderello." I handed him a canvas bucket. "Go fetch a pail of water." He was a nice, sunny, responsible, sincere kid. I hoped there were a lot more out there like him. I picked up Pete's ax and hacked some stove kindling from my damp pile of fallen pine limbs. The ax was beautifully sharp. I wasn't real swift with it, but I didn't cut off my toes, either, and the wood was dry enough under the wet bark to get the stove going quickly.

The rain fell patiently, as if it had all day. By 7:30, I was combed and coffeed, if not clean under my slicker. Brett made the rounds of the tents, passing in tin cups of scalding hot coffee. This to please Lucia, who had waxed nostalgic about how the "boy" on their Kenyan safari had woken them with tea at sunrise. Grateful groans rose from one tent after the other, all but Cyrus's. Lucia needed creamer, for which Brett happily trotted back through the rain. Then she needed her Equal, which she claimed she had left somewhere in my kitchen box. We couldn't find it. I felt like wringing her glamorous little Milanese neck, but Brett didn't seem to mind. As for Cyrus, he didn't drink coffee.

He was the first to appear under the cook fly, booted and slickered à la L. L. Bean, his lumpy, canvas fisherman's hat soggy on his head, his stainless steel Thermos in his hand. He wanted hot water for his Earl Grey, more hot water for a shave.

"First come, first served," I chirped. But he looked bad. Talk about skin sliding off one's bones. His eyes looked slightly bruised, as if rocks had found their way into whatever he was using as a pillow. He seemed to have difficulty moving.

"You look a bit saddlesore," Brett said kindly.

"It's my back," he snarled. "That fall yesterday. I must have twisted something. Goddamn!" he exploded. "A *nothing* spill, I just slid off that horse, and look at me! I'm creaking around like a cripple! Where the hell's Pete?"

Brett told him. I half expected a tantrum but Cyrus was philosophical about the stray mules and horses. The prospect of a morning in camp was perhaps a welcome relief.

Cory and Pete were back in time for pancakes. On their search, they had split up, Cory going on up the trail a couple miles while Pete backtracked. Cory found no sign of any stock, but Pete found windfalls of "apples" along the trail we'd ridden in on. He also found a pair of backpackers camped just above a fork in the trail who said they thought they'd heard bells during the storm. It was hard to tell, with all that racket, but if they had to guess, they'd say the sounds were moving north toward Big Prairie. They added that they'd come from Big Prairie the day before and there had been a large group camped there with more than three dozen horses. They'd assumed that some of that outfit's bell mares had gotten loose.

"So you think they're at Big Prairie?" Adrienne inquired. She, of all the group, looked rested and ready to go. The delay was a disappointment to her.

"Unless they've gone all the way back to Monture," Cory said. There was stubbornness in her voice, as if she were still arguing her point.

"We'll try Big Prairie," Pete said firmly.

"How far is that?" Adrienne asked.

"About ten miles. We should be back with them this after-noon. We'll stay on here tonight, then get an early start tomor-row." He glanced out at the drizzling sky. "You might be able to get some fishing in later on. Brett can show you where the holes are."

Brett tried not to look surprised.

"Ah," said Lucia, "here we are." She had taken her green topographic map, still crisp as a new dollar bill, out of its Ziploc bag and unfolded it on one of the kitchen crates. I peered over Henry's shoulder at our quadrant. The area called Big Prairie was a fat, blue-dotted worm bisected by a meandering vein of creek, which, further up, widened to become the Flathead River. There were two main trails (lines of black hyphens) leading into the area, and a ranger station (a tiny, hatted rhomboid) maybe half a mile south of a peak labeled Packrat Mountain.

Lucia ran a finger west, across the black line demarking the Continental Divide, to a spot circled in red Magic Marker. "Here's where we were supposed to spend tonight," she said.

"We can make it up tomorrow if we push a little," Pete reassured her.

"Oh no," she protested. "We do not need to kill ourselves for the schedule. It is very nice to have a—how do you say—layby?"

There was a general murmur of agreement.

Pete smiled. "Layover."

"Will we still see the Chinese Wall?" Adrienne worried.

"It's not going anywhere," Cyrus hurrumphed.

"*Esattamente*," Lucia chimed in, catching Adrienne's eye and warning her off with a shake of her head that was scarcely more than a tremor. "We could all use a little rest."

It occurred to me that Cyrus had not spared Lucia his bad night. Clearly, a ride over the Divide in the pouring rain was not what the chiropractor ordered. It was easy enough to imagine those high, narrow trails turned to brown soup, the sudden jerks as the steaming horses slipped and slid, the wet saddles, the relentless, dripping forest spiked with broken, shade-killed branches, the *pain*—though I had to admit, my crotch was feeling better. After breakfast, I might try a short hike up the hill behind us. Then again, I might hole up in my wet tent with my whiskey and try a paragraph or two of the paperback I still hadn't opened. And after that I might cook up a hot lunch. Chicken soup made from the leftover base of my fricassee, toss in a handful of rice, more on-

98

ions—maybe, just for fun, use those nodding wild ones Lucia had identified for us—and hot bread. I decided on my dear, dead granny's old-sod soda bread. The thought of her grumpy self cheered me. Had Cyrus, for all the Irish in his face, ever broken a crossed loaf of hot soda bread?

I asked him. "Yes," he said. His mother had an Irish maid who sometimes made it for herself. "It was never served at the table," he remembered. "My mother always had little dinner rolls." He was sitting on the ground, knees up around his chin, nursing his tea in both hands as he stared, unseeing, at the veil of rain dripping off the fly. It was brighter now, the rain was almost white. It erased the mountains, leaving only the smudges of pines, charcoal on oyster gray. My rinse water was starting to boil. I moved the basin off the stove and onto the ground. Squatting, I slid the soapy breakfast plates, one after the other, into the scalding water. "You need a hand?" he offered. I had the feeling it would take a major act of will for him to move even a toe. "No thanks," I said.

"I grew up in a New England mill town," he reminisced. "The Italians had all these bakeries, I remember the smell of their bread baking. I had a friend—Henry's father, actually—and his mother used to give us great slabs of the Italians' bread after school. We'd smear it with butter and sprinkle sugar on top." He took another swallow of tea, holding his cup in both hands. "I used to ask my mother to buy bread like Mrs. Flores, but she wouldn't have it on her table. She thought it was inferior, like the maid's bread."

The others had scattered, off to find fishing gear, hiking boots, bird and flower books, binoculars. Brett was going to take Nat and Henry upstream with their rods. Lucia and Billy and Adrienne set out for a stroll along one of paths that came and went through the woods around the camp. Gene retired to his tent to sleep off both his antihistamine and his hangover.

Over his tea, Cyrus rambled on about his upbringing. At the time, I figured it was the mention of soda bread. Like Proust's famous madeleine, a remembered flavor had popped Cyrus into his own private attic of childhood memories. A fine pastime for a rainy morning. (I remember exploring my mother's attic in our old house with the tattoo of rain on the eaves. What had happened to all that precious junk when she moved? The undistinguished pre-war pastel portrait of her at seventeen, or the seatless gilt ballroom chair, or the crates of old books, their thick, musty pages spotted brown? Had my ever-greedy brother appropriated these things? I found myself wanting them. (Right. No trouble to tote around with my backpack from mansion to mansion.)

Anyway, now that I look back on Cyrus, with his hurt back and his tin cup of tea, I believe he wasn't simply adrift in time past, in the nostalgia of *temps perdu*. I believe he was struggling, evaluating, working his way through to the decision he made later about his children. I believe he was judging them the way his own parents had taught him to judge himself. There he was, talking it all out and I wasn't home, I wasn't really *listening*. Not that I could have prevented anything. But perhaps things would be clearer to me now.

So. The man meandered, backtracked, repeated himself, and I nodded and said "hmm" and washed the dishes and considered the weather (which seemed to be lightening up) and plotted menus and revised Pete's shopping list for him (next time . . .). What I did hear, the bits and pieces of your basic poor-little-rich-boy story, made me impatient. For Godsake, get on with it, I wanted to scold. I was not disposed to kind feelings toward this man who had smacked his daughter, sneered at his son, and insulted us, "the help," with his big-white-chief bigotries. So when he conjured up this gangling, lonely boy in a big house on a hill, my heart didn't get squishy. I had the impression of dark porches and dark paneled halls and a long, dark banister down which he was forbidden to slide. The house is now a public library, Cyrus told me with bemusement. His father left it to the town in his will.

Cyrus had been the richest boy in town. His father owned the mill there, but allowed him no pocket money. He had earned it himself delivering newspapers on a bike bought by mowing other people's lawns. Their own grass was cut by an Italian gardener who grew zucchini and eggplant—exotic vegetables for his own use—with the carrots and peas for his employer's kitchen.

Cyrus clearly admired his father. He proudly told long-winded stories about how he, Cyrus, had "gotten the strap" for assorted transgressions I didn't quite grasp. It was as if he'd omitted the bottom line of these incidents. I made polite noises of pity. "Oh, I deserved it," he chuckled. "I was a handful. My mother just about gave up on me." The highlight of his youth seemed to have been the times his father took him along duck hunting. He described waiting for dawn in an icy blind with his father and a worker named Guido from the plant who had lost his left thumb and who had a way with the dogs.

He didn't speak in any concrete way about his mother. In my mind, she remained a refined sort of shadow, a woman who probably wrapped her Parker House rolls in monogrammed white linen. He mentioned a sister, now dead, and her three children, two girls and a boy, all "artistic"—which, in Cyrus's view, was well enough for the girls, but unacceptable in a grown man. (As Adrienne had complained more than once on the trip, the women in the family appeared not to count when it came to the family business.) "My nephew fools around with what he calls paintings. He's never shown the least interest in working. Like the rest of them. None of them has amounted to anything worth a damn. All they care about are their dividends." Cyrus's voice was bitter. "They have no idea of the sacrifices I've made," he said. Then he was quiet, as if reviewing a lifetime of offerings he'd lain on the altar of family prosperity.

"Sometimes things happen. . . ." He trailed off. I glanced up from the dishes, then quickly looked away. His weathered features were anguished. For the first time during his monologue, I felt the prickle of real sympathy. I wanted to hear him. I stopped rattling pots and pans. But the silence seemed to toll him back from his pain. His face cleared. In a conversational tone, he remarked, "For a long time, I hoped Henry would be able to take over." He studied the empty cup in his hand. "When I retire," he explained, including me in the conversation.

I made a listening noise.

"But there's no one. Not one of them is capable." It came out baldly, a decision still raw, still hurting, but nonetheless firm and final.

Sometimes things happen. . . .

I thought he was talking about King.

I can tell you that the grief of losing a child is not simple. You can hope that time will distill your loss into pure sorrow, but that hasn't happened for me yet. I still haven't gotten over the guilts. And neither, apparently, had Cyrus. His daughter Adrienne, shrewd in her fury, had pushed the right button: *It's your fault, Daddy. If you hadn't beaten up on King, he might still be around to run your precious plant.*

If only, if only. After a while, you don't allow yourself to finish the sentences. A little mental-health bell goes *ding,* and you turn your back on the vision of your child standing there in the ring, waiting.

If only. That rainy morning in the Bob Marshall Wilderness, I believed Cyrus was seeing his oldest son behind his squeezed-shut eyes. Now, safely back in my many chambered mansion, I wonder if the ghost flitting across his eyelids wasn't Tony Flores, Henry's father.

11

The rain stopped after lunch and, nonchalantly, the sun came out. Our tents steamed, pine needles glinted like prisms, the wet grass unbowed, sleeping bags and slickers were strung across lines. By late afternoon, when Pete and Cory rode sedately back into camp, the only sign of rain was the lack of dust under their horses' hooves. They had not found the lost stock. But despite the futile six-hour hunt, the riders and their mud-splattered horses looked scarcely worse for wear. Pete greeted us cheerfully and Cory smiled her shy smile.

There wasn't much of a welcoming committee: Cyrus had gone fishing with Brett and the others, Adrienne and Billy had disappeared with their towels and a bottle of biodegradable shampoo. So to greet them there were only Lucia, who was sketching away at the edge of the field, and I. I'd been trying to nap under a thick old pine that seemed to belong to a population of teeny, sap-sucking ants.

Under the cook fly, I made fresh coffee and put out a leftover wedge of my granny's soda bread and a jar of strawberry jam. Pete and Cory tore into it. "Well," Pete admitted, between mouthfuls, "Cory was right. They must have gone back all the way out to Monture. If those campers heard bells, they weren't ours."

The plan was, Pete explained to Lucia, to rest up a bit and leave around six. It didn't get dark until almost ten, so he'd be able to track pretty much all the way back to Hahn Pass. He figured he'd take Brett, and leave Cory, who knew the camp drill, with us. He and Brett would get to Monture around two in the morning, round up the stock, and get a couple hours' sleep. It would be slower coming back with the whole herd of them, but if they left Monture early the next morning, they should be back around five in the afternoon. "I'm afraid you are going to be stuck here another day," he apologized.

"I am very content to be here." Lucia gazed into his eyeballs as if he were Prince Charming locking the bedroom door behind him.

You couldn't really say her erotic current went over Pete's head. It was more like it parted and went around him, the way water divides around a boulder. Who knows? Maybe below the surface he was tickled, but on top, in the open air, he didn't budge a millimeter. He seemed benignly impenetrable, like the sun-warmed surface of an ancient rock.

Lucia worked a little harder. (Catty? Who, me?) She flashed him a conspiratorial smile. "It will be good for Cyrus to stay off his horse one more day. It will give his back a chance to heal."

"Oh?" A sharp edge to Pete's politeness.

"It is nothing. A little twist when he fell yesterday. I will work it out for him tonight in our tent." Another little smile. She looked terrific. Her blond lambsuede shirt was open at her neck (lightly tanned and just barely crepey) and cinched around her petite-sized waist with a plain silver-buckled strap. A pair of horn-rimmed glasses on the top of her head held her frosted, blond bangs off her faintly lined forehead and out of her large, gray eyes. They were smart eyes. They noticed that neither Pete, nor Cory and I, was interested in what she could do for Cyrus in his tent. She shrugged a small European shrug and shifted gears. "For me, another day here is perfect. I am not yet finished with my flowers. Here, I will show you."

She pulled her glasses down onto her nose and flipped open the sketch pad she was carrying. I was impressed. We were all impressed. Her drawings were meticulously correct. With a super-

104

fine pen and a swift hand, she had inked in bristles and bracts, clusters of tiny pistils and stamens, tendrils and filaments. But her underlying soft pencil transcended botanical virtuosity. The long sweep of stem, the enlarged, slightly distorted petals had emotional power. Lucia's cinquefoil and wild geranium, her yarrow, stonecrop, and lupines stretched and burgeoned, as if in the next blink, they might spurt off the page. But she had anchored them to her pad with taproots and rhizomes. Although only roughly sketched in, the roots were nonetheless startlingly sexual. And like their blossoms, their line was off—twisted a bit, as if writhing below their networks of skyward-shooting blooms. I wondered how such drawings translated into bed linens. Certainly there was nothing comfortably pretty about the preliminaries.

"Tomorrow I will work with my colors," she said, satisfied by our compliments. "Of course, I have my camera, but I cannot count on film for my palette."

I will confess I was surprised by her talent. I had not expected it in a woman who came across as an elegantly groomed Circe. I suppose I thought *real* artists should be messy, if not dirty, in their personal habits. The artists I knew generally were slobs. A self-fulfilling American stereotype?

Pete and Brett had an early supper of my gin-spiked elk stew, which had been simmering on the back of the stove since lunch. They rode out as the dudes were pulling out their flasks for cocktail hour. Only three of the trout fishers had caught anything, and of those, Nat and Gene had to throw their catches back—huge cutthroat trout, nearly two feet long, they estimated excitedly. But according to Montana game laws, keepers had to measure between eight and twelve inches. Henry presented me with an eleven-inch cutthroat to cook and passed it around as an *amuse-gueule,* as Simone Beck might say. He was excited by his catch. As he had pulled it from the water, he related happily, it had gleamed like a fish that could grant three wishes.

"And what did you wish, Henry?" Adrienne asked sarcastically.

Henry folded in upon himself. There was an almost ritual dignity in his withdrawal.

"For that, Adrienne," Gene pronounced, "you forfeit your bite of Henry's most marvelous trout!"

"Well, *excuse* me," she said. She rose to her feet and left the family cocktail circle in a huff ignored by all.

Well, Henry's trout was indeed most marvelous. I couldn't resist accompanying it with a vinaigrette of roasted peppers. I was sorry Pete had missed out on tasting his money's worth of the red and yellow peppers we'd debated in the supermarket. But he'd given my stew a surprised nod of approval. For the family, I did a polenta on the side (there was plenty of cornmeal) and that worked pretty well. If the meal needed a headline, it might have been: YUPPIES STRANDED IN WILDERNESS WAX LYRIC OVER PEASANT FARE. The only flaw was dessert: canned pears, speared directly from the tin. I hadn't had time for anything more. With four hands—or better yet, with Julia Child along, I might have been able to present them caramelized in maple sugar. Maybe even *flambé* in someone else's booze. I wasn't about to sacrifice mine. In fact, we all had begun to keep a jealous eye on our flasks. No more lavish offers of "Here, have some of mine."

After supper, Cory took the ax and Handsome Henry along to chop more deadfall for the campfire. I left the pots soaking and climbed the hill behind our tents. On the deer trail I followed up through the firs, it was deep twilight, too dark to distinguish individual fern fronds or identify the small, waxy blooms sprouting beside clumps of wet moss. The light was deep lilac, a fairy-tale hue that reminded me of the story I used to read my daughter about princesses escaping underground to dance the night away. I was climbing upward, not down a secret stone stairway, but in terms of light, the destinations were similar: the princesses wound their way through night forests to a ballroom exploding with golden light; I wound my way up through lodgepole pines to a high meadow bathed in a rosy alpenglow. I felt a sense of freedom and exhilaration. I felt like dancing. I took off my hat and dropped it in the flowers at my feet. I tried out a few Isadora Duncan moves that didn't work so well in hiking boots. Then, arms, hands, fingers yearning, reaching, I attempted a Dying Swan. Forgive me Anna Pavlova. I was hopeless. The sky was hard, a dome of judgmental blue. A single, epic-sized cumulus cloud began bulking

106

up over the treeline on the far side of the meadow. Its edges were tinged pink, but the sheer mass of it was threatening. I stood there a long time watching the cloud gather and grow like an atomic mushroom flowering against the blue wilderness sky. For reassurance, I broke off a bloom of cinquefoil. The soft petals were colorless in the fading light. The stem felt sticky, as if it leaked invisible blood. I stuck it into my hat band, then strode out across the meadow. On the far side, I bumped into Lucia and Nat making love.

To be accurate, I should say Nat was making love to Lucia. He was prostrate between her knees, his jeans still up but his belt flapping, and she was stretched out naked on their jackets, watching the giant cloud overhead and lightly directing his head with her hands down over her stomach to her sex.

I should also say that I didn't actually bump into them. I bumped into her black riding boots, neatly together in the grass, her socks draped casually across the open tops. When I looked up from this still life (it might have been torn from a Ralph Lauren ad), there they were, not twenty feet away. She saw me, but never blinked. Her gaze was as deep and steady as a doe's. Maybe she was having too good a time to be embarrassed. But it embarrassed me. I flushed and turned away, my cheeks burning like a twelve-year-old's.

It was dark at the bottom of the hill. Cory had a good blaze going and the firelight slid across our tents and flickered on the undersides of branches. Cyrus and Billy and Adrienne stood around the fire, cups in hand, not talking. Under the cook fly, Cory and Henry were building up a new stack of stovewood. I thanked them and set to work on the dirty stewpot.

"Did you see Nat and Lucia?" Henry asked. "Cyrus wants to talk to Nat. He's got some bee in his bonnet. They said they were going to explore that meadow above us."

"I saw them." It probably didn't come out as casually as I intended. Henry didn't say anything. I looked up from my dishpan. He had an odd expression on his face.

"They were—busy?" he asked, almost kindly. It was the sort of tone in which policemen question small children.

"You might say so."

I could feel Cory's interest prickling. She looked from me to Henry and back again. I ran my hand around the inside of the stewpot, scraped at a scab of burned food with my soap-softened fingernail.

"That's been going on a long time," Henry said quietly. "Don't worry about it." He sounded protective, like a knowledgeable older cousin.

"I'm not worried."

His face closed. I'd wounded him. What was the matter with me? It wasn't like I'd never heard of adultery before. I'd even participated in it myself. ("If you want to call it that," said a be-kind-to-yourself voice. "Oh?" I snapped back. "There's another name, maybe?")

I saw Lucia's passion-dark gray eyes gazing through me, innocent and uninterested as an animal's. If she and Nat had been deer or even squirrels or a pair of crows, I would have stayed and watched transfixed, without shame. I would have felt an awed sense of privilege. But they weren't deer. Or squirrels or crows.

Henry poured himself a cup of coffee and ambled over to the campfire.

Stupid! I cursed myself.

Cory said, "Nat and Lucia?"

Why not clue her in? "They're up there in the meadow going at it."

"Huh." She pushed her hat off her forehead. "Well," she decided, "you can't blame her."

"What do you mean?"

Cory glanced at Cyrus over by the campfire. "Her old man's a first-class shit. Here." She took the stewpot from me, rinsed it with water from one of our nylon buckets, then dried it with a terry-cloth towel printed with brown and orange butterflies. She said, "These kind of trips?"

"Yeah?"

"Every outfitter I know says the high country brings out the best in people. Take Pete. He ends up being best friends with everyone he brings in here. To hear him tell it, Cyrus is his bosom buddy. Then look at all the grief Pete takes—all this chummy heap-big-Injun shit! Cyrus don't give one about Pete! Just before

Pete rode out he asked Cyrus about his back. Like, as long as they were going out, did he need anything for it? And Cyrus let him have it. I don't know why Pete doesn't tell the old man to go—" she stopped and searched my face. "To go screw himself," she amended.

"It's the money," I said sourly. "Pete owes him."

"Yeah, well he said he was going to foreclose on Pete. All Pete did was ask if he wanted a doctor. There's not enough *best* in the guy for this country to bring out." She was enormously angry. Her eyes were pinpoints of steel. "I thought it was going to be different," she said.

"What, the trip?"

She didn't answer for a moment. Then she ducked her head. From under the brim of her hat, she said in a small voice, "Cyrus Strand the Third. I thought he'd be different." She stopped.

"Different how?" I asked.

She didn't answer right away. Then she raised her head. There was pain in her eyes. "Like, he'd be okay. One of the good guys."

I nodded.

She flushed. "I mean, after all Pete said." It came out awkwardly, as if she were lying.

Lucia and Nat strolled companionably back into camp. Lucia was carrying a specimen bouquet. She showed the flowers around the fire, brushed them teasingly under Cyrus's nose for a smell. No one was interested. Unbothered, she carried the bouquet over to her tent. Next time I looked up, she was hunting for something with a flashlight, raking the grass beside the tent with its beam. Had she lost an earring? A contact lens?

"Cy, darling," she called. "Where are my flowers?"

But Cyrus and Nat had withdrawn from the fire to talk out of earshot. They stood together under a pine, a pair of dark shapes with orange-lit faces. Cyrus, whose shoulders and head moved in sharp, puppetlike jerks, was doing all the talking. Nat stood still, listening with lawyerly nods.

"Cyrus!" Lucia called, less sweetly. "What has happened to my flowers? Cyrus?"

"What's the matter, Lucia?" Nat demanded.

"I can't find my flowers."

"You had them in your hand."

"Not those. The ones I had this morning. I am not finished with them!"

"Pick some more!" Cyrus barked in annoyance. He turned back to Nat.

But Lucia kept on fussing. She questioned the younger Strands around the fire. Maybe a bear stole them, they joked. For his honey, Billy Caton punned to a chorus of groans. She marched over to Cory and me, her flashlight bouncing. "Have you seen them?" she accused. "Did you clean up around the tents?"

"Lucia, there's no maid service on this trip. No Godivas on the pillow," I told her. "We haven't been near your tent."

She looked at us. "I am sorry," she apologized. "I am in the middle of my drawings and the flowers I am using for them have disappeared. I need them to finish. I had them in that tin you gave me."

I had given her an empty grapefruit-juice can after breakfast. "I haven't seen it," I told her.

She looked at Cory.

Cory shook her head.

"Oh, this is very annoying!" she said crossly. "I was not yet finished with the valerian. I had it with a monkey flower—you know this one? A little yellow figwort?"

We shook our heads.

"And a nice wake-robin. I found them by the stream this morning and put them in your tin. Now they are gone. And my roots have also disappeared. I had them drying on one of Cyrus's handkerchiefs. A big white one. It has his initials in the corner?"

"Sorry."

"I had biscuit-root with the valerian. And the root of the water hemlock as well. I was saving them to draw at home. There is so much here that cannot wait, so I am thinking, well, I will take these lovely big ones home to my studio."

"Can you find some more?" Cory suggested.

"They will not be the same. But who has taken them?" Her voice rose in a tragic wail. "Roots and flowers do not fly away like birds!" She marched off with her flashlight to renew her search. Clearly she was not a woman to give up easily.

I felt sympathetic to her loss. Early on in my marriage, my former, compulsively neat husband cleaned up our bedroom where I worked at a desk made of a hollow-core door and a pair of secondhand filing cabinets. (The decor in our apartment was Early Academe: wall-to-wall board and cinder-block bookcases.) In addition to scrubbing half the plaster off the ceiling moldings, he threw away an ankle-deep sea of lined yellow paper I had flung on the floor. It was the only extant copy of an epic poem I had thrown aside in a flamboyant gesture of artistic distress. Clint probably did me a great editorial service. But I remember the sinking feeling, the despairing sense of betrayal, the frustration laced with flashes of hatred. If someone was playing a joke on Lucia, it was a mean one.

Why did Adrienne come to mind? Perhaps because she had so unerringly jerked her father's chain: *If you hadn't beaten up on King. . .* Did Adrienne, like her adopted brother, Henry Flores, know about Nat and Lucia? Was she making her stepmother pay for her pleasure in the way it would most hurt?

It was warm next to the cookstove, but I felt a chill prickle down my back. I wished Pete were back. The darkness out there under the trees seemed alive and not friendly. I gave myself a shake. "Sabotage?" I said lightly to Cory.

"Maybe it was an animal." She sounded dubious. "The bears go for that biscuit-root."

"Wouldn't a bear have gone for the leftover stew as well? I left it sitting out on a crate to cool."

"We were all around making noise, though. And I had the campfire going pretty good." She paused. "But I know one guy who had a bear come running right into his cook tent." She chuckled. "He chased it out with a stick of stovewood."

"A black bear?"

She nodded. "A young one, he said. You aren't likely to bump into a grizzly here. There aren't that many of them—not like at Glacier. And they stay higher up this time of year. But black bears, they're around. That's why Pete likes an open kitchen. A fly lets all the cooking smells disperse. A tent gets saturated with them— especially bacon grease. And those black bears, they can bat a

111

fifty-pound pannier around like it was a balloon! You wouldn't believe the mess they can make. One little knock and your whole kitchen's flying through the trees—pots, pans, busted bags of flour, sugar, you name it. They'll even rip open all your cans with their teeth."

I thought of the black bear that had walked through my dream. My mother, the dream-eater, had swallowed it whole and regurgitated a guardian spirit for me, rather the way a bird feeds its young. Granted my mouth was wide open. I was still as hungry at forty as I had been at four. But her morsel didn't sit well. There had been nothing protective about the bear in my dream. It had no idea who I was. It did not recognize me as its dreamer. Claws clicking on the platform tiles, it had moved through the crowd as if they were trees. When it sprang at my heart, its small yellow eyes had been utterly indifferent.

The beam of Lucia's flashlight bobbed in the trees behind her tent. "Maybe we should say something to her," I suggested. "That it could have been a bear."

Cory raised an eyebrow. "You mean give the dudes a thrill?"

"If I were her, I'd rather it be something fourlegged."

"Me too," she said sincerely.

We surveyed the camp. Cyrus and Nat, still deep in conversation, had moved closer to the dying fire. The others had drifted off to their tents. Against the insides of the green nylon, flashlight beams wavered erratically, like moths battering themselves against a screen.

"I reckon there's not much point in getting things stirred up again," Cory observed. "Bear stories at bedtime work better than coffee. But go ahead. If you want to."

I didn't. We battened down the kitchen with extra care—just in case. Then Cory took her bedroll to sleep out under the stars. It was a clear night and the stars seemed close enough to pluck, but I was content to have the tent to myself again. Still, I found it hard to drift off. It wasn't bears that kept me tossing in my bag. It was the image of Nat and Lucia in that meadow floating with flowers high above our tents. The radiant pink dusk had given his white hair an elfin strawberry gleam, but there was nothing whimsical about his lovemaking. His lowered head and the curve of his bowed spine had the weight of worship, as if her body were a prayer rug and he a convert whose hands trembled slightly in an act of adoration.

Is that what I wanted? To have love blow the dry leaves out of my heart? To have my life become new and wondrous, every picayune detail of it gleaming like a gift for a beautiful, long-limbed lover? Sure. Yes, please.

But I was beginning to think I wanted something else as well. After ten years of being single, I wanted to try again. For the long run. And not with some flake who's learned the knack of looking into a woman's eyes. With someone as solid as Pete Bonsecours. Someone who wasn't out to save the world and its mother. Someone who would hold my hand whenever necessary. Like the song says, sweet dreams.

12

The next day, our fifth day in the wilderness, Cyrus died at 1:35 in the afternoon. Or thereabouts. Actually, it was probably some minutes earlier. What with all the confusion, I doubt I looked at my watch at the exact moment of death. There is always that uncertainty: Is that it? Is it over now? Then a small hiatus of surprise. We gaped like fish on a riverbank, stunned by a sloppy blow from an angler's "priest." When it occurred to me to note the time, my Timex read 1:35. The time of his death seemed important, something to save for the authorities. Maybe I believed they could scry a pattern from it, the same way astrologers draw charts from the time of birth.

It was a perfect day, sunny and just warm enough to roll up the sleeves of a flannel shirt. The sky was deep blue and almost painfully clear. There was the illusion that if you reached, stretched a tiny bit farther with your eyes, you might be able to make out each boulder on the distant, snow-capped peaks that cut the horizon like jagged teeth. I had a long prebreakfast jog around the high meadow and realized happily that the mountains around me were beginning to become less like scenic postcards and more like reliable and familiar faces. I descended with soaking wet sneakers, a wildly pounding heart (the altitude, the altitude) and the sense of renewed virtue that follows penance. Cory rekindled the campfire, and the family ate a late pancake breakfast around it while I, still disgustingly high from my run, mixed up a celebratory batch of sourdough bread for Pete and Brett's return supper. I had brought my starter along with the idea of sourdough pancakes, but soon discovered that by the time I'd cleaned up after supper, the notion of whipping together a batter for the morning had lost its romance. The ready mix Pete had provided worked just fine. By this time, however, without refrigeration to halt fermentation, my starter had gotten extremely ripe. When I unscrewed the lid, the blast of cheesy fumes made my eyes tear. Nonetheless, in the interest of historic authenticity, I added a full dose to my "sponge."

Cyrus and Nat Rosenfeld, head to head again, left the group around the breakfast fire and wandered over to the cook stove. Nat poured himself a second cup of coffee. Cyrus refilled from his tea Thermos, which he kept parked on the "counter" of my kitchen box. Then they moved off together and stood a few yards from the cook fly.

I was kneeling over one of the plastic crates, kneading cool, now acceptably fragrant sourdough in one of the stainless washbasins. My back half was turned to them, so they were out of my sight line but not out of range of my big ears which, for lack of anything better to do, flapped in the still morning air. Cyrus I couldn't make out. He rumbled stubbornly now and again. But mainly it seemed to be Nat's turn for talking and his voice, trained for the courtroom, carried clearly.

"Cyrus," he urged, "listen to me. Someone got angry, exercised bad judgment in the heat of the moment. We've got no reason to think it's anything more than that. You're overreacting."

Rumble.

"Yes, I think Pete knows what he's talking about. But even if your latigo *was* in fact cut—"

Rumble, rumble.

For a long moment, Nat was silent. "Your will is, of course, your own business." He paused. I imagined him giving a small tug to a pinstriped vest. "But as a lawyer, as *your* lawyer, Cyrus, and

115

as your friend, I must point out that what you propose will prove counterproductive to your stated aim. I don't foresee this new will of yours as an instrument which will encourage self-sufficiency and maturity in your heirs. I see it fostering division and bitterness. And—if you will allow me a cynical observation—I see it endowing several braces of attorneys with new BMWs. You can't think it won't be contested."

Cyrus snapped something.

"Yes, I believe it will stand up in court. But that doesn't mean they won't contest it. What have they to lose? Fifty, a hundred thousand in legal fees? Peanuts, compared to an estate the size of yours. People go to court for a whole lot less. I've seen families fighting tooth and nail to get their hot hands on things they wouldn't look at when dear old Mom was alive. Believe me, it's not a pretty sight."

Unyielding silence.

"Damn it, Cyrus," Nat burst out, "I'm telling you, when you try to control things from your grave, nine times out of ten, it backfires!" He took a swallow of coffee. More calmly, he added, "Certainly, there's no rush about it."

Cyrus raised his voice in determination. "I've made up my mind. They might as well know."

"You really think it's going to change anything? At least think of Lucia!"

"That's exactly who I *am* thinking of."

Nat let out a sigh of exasperation. Then, with carefully measured pomp, he announced, "For your own welfare, I advise you to refrain from making the contents of this will known. There is absolutely no reason to inform them of your decision right here and now out *in the middle of nowhere*. Do you understand what I'm saying?"

Cyrus mumbled something and began to move away.

"Wait! For Godsake!" Nat called after him, "if you're so concerned about malicious mischief—"

Over at the campfire heads turned in their direction.

Cyrus made a gruff noise. A dismissal. He walked off in the direction of the latrine. He was still moving as if his back hurt more than he wanted to admit.

116

I set my bread to rise in an oiled pot atop my kitchen box. I figured the air temperature was about right for the kind of long, slow rise that gives the yeast a chance to maximize the sour flavor of molecules inherited from the 1870s. I fed my starter more flour and water and screwed on the lid. I cleaned out the stainless basin and set it down on a patch of pine needles. Then I made more tea for Cyrus's Thermos, poured the rest of the hot water into the basin, and added liquid Joy.

Cyrus reappeared as his family clustered around the basin, dunking their hands in the hot soapy water along with their forks and plates. He had strapped his trusty cannon onto his hip. It looked like a .45 long Colt, a classic revolver of the American West. Its plain brown holster had U.S. stamped on it. The belt was loaded with enough cartridges to keep Billy the Kid in business.

"Time to circle the wagons, Cyrus?" Billy Caton inquired dryly.

"Is that a gun in your holster or are you just glad to see us?" Henry cracked.

Adrienne rolled her eyes skyward, like a Victorian martyr.

"Is everyone here?" Cyrus demanded.

They looked around at each other. "Yes, Daddy, everyone's here," Adrienne said. Like an obnoxious adolescent, she managed to sound bored and snide at the same time.

"I have an announcement to make. It won't take long." He studied them as if they were a group of strangers. Henry, who was refilling coffee cups, banged the pot back on the stove in a show of annoyance. Nat, who had been studying the lizard-skin toes of his cowboy boots while Cyrus called the family to attention, now moved around to Cyrus's right and stood slightly behind him. When the lawyer looked up, his expression was impassive. But there could be no doubt whose side he was on. Gene caught Lucia's eye and raised a questioning eyebrow. She gave a minute shrug that said, "I have no idea."

I signaled Cory with my chin. We started to move away. "Stay put," Cyrus commanded. "Yes, both of you. I want outside witnesses to this."

"It's not necessary," Nat instructed, his voice carefully neutral.

Cyrus ignored him. "You said you lived in Washington?" he asked me.

"That's right."

"Okay, Lee Squires of Washington, D.C., and Cory—?" He waited for her to supply her last name. She stared at him.

"What's your last name?" he demanded.

"Johnson." Her eyes were intent on his face. "My last name is Johnson."

"Cory Johnson of Missoula. Is that right?"

"That's right. Cory *Ann* Johnson." She stressed the "Ann."

Cyrus ignored her. He turned and glanced at Nat to make sure he'd taken in our names. Nat gave him a tight-lipped nod.

The family stirred impatiently. "I have decided," Cyrus said levelly, "that when I retire as president of Strand Textiles this fall, neither Billy, nor Henry, will succeed me. In my judgment, it is in the best interests of the company to bring in an outside CEO. I'm sorry if this comes as a disappointment to either of you. But it shouldn't surprise you."

Billy Caton looked surprised. He opened his mouth, then shut it firmly. He glanced from his father-in-law to Henry and back again. His bloodshot eyes and the two-day wilderness stubble on his jaw gave him an air of menace. As he folded his arms across his chest, the swinging fringes on his jacket no longer seemed comic.

Henry stood still, his eyes veiled with an unruly fall of dark hair. There was an embarrassing silence.

Gene broke it. "Are we dismissed?" he asked coolly.

"No."

They waited.

"I have written out a new will." He patted the buttoned pocket of his shirt. "Nat has corrected the language and, as it is written in my own hand, I'm told it is legally binding." He turned to Nat.

"A holographic will," the lawyer confirmed.

"Being of sound mind," Cyrus continued, "I have written you children out of it. Upon my death, my entire estate, including all my stock in the company, will be held in trust. Lucia is the trustee and my executor. She will have use of the income during her lifetime. When she dies, it will go to the National Wildlife Federation."

"Cyrus," Lucia protested in a shocked murmur.

"But you can't do that!" Adrienne cried. She looked to Nat for help. Nat said nothing.

Cyrus held up a hand. "I have given you the best education money can buy. You never had to lift a finger for it. Moreover, you had the guarantee of a job with, as it happens, undeservedly handsome salaries, in the family company." He glanced at Gene. "If you were so inclined.

"And as if that weren't enough, since you were twenty-five, you have each had the advantage of a trust fund set up by your grandfather—in your case, Henry, half the capital came from your father's life-insurance policy. As you know, I made up the difference out of my own pocket. I felt it was only fair that your fund be equal to those of my own children. When King died, I dissolved his fund and divided it equally among you and Adrienne and Gene."

Cyrus pressed his lips together in resignation and surveyed his children. "Well, you ran through King's money fast enough. The same way you squandered your trust funds."

The group didn't flinch. I had the feeling they had heard this speech before.

"But I'll be damned if I'll give you a second fortune to waste! You're spoiled rotten, every one of you! No wonder your children are drug addicts."

"You call buying a decent roof over our heads *squandering* money?" Adrienne spat out. "You call tuition payments *squandering*?" Her face was scarlet. "And tell me, who spoiled us? It sure as hell wasn't you, Daddy. I suppose you blame that on mother—like everything else. You weren't even *around*."

Gene and Billy closed in on her with small shushing sounds, as if the situation were still salvageable.

"It's her fault," Adrienne said to them. "Lucia's put him up to this."

"Darlin'," Billy objected. He put a comforting arm around his wife. But his hazel eyes were cold.

"Cyrus?" Lucia asked, her voice tentative.

119

"I have nothing more to say. I'm going fishing now." He hobbled over to his tent, picked up his vest and rod, and set out in the direction of the creek.

"I don't believe it," Adrienne said. "He's going fishing now."

Lucia turned to Nat. She was wearing a man-sized blue chambray work shirt, belted like a peasant's smock over her khakis, and rolled up at the elbow. The volume of material made her look frail. For the first time, I realized she was older than she looked—closer to Cyrus's age than his midlife children. She steadied herself on Nat's arm. "Why is he doing this?" she wondered. "What has happened?"

"Good show," Gene applauded. "Lucia the Innocent."

Nat and Lucia ignored him. "Someone cut Cyrus's latigo," Nat said. He included them all in his answer, making eye contact with each of them, as if they were members of a jury. "He didn't think it was funny. That's what happened."

"Jesus," Billy muttered. "I need a drink." He produced a wallet-sized pewter flask from somewhere under the fringes of his jacket, unscrewed the top, and said, "Cheers." He took a pull, then passed it to Henry, who followed suit.

As my mother would diagnose blandly, there were a lot of issues floating around. A lot of anger. I felt slightly nauseous, as if somehow I too were under attack. I thought of my own father. He had shared Cyrus's values: self-sufficiency, thrift, hard work, clean living. He would not have approved of my recent career as freelance freeloader.

Henry offered the flask to Cory. "You look like you could use something," he observed.

Her skin had an ashy color. She took a breath. It came back out shakily. She tried a smile. "No, I don't think so," she said to Henry.

Henry's dark eyes were concerned. "Sorry about all that," he apologized to Cory and me. He clapped a weighty hand on my left shoulder, true-pal style. I felt a silver tingle of pleasure shoot from under my armpit to my left nipple and trill all the way down to my big toe.

"Did you just get fired?" Cory asked.

"I hope not. I'm kind of attached to my 'undeservedly handsome' salary. Hey, Billy. Did our jobs get axed in that little episode?"

"No, just our futures. You aren't going to get to sit behind the big desk, Henry."

"Reckon not." He grinned at the phrase. "This Wild West stuff seems to be catching."

"Has he done this before?" I asked, disconcerted by Henry's nonchalance.

"You mean disinherited us? No. Just the Worthless Ingrates routine."

Cory said, "But he'll change his mind."

Henry raised his straight, dark eyebrows. I wondered what it would be like to live with a man who looked like a movie star. After a while, would his manly beauty go flat? Would he lose his sparkles, like champagne left out overnight?

"What do you think, Nat?" Gene asked sarcastically. "You think maybe Dad will back down?"

Nat looked at Lucia. Lucia said nothing. "You know your father," Nat said.

"I hate him," Adrienne announced fiercely.

"Look upon it as opportunity knocking, baby doll," her husband said. "Here's your chance to put your money where your mouth is."

"What do mean?"

"You've always felt you had more potential than me out there in the business world." He took another swig from his flask and screwed the top back on. "And if you're planning to keep Paul in that fancy rehab school of his, our coffers are going to need an infusion of something more than hot air."

We spent the rest of the morning in separate corners. I took my paperback up to the high meadow for a couple of hours. Lucia went hunting for replacement roots, and Gene took his binoculars and wandered out across the old Indian battleground where Cyrus had hit the dust on the way in. The rest took up fly rods and found their own private holes up and down what the map called a creek—never mind that it was big enough to qualify as a river back East. As it happened, the trout were rising. Everyone with a rod brought back at least one keeper for lunch. Cyrus returned with three. The winner. But there were no celebrations. The group mood was cool. Cory, who had spent the morning dozing under her hat in a patch of sun, emerged sullenly from her nap to help me grill the fish over the campfire. I did a new batch of Dutch-oven corn bread in the coals and cut up a brick of sharp cheddar to go with the apples for dessert.

Cyrus seemed more restless than usual. He hovered over our shoulders, inspecting the fish on the grill as he sipped tea from his enameled cup. The others drank lukewarm martinis from their cups. (Lucia politely volunteered the vermouth to enhance Billy's gin. He accepted, making it clear that she got no points for her contribution to the common weal.) Cyrus kept working his mouth and swallowing. "I must be hungry," he joked. "Those are mouth-watering trout all right!"

We turned the trout. Cyrus nodded approvingly. Then his hand jerked, spilling his tea on my shoulder. "Goddamn," he swore under his breath. "Excuse me." He stepped away from the fire, hawked, and spat out a great mouthful of saliva onto the ground. He spat again, another full mouth. "Goddamn," he repeated more loudly.

His family looked over at him. "What's the matter now, Cyrus?" Lucia asked. She sounded like an overworked nun keeping the lid on her testiness.

"Nothing," he growled. His cup fell out of his hand and landed with a *ping* on the ground at his feet. He began to shake. He crossed his arms and held on his elbows in an effort to control it.

"Cyrus," she said in alarm. She set her martini cup down on the ground and strode over to him. "What is it?"

"It's nothing," he said. "I must have caught a chill in the river." But he didn't sound convinced.

"Henry," Lucia called. "Please bring me a sleeping bag."

The others watched dispassionately as Henry went to Cyrus's tent, fished out an ochre-colored down bag, and presented it to Lucia. She wrapped it over her husband's shoulders. "Sit down," she instructed.

He obeyed.

She knelt beside him, frowning. He was seized again by the shivers. "Cyrus?" she asked. He coughed, spraying saliva over her. She turned her face away with a sharp "Oh!"

The fish were done. Cory and I lifted them off the grill onto the plates. "Come and get it," I said to the rest of them.

They drifted over, cups in hand, and picked up their plates. "Do you think some Advil would help, Lucia?" Adrienne offered.

Lucia felt her husband's forehead. "He has some fever, I think," she said worriedly.

"I'll get you the Advil," Adrienne decided. She put down her plate of trout and strode off to her tent.

Cyrus continued to shake. Saliva drooled abundantly out of the corners of his slack mouth. I put down my spatula and went over. There was something odd about his eyes. I squatted down beside Lucia and looked at him. His eyes were no longer pale blue. They were black and empty. "Your pupils are dilated," I told him. No response.

"What does that mean?" Lucia demanded.

"I don't know," I said helplessly.

Adrienne brought the Advil. Nat brought an inflatable pillow. The sleeping bag draped over his shoulders quivered like a running motor. He retched, but nothing came up. Lucia clutched his hands. "He is so hot!" she exclaimed. "He is burning up!" In one swift gesture, she swept away the down bag. "What is the matter with him?" she entreated the group.

No one had an answer. Their faces were solemn. Nat stepped forward out of their loose circle. "Perhaps we should move him into the shade," he suggested.

"No," Cyrus said loudly.

"Cyrus?" Lucia asked.

He made a frightening noise, more birdlike than human, then his eyes rolled white and his body jerked horribly—as if he'd been shot from behind. His head flew back, his back arched, and he landed on his side, writhing in the dust.

"Oh my God, my God, what is the matter?" Lucia cried in panic. Instinctively, she moved to hold him, but a flailing arm sent her flying backward with such force that it knocked the wind out of her. Gasping, on all fours, she crawled back toward him. Cyrus's leg missed her head by inches. "Don't!" Billy warned, pulling her back.

"Christ Almighty, he's having a seizure," Gene said, his voice shrill.

"Give him room," Nat ordered. Cyrus's head banged on the ground with a sickening, melon-thumping sound. Cory and I bundled up the sleeping bag and slid it under his head, but it didn't do much to cushion the blows. Pink foam bubbled out of the rictus of his mouth. I was aware of the others crowding over us, peering down. At one point, I heard Lucia sobbing.

I don't know how many convulsions wracked Cyrus's body. During one spasm, his jaw clamped shut with the violence of a sprung trap and he bit off the end of his tongue. Blood spurted brightly all over us. It gurgled in the back of his throat. To prevent him from choking on it, Adrienne and Cory turned his head to the side and let it drain out onto the ground. I picked the lump of tongue off his blood-soaked shirt—but there's no point in going over that again. The seizures came and went, banging us back and forth between fear and hope. But after each one, his breathing became more and more irregular.

When it finally ended, Lucia said she wanted to be left alone with him. It was very quiet. The sun was high in the blue sky, the pines around the camp were still, no one talked. I began picking up the plates left on the ground. My hands were shaking. I noticed that no one had eaten more than a bite or two. Some of the grilled trout were still whole, but had been invaded by armies of tiny ants. I dumped the fish in the fire and piled new logs on top. After they started crackling, I stood and watched the flames. Then I remembered the corn bread. Its cut edges were dry, the crumbs hard. I carried it back to the cook fly along with the cheese and apples.

Along with a barrage of instant replays of Cyrus's seizures, the term *brain fever* kept running through my head. Where had I read that? It had a nineteenth-century ring to it. I nudged it out of the way. "Epilepsy?" I tried. "A brain tumor?" I punched down the bread for supper. I noticed that moving seemed to help. I circled through the lodgepoles behind the kitchen several times.

Then I walked over to Lucia, slid between the family's elbows, and knelt down beside her. She had already closed Cyrus's eyes.

"It might be a good idea to move him out of the sun," I said.

"Of course," she said.

"I'll ask Cory to get you a manty."

"He would like that. To be wrapped in a manty. Better than a box." She stroked his hand. "But he must be washed." She shooed a fly away from the blood drying on his throat.

"Would you like me to help?"

"No. I will do it myself."

"Lucia, I'd like you to let me have his gun. To keep it safe."

She unbuckled the belt. I lifted up his shoulders. His head lolled, mouth open. His teeth were bloody. The sweat-soaked back of his shirt was still warm. Lucia pulled the gun belt out from underneath him. I lowered him down.

She gave me the gun. The grip poking out of the holster was worn, dark-grained wood with hairline cracks at the butt. It was the kind of lovingly maintained, old revolver that a collector like my brother would drool over. I left it holstered and stood up with it. Perhaps there's a casual way to carry a weapon that size—slung over the shoulder like a purse or swinging from the hand like a pail. But it didn't feel casual. I bundled the macho-looking cartridge belt around it and walked away carrying it in both hands like a UPS driver delivering a package.

The family drifted after me. Their faces were shocked. I told them Lucia needed water, a washcloth and towel, a clean shirt from Cyrus's duffle, and help moving his body. They seemed relieved by the small chores.

Gene looked at the gun in my hands. "You know how to use that?" he inquired.

"I think so," I said. "But it's been a long time. My aim's probably rusty. If I had to fire a warning shot, I might get one of you by mistake."

No one chuckled.

13

They moved the body into the shade of the pines behind the line of tents. I went back to the campfire and cleaned the area as best I could, scraping up the clotting blood without looking too closely at it and throwing dusty handfuls of it into the fire. I rinsed my hands in a bucket of creek water, then poured it out over the stained tufts of grass and broken wildflowers. I sprinkled pine needles around. I noticed Cyrus's khaki hat lying behind one of the logs used as a seat. I picked it up and carried it back to the cook fly with the dirty plates.

The dishes I let soak in a basin. But what to do with a dead man's hat? Leaving it lying casually on top of a kitchen crate seemed insensitive. Nor did I want to present it to Lucia while she was washing her husband's body. My yellow slicker caught my eye. I'd left it hanging out to dry on a dead limb behind the kitchen. I rolled up Cyrus's canvas hat and stuffed it into one of my slicker's large, Velcro-latched pockets. I'd give it to Lucia later.

I settled down under the cook fly with my dough, Cyrus's gun, and two stacks of defrosting elk steaks. My shoulder kept itching. I didn't even attempt my book, an out-of-print Elizabeth Spencer novel that I'd been looking forward to reading. It just didn't go

126

with the scenery. Instead, I picked up the classified section from a Sunday *Missoulian* unwrapped from the steaks. It was only three pages. For something over a hundred thousand you could buy a "partially-restored Victorian in the University area" or a "luxurious townhome on the Rattlesnake." For something over six thousand, you could buy a mobile home with a wood stove and a Jacuzzi or a 1987 Toyota pickup with 30,000 miles and an "Alpine stereo cassette." I found it reassuring to think that some thousand feet below us, people were buying and selling. I wondered how much a mule cost. There were Appaloosas and Arabians advertised, but no mules for sale.

My shoulder started to sting. I wondered if I'd been bitten. When I reached back to rub it, my shirt seemed oddly damp. Then, through the fog that I seemed to be floating around in, I saw I had Cyrus's blood down my front. This gave me a jolt. I crawled inside my tent. It felt like 101 degrees Fahrenheit. I peeled off the offending shirt, sniffed my underarms, and pulled on an old Brooks Brothers blue button-down. The frayed threads at the points of the collar had been starched into respectability by my friendly neighborhood Cambodian laundry. I took out my comb and rebraided my hair. Then I looked at myself in my pocket mirror. Despite the fact that I hadn't spent much time out in the sun, I had turned a pinkish tan. I grimaced at the mirror, then snapped it shut. I gave myself a squirt of Chanel No. 5. For an instant, I felt glamorous and worldly, as if I were the sort of woman who might wear red lipstick and a huge, black, floppy-brimmed hat with my bathing suit.

Then the skin on the back of my shoulder started burning again. I slipped my shirt off my shoulder, and twisted around in an effort to inspect it, but all I could see was my bra strap. I rebuttoned my shirt.

Cyrus, I remembered, had slopped his tea on me just before his fit. I felt the shoulder of the flannel shirt I'd been wearing. It was damp. I balled it up into the white plastic garbage bag I was using for dirty clothes, crawled out of my tent, and stood up.

Under the cook fly, Cyrus's tea Thermos was sitting where he had left it: on top of my cook box. It had been there since the morning. Anyone could have gotten at it while I had been up in the high meadow trying to read. For that matter, the lot of them were milling in and out of the kitchen while Cory and I were grilling the trout over the open fire. I shook the Thermos. There wasn't much left in it. Cyrus must have come back from fishing thirsty. He had polished off nearly the whole quart—with the exception of the half cup he had spilled on me.

I screwed the top of the Thermos on tight, wrapped it in a green garbage bag, and buried it in the bottom of a crate full of cans: peaches, succotash, tomatoes, boysenberries, peas. I soaped up my hands with Joy, then poured half a bucket over them. I sat down, using the crate as a backrest, and stared at the rusty pine needles on the gray ground between my legs.

Cory came over and sat down cross-legged. "You okay?" she asked.

"I think so. How about you?"

"I'm all right." We were both lying. "I gave them the manty," she said.

I nodded. "Good."

She sat facing my direction as if we were sitting on the same bench. I had to turn my head to see her face. There was a puffiness around her eyes. We gazed out across the campground, a large apron of open field with the guests' tents pitched down one side, and a wooded draw down the other. The hem of the apron was a curving line of bog birch and shrubby willows that hid the creek from view. Our kitchen and my tent were located near the top of the apron, in the lee of the tall, skinny pines that climbed steeply uphill to the "bench" above us.

About a hundred yards upstream, on the other side of the wooded draw, the creek had carved a border of the ancient battleground where we expected Pete and Brett would ride in with the horses. We could not see this broad, mountain plain from where we sat, nor could we see Cyrus's body, which was screened by Nat Rosenfeld's tent, but we did have a clear view of all the comings and goings between his body, the tents, and the creek.

Cory bobbed her head a couple times, but whatever she wanted to say seemed stuck in her throat.

I picked up my rumpled sheets of newsprint and read about a Sears air conditioner in excellent condition and a "like new" electric wheelchair, narrow adult, paid $6,800, will sacrifice. I squinted at the price. Two zeros, not one. Six thousand, eight hundred. Either the machine was made of solid gold or it was a health industry rip-off. Barrel cactus, $25. I felt as prickly as. I put down the paper.

"Cory," I said, trying to keep the sharpness out of my voice. "You cut Cyrus's latigo, didn't you?"

She didn't answer.

"I'm just trying to sort things out. Was King your father?"

She looked at me as if I were crazy. "Who?"

"King Strand. Cyrus's son. The one who was killed in Vietnam."

She studied me with bemusement. "Why would you think that?"

"Your mother came from virtually the same town. Both your father and King died in the war." I hesitated, then blundered on. "And you look like a Strand."

She sat quite still.

"I mistook you for Gene from a distance," I told her. "Once I saw the resemblance, it kept hitting me between the eyes. You've got Cyrus's nose, his chin—even that little bend on the top of your ears is the same."

She touched the rim of her ear with her forefinger, as if to confirm it was still there. She shook her head. "You've got it wrong," she said bitterly.

I waited.

"It wasn't his son. It was him. Cyrus." Her voice was like homemade vinegar, cloudy and sour.

"Cyrus is—was your father?"

"My mother worked for him. She was his secretary at the mill. He knocked her up and then he fired her and gave her money to go have an abortion. Instead, she bought a Trailways ticket out of High Point. She was planning to go to San Francisco and stay with a girlfriend. But she met a bunch of hippies on the way and ended up in Missoula instead."

"Her name is Ann Johnson?"

"Was. She died of breast cancer right after I graduated from high school. In June, 'eight-six."

129

"That couldn't have been easy."

Cory went on brusquely. "She was six months pregnant when she got out here. She lived in some kind of commune south of Missoula and changed her name to Maya. She said it meant *Mother* in Greek. Then the commune folded, and she became Ann Johnson again and started working in a vet's office. I grew up thinking my real father was a hero of the Vietnam war. She never pretended she'd been married. Then when I was five, she married my stepfather." She paused. There was something grim about her silence. "Anyway, she gave me her name. Cory Ann. That's what she used to call me." She studied her hands for a moment, then burst out, "He never even remembered her name!"

"What about your stepfather?" I asked.

"What about him?" she said sharply.

"Did you like him? Was he good to you?"

She stared at her knees. Finally, she said, "I hated him. He used to make me touch him. And other stuff. Mom never found out." She fiddled with the lace of her boot. "I kinda thought my real dad might be different. You know. Like maybe he'd turn out to be okay."

A jay squawked loudly somewhere above the green plastic cook fly that made a green shade for our thoughts. Gene crossed the campground with a yellow nylon bucket dripping creek water. The afternoon sun tarnished the needles of the lodgepoles where Cyrus's body lay. Adrienne appeared from behind the tents and walked purposefully down the row to the tent her father and Lucia shared. She unzipped the insect netting and crawled inside.

"So you knew he was your father all along?" I asked Cory.

She shook her head. "When Pete was looking for a bankroll, he mentioned he was talking to this guy from North Carolina. But I didn't know who it was until they started setting up this trip and Pete said his name. Cyrus Strand, he said. You coulda knocked me over. My mother had told me about him before she died. She said she thought I ought to know. I wasn't living at home then, but when I heard she was sick, I went to see her in the hospital and she told me. Anyways, like I said, this was all a while back. And then Pete comes out with his name. I thought, maybe there's two of them or something. I mean, it was kinda hard to believe."

130

"You didn't say anything to Pete?"

"You kidding? Besides, I wasn't sure till I saw him in the corral at Monture."

I didn't say anything.

"I found a picture of them in her things. Him and my mom."

Adrienne crawled out of Cyrus's tent with a navy blue shirt and a pair of khakis. Henry walked out of the pine wood, carrying Cyrus's bloody clothing toward the creek.

"Who else knows?" I asked.

"Maybe the lawyer. Nat. At least he looked like he knew. When I said 'Ann Johnson.' "

"Did you tell Adrienne?"

"No." She blushed, stared stoically ahead. "Why should I tell her?"

"She's your sister. Half sister, anyway. And you seemed to get on."

"He thinks I'm hitting on her," she blurted out.

I didn't correct her tense. "Some men get off on it," I said.

Her oval gray eyes widened. "What do you mean?"

"The idea of women making it together gives them a charge. Take a look at some of those pink magazines, *Hustler, Penthouse*."

She turned her head and stared at me. I watched Gene conferring with Adrienne at the edge of the pines. She was shaking her head repeatedly. He set off for the creek, then changed his mind, walked back to the tents, and stopped in front of his father's. He tied back the flaps, knelt, and crawled inside.

"How old are you?" I asked Cory.

"Twenty-three."

She seemed younger. "Did you go to college?"

"I wasn't much good at school."

"Cory?"

"What?"

"Did you do it?"

"I didn't do anything!"

"Forget the latigo business. Did you poison Cyrus's tea?"

Her mouth dropped open in astonishment. "What?"

Gene crawled out of Cyrus's tent, dragging Cyrus's duffle behind him. He raised an arm to wipe his forehead on the sleeve

131

of his kelly green polo shirt, unzipped the duffle, and began un-packing it, frisking each item, then carefully refolding.

"Lee!" Cory demanded. "What are you talking about?"

"I think maybe he was poisoned."

"Christ."

"People just don't start having fits out of the blue and die. If there was something terminally wrong with his nervous system, there would have been previous symptoms. The shakes, stumbling, headaches, other seizures. Unless he was keeping it a secret. I suppose that could explain why he was in such a hurry to rewrite his will."

"I heard a story like that," Cory said. "The couple Pete and I used to work for, they knew this guy, an old-timer like them, who'd been taking hunters into the Bob all his life. Sometimes he'd come around and tell these stories. Didn't take much to get him going, a couple beers was all, and he'd go on past my bedtime, I can tell you! Anyway Dave said—that's this guide's name, Dave—he said how one time he got a call from this trophy hunter who said he'd hunted all over the world but he'd never gotten a big elk. So Dave said, 'Sure, no problem,' and they set it all up. Well, turns out there's only three of them in the party, the client and two younger guys, who said they weren't shooting. So Dave says, "Well, you'll have to pay full fare for them anyway," and the client says, 'No problem,' and writes out the check and off they go. Well, they get their bull, but all the while they're up there, the client keeps collapsing and every time it happens, the young guys open up their packs, pull out an oxygen tank and mask and hypodermics, and pump the client back up. Turns out the client had cancer and he wanted to bag his elk before he went. One of the young guys was his doctor and the other was his butler."

Cory shook her head. Clearly, having a butler was the part of the story that amazed her. "The way Dave tells it," she went on, " 'round about Christmas, he gets this card from the butler. The client died the night they hung the elk head on the wall of his trophy room. The butler got him settled in his chair so's he could admire it, then turned his back to pop some champagne. A minute later, he brought a glass over for the toast and found the old guy dead with this smile on his face."

A happy ending. But there had been no smile on Cyrus's face. I glanced at Cory. She winced. She must have been thinking the same thing.

Henry came back from the creek with Cyrus's clothes twisted into wet screws. He gave them a couple more turns, shook them out, and spread them to dry on a bush behind Cyrus's tent. Then he came around to the front. He stood over Gene. Gene shook his head. Henry squatted down and looked at the piles of clothing. Then he crawled halfway into the tent and came out with the long aluminum tube that held Cyrus's fly rod. He took out the rod, shook the tube, peered inside. Adrienne joined them. She pulled Lucia's duffle out of the tent. Hastily, she checked the outside pockets. She looked around, then unzipped it.

"You going to tell Pete?" Cory asked.

"About what?"

"About Cyrus being my old man."

"I think so," I told her.

Abruptly, she stood and strode over the edge of the fly.

I got to my feet. "Cory. Stick around."

"Why?" she challenged.

"For your own good, you little idiot." It came out nastily. I let out a blast of air between my teeth. *Breathe,* I heard my mother say. I inhaled. "Sorry," I apologized.

To my surprise, she grinned.

"I'll make a new pot of coffee," I offered.

"No thanks. But it looks like Billy could use some." He was weaving his way along the line of tents toward Henry and Gene. They looked up. Billy tripped on a tent peg and fell face forward on his belly. Then, to everyone's astonishment, he did three push-ups and on the last one rebounded to his feet like a kid's inflatable punching bag. He hooted loudly. Henry left Cyrus's piles of belongings, caught Billy by the arm, and started steering him toward us.

"Cory," I said urgently. "This is deep shit we're in. If you don't want it running down the inside of your boots, stay away from them. Adrienne, too."

"Why should I?" she bridled.

"They aren't *nice.*"

133

Cory looked at me as if I were crazy. "Look," I tried. "If you can prove you're Cyrus's natural child, you can probably lay claim to a share of his estate. Which gives you a motive for murder."

"Hold on." Her vowels had a long western sound, as in "whoa." "Just hold on a second. In the first place, you don't know someone did him in. In the second place, he left everything to *Lucia*. The others got zip. You were there. You heard him as well as I did."

"Keep it down, for Godsake."

"I am keeping it down."

But Billy and Henry had stalled out. They stood arguing in the middle of the field, muscling each other back and forth like buddies on the edge of a fight.

"Lee," Cory said with the superiority of her youth. "If anyone has a motive, it's Lucia. She gets the pile."

"If the new will survives," I hissed. "What do you think they're doing over there? Hunting for Easter eggs? Stay away from them! Go get me some more wood. Go on." I picked up the ax and thrust it into her hand.

She stood there, frowning under the brim of her pearl gray Stetson. The band was woven of black horsehair. The felt seemed miraculously clean, considering what we'd been through.

"Your hat new?"

She flushed. But her voice was ironic. "Figured to put my best foot forward. Cost me twenty-five bucks to have it cleaned and reblocked."

I put my hand on the small of her back and gave a slow shove. "Go on," I said. "Bring me some more kindling. Please."

She walked off swinging the sheathed ax at her side. From behind she was waistless, as straight as a child in her slim-cut, K Mart pearl-snap shirt, her faded Levi's, her White's packer's boots. It was an uncanny sight. I might have been watching the ghost of a teenaged Cyrus Strand striding across a field of pink geranium, yellow cinquefoil, and coppery sprays of grass.

Henry and Billy stopped their push-me-pull-you game and looked at her passing. I picked up Cyrus's long six-gun and slid it out of the holster. The browned steel was bright along the barrel. There was no safety. Cyrus had loaded five cartridges in the cylinder and left the hammer on empty. I took out the bullets, slid them into my starched breast pocket, and shoved the gun back into its holster as Billy Caton, steadied by Henry, stepped under the cook fly.

"We thought we'd pay you a visit," Henry said. His eyes traveled from the gun in my hands up to my sagging shirt pocket. He met my eyes as he reached out and lightly tapped the bullets under my breast. "There's more where those came from," he said. "We found the box in his tent. I guess they didn't all fit in his belt."

"Henny," Billy slurred. "Not nice. You leave the lady alone." He clutched my arm. "Is he bothering you?" His red-rimmed eyes were enormously sincere.

They were standing too close. I twisted out of Billy's grip. "Give me a little space, guys." I was damned if I was going to give ground. But they didn't budge.

"Hey," Billy said. "Hey. The last thing in the world I wanta do is hurt you."

I felt a tingle. This time, it wasn't the fun kind. It slid down my spine like a drop of ice water.

"You know that, darlin', don't you? The last thing—"

"I'm just about to make a new pot of coffee," I announced. I looked at the gun in my hands.

Henry admonished, "You know it's worth some money?"

I turned and put it down on the kitchen box behind me. I turned back to them. "I guess it's part of his estate, now." They stood there pondering me. Billy's face was earnest and worried. Henry's was thoughtful.

"Tell you what," he suggested. "We'll take a couple laps around the battlefield and come back when your coffee's done." He put *coffee* in quotation marks, as if I were faking it. But he caught Billy under the arm. "Come on," he said. "Time to walk it off."

"Wha' for?" Billy demanded.

Henry let a click out of the side of his mouth. "Maybe you've got a point there." He winked at me. "How about a nice nap under those bushes by yonder cool, clear water? Come on, pal."

"And miles to go before I sleep," Billy mumbled good-naturedly.

135

I watched them walk toward the creek, Henry patiently adjusting his step to Billy's. Henry the Helpful. Clearly his good looks hadn't given him any leverage in the bosom of the Strand family. But his willingness to please didn't seem to have worked any better.

I toyed with the idea of leaving Cyrus's gun displayed atop my kitchen box, then decided "out of sight, out of mind" was wiser. I really didn't want to test my brawn and/or agility wrestling one of them for the thing. After scanning the food boxes under the fly, I settled on my tent. It would be easy enough to keep an eye on it from the kitchen. I shook the holstered gun down into the toe of my sleeping bag. That was about as clever as I could manage. The five bullets I zipped into one of the plastic-lined compartments of my Bloomingdale's Provençal-print cosmetic bag.

Cory hauled her bucket of water back from the creek. We poured it into our plastic water bag and hung the bag back on its tree, a lodgepole spiked with dead lower limbs. A plastic tube ran out of the bottom of the bag. It fed the creek water (at a painfully slow rate, if you were thirsty) through a charcoal filter and into a collapsible plastic jug equipped with a spigot. The water coming out of the spigot was supposed to be *Giardia*-free. *Giardia,* Cyrus had explained, was a dysentery-producing protozoa that flourished in even the highest, clearest streams. He had been extremely careful about it, even brushing his teeth with filtered water. Pete, on the other hand, drank directly out of streams. "He's a native," Cyrus had said, as if that explained the mysteries of immunity.

I put the coffee on and tried to think what to dish up with the steaks for supper. We were getting low on fresh veg, and the generic cans of peas and lima beans and carrots and corn weren't inspiring. I suspected that in the minds of native Montana campers, veggies were an afterthought, a frill laid on for the dudes. However, I found a can of mushrooms and thought a *risotto con fungi* might not be bad with the steaks. There was even Parmesan, albeit the cardboard-shaker variety. Then I hit on the idea of passing off the canned carrots in a garlicky, herby, tomato sauce. After all, the Italians used diced carrots to sweeten up their tomato sauces. Why not the other way around? If it didn't work out, I could chuck it into a soup. (To jump ahead here, it worked out *mezzo-mezzo*. The texture of the canned carrots was still disgusting, but the flavor was passing fair. In any case, they got et, as the Brits say.)

Cory became restless while I worked in the kitchen. She walked off through the woods behind us, down the draw to wait for Pete at the edge of the battleground. Twenty minutes later she marched back up with Henry in front of her, as if she had taken a prisoner. Her narrow face was hot. Henry looked amused in an urbane, bored sort of way. They skirted my tent. Henry tipped his Stetson to me, flashed his white teeth at Cory, and crossed the open ground to Adrienne and Gene, who sat together in front of their father's tent. Billy, I presumed, was still passed out under the cottonwoods. There was no sign of either Lucia or Nat.

"Henry was into the saddles!" Cory exclaimed angrily. "He had the tarp off and my whole pile torn apart!"

"What did he say?"

"He said he was looking for something. He was going through Cyrus's saddlebags." Clearly she expected me to share her outrage.

"And?"

"I told him he couldn't do that, and he said that he could, Lucia had asked him to, and that as long as I was there, why didn't I show him which was Lucia's saddle. He wanted Nat's too." Her voice wavered. "I didn't know what to do. I told him we didn't want any more porcupines, that they'd already cost us a lot of damage. And he said he'd help me put everything back, if I'd show him how."

"He find anything?"

"I don't know. I couldn't tell. He kept his back to me."

I realized none of us had seen Cyrus's impromptu wilderness will. He hadn't waved it under the noses of the heirs he was disinheriting. He had simply patted his pocket. He could have used lined yellow paper, or the back of a map, or an end page of a paperback. For all the searchers knew, he could have written it out on a long, fragile ribbon of toilet paper.

The afternoon seemed to be taking a long time, as if Cyrus's death was a red pushpin that had fixed the sun to the sky. Lucia stayed with his body in the woods behind the tents. Every so often, one or two of the young Strands, in varying combinations, would interrupt their searching and wander over for a brief visit. Cyrus's body seemed like a magnet that repeatedly drew, then released his survivors.

Henry walked over to the cook tent with the box of leftover bullets for Cyrus's Colt. He squatted down next to me and slapped them on a food crate like a deck of cards, but didn't immediately remove his hand. I wasn't sure I wanted to play. I didn't even know the name of the game. His fingers were square and sturdy like a laborer's, and his nails were square too, but the tops of them had been manicured into white crescents, as perfect as slivers of a new moon. He took his hand away. *Magico presto. Bullets for you, pretty lady.* I frowned at him.

He smiled back charmingly. "You might as well have these for safe keeping, too," he said.

Had he brought the ammo over on his own, or had it been deliberated in a group conference? I felt as if one of a group of failing students had stepped forward to present me with a polished apple. An honest trifle or bribe?

"Thank you," I said, playing it straight and crisp, as if the .45s were mine by divine right. I used an over-the-desk voice that worked with the semiliterate, nineteen-year-old males who giggle together in the back row of every English 101 class. It seemed to work on Henry as well. The slyness on his face was replaced with a show of sincerity.

"I'd like to borrow a wildflower guide," I told him. "I didn't think to bring one."

"Sure. Adrienne's got one."

"I'd also like a look at Lucia's sketchbook. Do you think she'd mind?"

He looked taken aback. Evidently, he hadn't checked out her sketchbook. "Oh. I don't think so," he said. He stood up.

"I don't want to bother her."

"No, of course not," he agreed quickly. "I'll bring it over."

Hurriedly, he walked off toward Cyrus and Lucia's tent. Cory and I watched him crawl in. As if he'd sounded an invisible dinner gong, Gene and Adrienne gathered at the flaps. Like hungry dogs, they stuck their noses inside.

Cory stood up. She picked up the box of bullets, weighed them in her hand, then looked around for the gun. "Where'd you put it?" she wondered.

I didn't answer.

She shrugged. Then she asked, "Whose team are you on?" She sounded like she really wanted to know. "Lucia's or Adrienne's?" she persisted.

I thought about it. I realized I didn't care about Cyrus's millions or who got how much of them. My primary concern was keeping poison, if that was indeed what had killed Cyrus, out of my kitchen.

"How about Pete?" I asked Cory. "Does he have a team?"

14

Adrienne crossed the campground with Lucia's sketch pad and her Audubon field guide to western wildflowers, a small, thick tome bound in yellow vinyl. She was wearing large dark glasses, hammered silver earrings, and no hat. Her unset dark hair was straight and wispy, but she had pulled it off her face with a navy bandanna whose cotton looked too fine for the army surplus store. On her navy-and-white-striped shirt, spots of her father's blood made small, dark continents. The rest of the group had changed. But Adrienne seemed to wear her father's blood like her sunglasses: both were badges of grief. Perhaps holding his head as he died was as close to him as she'd ever come.

She nodded at Cory. To me she said, "Henry said you wanted these?" Like an accusation, she thrust the guide and the sketch pad at me.

"Thanks," I said, taking them. "I wanted to look up some of the things we've been seeing—unless there's something I can do?"

"I don't think there's anything anyone can do," she said despairingly.

I offered her coffee, an apple, cheddar cheese, a cookie, soup, anything.

"Maybe a cookie," she said.

I excavated a bag of Oreos. She took three, hesitated, and took two more. "What the hell," she said.

"Emergency rations."

"Right." She split one of the double wafers in half and began gnawing at the icing with her front teeth. I thought of a beaver—a sort of Saturday-morning-cartoon beaver wearing shades. Then she stopped scraping. In the next instant, she hurled the handful of cookies into the woods behind us. "I'm too fat!" she explained angrily. She added in a small, watery voice, "I don't think I can stand this. Where's Billy?"

Cory, who had discreetly retreated under her hat (oh, wondrously useful object!), perked up. "Would you like me to go get him for you?"

"Where is he?"

"Down at the creek. Sleeping, probably."

Her mouth tightened. "Go wake him up. Please," she added.

Cory quickly unfolded herself and ambled off to the line of cottonwoods.

"Adrienne, was your father sick?"

She snorted. "Depends what you mean."

"I mean, did he have a brain tumor, something that could account for his death?"

"That's exactly what we were wondering." She sounded awed that I'd thought of it too.

"No?" I prompted.

"Lucia says no. She says there was nothing wrong with his health. She says that they'd both had their annual checkups just before they came out here." She looked out across the campground toward his tent. "There wasn't any kind of medication in his toilet kit. You think it could have been an aneurysm? I had a cousin who had one. She was only thirty-eight. She got up to change the TV channels and fell over dead."

"Did she have convulsions?"

"I don't know. No one mentioned it."

"Had you noticed any changes in your father's behavior?"

"This is the first time I've seen him in over a year. Make it three for Gene." Her relaxed, North Carolina–flavored drawl

141

turned icily formal. "My father and his third wife had no interest whatsoever in spending holidays with any of his children. Every chance he got, they flew out to their place in Cody."

"Lucia's number three?"

She looked around, tested a food crate with her boot, and sat down on it. "My mother was number one. They were married for twenty-six years. Then after my brother King was killed in Vietnam, Daddy started running around with this bimbo. She wasn't the first one. But after the divorce, he married her. She was twenty-three—two years older than I was—and *built*, you had to give her that, but without one brain cell in her perky little body. She didn't even have the sense to get her own lawyer when they split! You almost had to feel sorry for her. Anyway, it didn't last long. He married her in June, 'seventy-four. The same day I was supposed to graduate from Chapel Hill. I'd dropped out after my sophomore year to marry Billy. I didn't go to their wedding. Instead I went to see my sorority sisters get their sheepskins."

I nodded. "When did he and Lucia get married?"

"A couple years after that. He met her on a business trip to Milan. We didn't go to their wedding either. That was twelve years ago. I had two kids under four, was pregnant, and studying to get my real-estate license!"

"You're a realtor?"

She was sitting up straighter now, as if energized by the memory of work in the "real" world. "Not anymore. I worked for one for a while. But now I'm working on a degree in architectural preservation. Billy and I bought this historic property, just outside High Point. I've been working on the restoration for the last ten years. You heard Daddy talking about squandering money on houses?" There was a squeak in her voice.

He had talked about an addicted son, too. I changed the subject. "How old was your father?"

She exhaled. "Sixty-five. His birthday was in August. He was a Leo. Same as me. I was the baby of the family. Gene came after King. The middle child," she commented dryly. "Gene's big on birth orders. The therapist's latest toy. Tell him your birth rank, and he'll tell you your problems. If you're interested."

"No thanks."

Behind her dark glasses, she smiled weakly.

There was still no sign of Lucia. I wondered if I should check on her, bring her coffee perhaps, but I didn't want to leave the kitchen untended. Cory came back with Billy, his hair dripping creek water onto his shoulders, his movements sober. Adrienne reached for his hand. He gave it an absent squeeze and asked for coffee. I gave him a hot tin cup. He blew on it. With his round, sun-reddened cheeks and curling wet hair, he reminded me of one of those cherubs that blow wind across old maps—albeit an unshaven, middle-aged cherub.

"Billy," Adrienne asked, "at the office, did you notice any changes in my father? We're all wondering if it could have been a brain tumor?"

He shook his head. "You're going to have to wait for the autopsy."

"Oh," she said, slightly shocked. An autopsy hadn't occurred to her. "But—how do we get him out?" She looked up at Cory and me.

Cory said, "As soon as Pete gets back with the horses, I can ride out and get some help."

Adrienne turned her head away like a queen in distress.

Billy studied her. "Darlin', you look like Jackie Kennedy at Dallas, showing off the blood on your clothes like that."

She whipped her head around. "He was my *father!*"

"It's hardly a tragedy, Adrienne," he said reasonably. "At least not yet. It all depends on that will. . . ." He trailed off thoughtfully.

Perhaps it was Billy's denial of the possibility of her grief. Or perhaps it was simply the snapping of tension. Whatever the trigger, she began to sob, rocking over her knees in the age-old movement of loss. Billy walked off disgustedly. Cory stood shifting her weight from one boot to the other. Her hands, which knew how to soothe a horse, dangled helplessly at her side. Under the dove-gray brim of her hat, Cory's eyes were dark with the acute, world-sized pain that only the young can suffer.

Marion Rombauer Becker, co-author of the *Joy of Cooking*, defined eternity as "a baked ham and two people." Here's another definition: watching someone else cry. Like a leftover ham, other people's tears always seem to last too long. I don't know how long Adrienne sobbed, how long Cory hovered hopelessly behind her. I felt stupid, cross, sad, and stupid. Eventually, Adrienne stopped sobbing in jerks, like a car running out of gas. She took off her sunglasses and wiped her reddened eyes and the glasses with a dish towel Cory gave her. She put the glasses back on. "I'm sorry," she apologized.

"You're supposed to cry when your father dies," I said. I glanced at Cory. She glared back at me, as if I'd insulted her.

Adrienne and I hugged. Then Adrienne reached out to Cory and hugged her. Cory remained as rigid as a board. From behind her shades, Adrienne gave us a kind, sad smile and walked back to the will-hunters. The sun had moved around so that the patch of ground in front of Cyrus's tent was now in the shade. Henry and Gene were still sorting through his belongings, maybe for the third time. Adrienne sat down in the grass beside them, her back slumped, her legs stretched out in front of her, like a discouraged doll.

"Will you keep an eye on things for a minute?" I asked Cory. "I need to pee."

"If he was poisoned like you think, it wasn't her!" Cory's chin rose defiantly.

"Why not?" I countered. "You think you can't kill someone and then cry?"

"But you hugged her!"

"She needed one."

Lucia's sketchbook drilled another hole in my stereotyped portrait of the artist as a spontaneous slob. Her studies were as meticulously organized and practical as her wilderness wardrobe. The wildflowers were labeled in her small, rounded, European hand and the pages were dated, the "sevens" for July crossed on their stems. (Later, Lucia told me she dated her drawings in order to match them with her photos: her camera had a device that dated each shot.) Notations on color ran neatly down the sides of the pages. They were written in Italian with her soft sketching pencil. The colors I managed to decipher sounded far more poetic in her language than in mine. Take *azzuro profondo*. In English, the "deep azure" becomes a prosaic dark blue. At first, I thought she had also written the flowers' names in Italian. Then I realized she was using their Latin names. Given the bewildering variety of English common names, it was an eminently logical approach, but I was again impressed by her botanical expertise.

I skipped over the morning's sketches and wrote down the names of the flowers she'd been working on yesterday—when someone or -thing had stolen her specimens. I remembered her mentioning monkey flower and valerian, but there were twelve others on the list, including two kinds of cinquefoil.

The Audubon guide offered lavish, color photographic plates, but its index stank. (Alfred A. Knopf, please take note.) Some names were indexed in English. Others in Latin. Some in both. The two cinquefoils, for example, were not listed under C, nor under S for "sticky" and "shrubby." They were listed under P for *Potentilla*—little power? If it hadn't been for Lucia's Latin, I never would have found water hemlock, a.k.a. *Cicuta douglasii*. It was a member of the carrot family. The description stopped my heart for three or four beats:

> The swollen bases of the stems and usually thick roots have horizontal chambers inside, a feature which helps identify this deadly poisonous species. Its toxin rapidly affects the nervous system, causing severe convulsions and usually death.

Of all Lucia's missing specimens, the only other plant with any potency was valerian:

> . . . extracts were used as a nerve tonic and are said, under certain circumstances, to relax better than opium. Valerian was one of the 72 ingredients Mithridates, King of Pontus, compounded as an antidote to poison, using poisoned slaves as test subjects.

The colored plates showed both plants as white, rounded clusters. Perhaps they had wilted sitting out the afternoon in

Lucia's can of creek water. Had someone made a mistake? Lucia was too knowledgeable to mix them up. If she had poisoned her husband, it wasn't by accident. But what about Nat? Suppose he'd decided to give Cyrus a nice valerian nap so he and Lucia could have their own sweet siesta? Suppose he'd picked the wrong plant and ended up killing his client instead of sedating him? I was surprised how easy it was to imagine Nat the lawyer as a murderer. I wasn't big on lawyers. Or was it my prejudice against pompous men rearing its snaky head?

15

Around five that evening, we heard distant, victorious whoops floating through the pines. Pete and Brett were right on schedule. As they trotted in from the south across the open battle-ground, the errant horses and mules broke their long line and bunched together, rumbling along in a knee-high cloud of ochre dust. Cory's willful pinto, Joker, was in the lead. I picked out tweedy Rex and the "blue" mule named Smokey and the big black one called Harley. The others merged into an earth-toned herd, shoulders and flanks glistening, the horses' jouncing manes and tails dark against the slanting sunlight. (The mules' manes were clipped into brushy mohawks.)

Brett, grinning like a hero, led them past us, saluting with his hat. Pete brought up the rear. He looked triumphant on his big horse. His barrel-shaped torso seemed to radiate energy and strength. I had forgotten, in the short space of his absence, how exotic he looked: his large, flat face set with a powerful, straight nose; his brown, pocked skin; his sharp, black eyes. If a pair of black braids had flapped on his wide shoulders, I might have started to worry about holding on to my own. Was it his Indian-ness, the differences of color and culture, that unsettled me? Or

147

simply his size? His stocky build was massive. He had the kind of presence which, on first impression, prompts members of both sexes to tread just a hair more carefully.

And how did Pete see us as we stood along the bank? How did he take our lukewarm waves, our strained smiles? Brett, sure of his welcome, looked puzzled. But Pete's broad face closed. Did our white faces suddenly all look alike? Were we no longer "his dudes," but a disorganized row of pale-faced judges? He rode over to where we stood and dismounted. Cory took his horse.

"Hey," she greeted.

"We're back," he said cheerfully. But it sounded forced. He surveyed us with tired, guarded eyes. "How's it going?" His voice was even, pleasant.

"I'll go help Brett with the pickets," Cory volunteered.

He nodded.

It was Adrienne who told him. "My father," she said, then hesitated. "My father's passed on."

Nothing registered on Pete's face, but his eyes took in the blood on her shirt.

"She means," Gene offered bluntly, "that he's dead."

Pete looked at me. "Cyrus? Dead?"

I nodded. "About four hours ago."

Shock dawned in his eyes. "What happened?"

"He had some kind of seizure."

"You mean a heart attack?"

"No. He went into convulsions."

He stood there as if a wicked witch had turned him to stone. "Come on," I said. "You'll want to talk to Lucia." I guess I was waiting for him to take over, to straighten up and say, 'Here's the plan, folks,' to let me retire to my kitchen. It didn't happen. Adrienne and Billy, Henry and Gene stood there watching us. I wondered if they'd been waiting out the afternoon with the same expectation as my own: everything will be okay when Pete gets back.

I took Pete's arm, digging my fingers between bone and biceps. "Come on," I repeated. He didn't budge. I pulled, then shifted my weight and moved against him sideways, knocking him off balance. As he moved his feet to regain it, I started forward. He

148

came along. "You probably could use a cup of good, hot coffee," I babbled. "Did you eat any lunch?" I sounded as obnoxious as a hospital nutritionist quizzing a patient. The others gave us plenty of space. For a short distance, they followed us in a loose pack. Then they dispersed.

I decided to come at it sideways. "Did you see your wife?" I asked Pete.

"Oh. Yeah," he said.

"Everything okay?" He didn't answer. I could almost hear the gears in his mind whirring. I tried again. "Dolores hasn't started labor, has she?"

"No." He peered at me. "The doctor says another two weeks. She had an appointment while we were gone."

"Good. Her leg's doing okay?"

He frowned. Maybe it hadn't occurred to him to ask.

"What the hell happened?" he demanded.

"I'm not sure." I told him about Cyrus's new will and I told him how Cyrus had died and I told him how and why I was wondering about poison. He drank two cups of my hot coffee under the cook fly, and I drank two ounces of my warm bourbon. I told him about finding Lucia and Nat *in flagrante* in the high meadow, but I didn't tell him about Cory being Cyrus's daughter. Enough is enough, already.

Pete's first worry was about his note. What would happen to the $100,000 loan Cyrus had made him? What effect would Cyrus's death have on that loan?

"Wouldn't that depend on his heirs?" I asked. "I should think your note would go into his estate."

Pete nodded. "So it would be up to his executor whether to foreclose or not. Do you know who that is?"

"Lucia, he said. But he didn't go into a lot of details. It was mainly the bottom line: his kids weren't getting any."

"And you're pretty sure they haven't found the new will yet?"

"That's how it looks."

"Fuck it!" he exploded angrily.

"Fuck what?"

"All of them! It doesn't matter who gets his money. Any one of them could bankrupt me. Even if Lucia doesn't call in the note, the rest of them could take me to court for wrongful death. Look at them and tell me they won't sue at the drop of a hat. They probably teethed on lawsuits along with their silver spoons!"

I felt encouraged. At least he was waking up. We went round in circles several more times. One thing he said, I filed away under *P* for poison: he remembered hearing a story on the reservation about a child who had died from using a peashooter made from the hollow stem of water hemlock. I wondered how long evidence of poison would remain in a dead body.

"We ought to notify someone pretty soon," I suggested.

"Cory can ride up to Big Prairie. There's a radio at the ranger station there." He thought a minute. "We're in Powell County. She'll have to call the Powell County sheriff."

"What about the Forest Service?"

"They just administer the area. They don't have any civil authority. Down at this end, the Bob's made up of land in three different counties. Each county has its own jurisdiction." He checked his watch. "I better go tell her. If she leaves now, she might get back by midnight. She'll have a half moon. We had it last night and it's supposed to stay clear. Which means they should be able to get a helicopter in here first thing in the morning." He handed me his coffee cup.

"Wait. I wouldn't send Cory, if I were you."

He turned his head. "Oh?"

"If it was murder, we're all suspects."

"What are you saying?"

"If Brett can handle it, it might be better to send him."

"So Cory's a suspect. You think she's gonna hightail it off into the sunset?" he said sarcastically.

"Cyrus could be pretty offensive, in case you didn't notice. He and Cory had a run-in."

"When was this?"

"I'd rather you ask her. All I'm saying is, she had as much—or little—reason to do him in as any of the others."

"Including yourself?"

I shrugged. "Where I come from, thirteen-year-olds kill each other for their sneakers."

He didn't buy it.

150

I tried again. "You're the one who's worried about being sued. If that happens, every decision you make is going to come under scrutiny. They're going to ask questions like, 'You mean you rode off and left your clients with an inexperienced woman you'd just met and a twenty-three-year-old girl?' "

Pete's jaw tightened.

"All I'm saying is, if I were you, I'd play it safe. Cory and I are witnesses—if nothing else. Suppose she freaks and pulls out? You're going to be the one left holding the bag in the courtroom."

It was probably the word *sue* that did it: the "open sesame" of the late twentieth century. "I'll see how Brett feels," he conceded.

"Before you send anyone out, you might want to pay your respects to Lucia."

He looked at me.

Glory be, the man was dense! "You want to be politic. Include her in any decision making. Get her approval."

I steered him across the campground to the wood behind the tents. Cyrus's body lay wrapped in a white manty on the pine-needle-covered ground. Overhead, the light was liquid and golden through the scraggly tops of the pines. But at ground level, their narrow trunks were indigo-washed, a hue from an early Florentine fresco. The heavy folds of the canvas manty were shadowed like a Giotto-painted shroud. I half expected to see Lucia and Nat in attendance, their antique gray profiles surrounded by heavy gold-leaf halos. But the body lay alone, a mysterious, solitary package under the pines. It looked smaller than Cyrus had been in life.

Pete walked up to it and folded back the top flap for a look. There was a rustle in the trees to our left. Lucia appeared, brushing off the seat of her pants. She gazed down at her dead husband, then stooped and smoothed a thin strand of gray hair back off his forehead. "You see?" she said tenderly. "How handsome he looks?"

"Yes," Pete said. Gently, he let the flap down. "I'm sorry."

"The animals, they will come at night? I do not wish—how to say it? I do not want him to be disturbed by anything." She hugged herself in an oversized beige cardigan. I wondered if it was Cyrus's.

151

"He'll be okay in a tent," Pete told her. "We'll move Lee's over here for him. Or wherever you like."

I nodded.

"It is nice here. I have been meaning to pick some flowers for him, but I did not like to leave him alone."

"Where's Nat?" I asked.

"Here." Twigs snapped behind us as he stepped forward. He had changed into a black T-shirt emblazoned with turquoise and hot pink coyotes that sat on their haunches howling above the bulge of his belly. It was the sort of T-shirt his grandchildren might have given him for a birthday.

Lucia was not happy to see him. "I told you to go away! How long have you been here?"

He settled back on his heels. "Go get your flowers. I'll help get the tent set up."

She made a little noise of irritation, as if torn between ordering him away and acceding to his plan.

Pete intervened. "I'd like to talk to you about the—arrangements."

It was a way out. "Of course," she said. "You can come with me. We will see what we can find for him. I am thinking maybe the arnica." She gestured toward a patch of yellow in the pines behind her. "There is more further back. I think it is more masculine than some of the others, don't you?"

It wouldn't be completely fair to say she was flirting with Pete. Call it an exercise of wistful charm. Pete visibly relaxed. As he followed her into the trees, Nat's face remained impassive. He smoothed the pink coyote over his pot belly.

I moved my gear out of my tent into a pile beside the cook fly. Nat and Henry struck the tent and carried it over to the pines where Cyrus lay. I rekindled both the campfire and my stove and started supper. While the family was uncorking flasks around the campfire, Brett and Cory came in from picketing the stock and Pete returned from his stroll with Lucia. I made them powdered lemonade in a plastic jar.

"Everything go okay?" I asked.

He gave a dubious shrug. "She got her arnica."

I tasted my tomato sauce on the stove. A blop of it fell and hissed on the hot metal. The evening was still. Then, eerily, a muffled drumming started in the woods behind us.

"What's that?"

"Just a grouse," Cory said.

The drumming continued insistently.

"She wanted to go out with the body," Pete said. "I told her it would depend how big the helicopter was."

"Could they make two trips?" I wondered. "Money doesn't seem to be an object here. Especially if she manages to hold on to the new will."

He grunted, then asked Brett if he could manage the ride to Big Prairie. "Lee here thinks Cory should stay put." He managed to make it sound like a question.

Brett was stoic. "Whatever you say," he said.

Pete looked at Cory. She didn't object. He seemed surprised. "What was going on between you and Cyrus?" he asked. She met his eyes, but gave no answer. Her resistance was deep, but not hostile. Pete waited patiently, as if he were listening to a piece of bent grass, an overturned stone.

Brett shifted uncomfortably and interrupted. "When do you want me to leave?"

"The sooner the better."

"He's got to eat first," I said firmly.

I gave him two steaks. Had there been enough, I suspect everyone else would happily have eaten two as well—with the exception of Lucia, who ate by the thimbleful even in the best of times. No one complimented the steaks, as if it were unseemly to enjoy meat provided by a dead man. Nonetheless, Cyrus's wild elk, running red juice, redolent with the resinous scent of the wood fire, gave me profound, primitive pleasure. I fancied I could taste autumnal acorns, the tang of grass, the sweet core of thistles in the grilled flesh. My doctored carrots and canned mushrooms in rice were indeed superfluous. Only my round, sourdough loaf stood up to the meat's richness. As I mopped up its juices with torn hunks of the bread, I not only felt more kindly toward Cyrus, I felt in earthy communion with the entire state of Montana.

153

The group mood was appropriately subdued, yet underneath, among Cyrus's children at least, I felt a current of relief, as if they'd all been let out of school early. Perhaps I'm making that up, dredging up a hitherto unadmitted feeling from my own father's death. It is hard to be pure in one's rememberings. What was certain, however, was the distance between Lucia Strand and her lover and lawyer, Nat Rosenfeld. They served themselves separately, sat apart to eat. It was as if their relationship had in some way depended on Cyrus and now that he was gone, they were floundering.

I poured coffee refills around the circle. Everyone had finished eating, but despite the awkward silences, no one moved to break up the circle.

"There will have to be some kind of memorial in High Point," Adrienne observed.

No one responded.

"Maybe you could get your choir," she said to Henry. "What about the Mozart *Requiem*? Didn't you do that last year?"

"That's a little grandiose, don't you think, darlin'?" Billy said.

"He'd probably rather have a couple old Tex Ritter tunes," Gene observed. "From this valley they say you are going—"

"Shh!" Adrienne hissed. She glanced across the circle at Lucia. But Lucia seemed not to hear.

"Ain't you got no respect, boy?" Billy drawled.

"Respect?" Gene wondered. "You want to talk about respect?"

His words were mild, but a clinical nastiness blistered beneath the surface. I decided I didn't want to hear him talk about respect. I turned to Henry. "You sing in a choir?"

"Tenor," he confirmed.

"Henry's never gotten over having made glee club in eighth grade," Gene pronounced.

"That's true," he admitted with a rueful smile.

"What would you choose, Henry?" Adrienne asked.

"For a memorial service, you mean?"

"Yes."

"I'm not sure. I'll give it some thought."

But Lucia had tuned in. *"Pie Jesu,"* she said. She hummed a bar or two—a high, quavering hum.

Henry raised his eyebrows. "Webber's?" He hummed along for a couple measures.

"Yes, that's it."

"That would be nice," he approved.

"Will you sing it?"

"At a memorial?"

"I would like to hear it now."

He hesitated, but no one seemed surprised when he cleared his throat and stood up. He collected himself, rocking slightly on the balls of his feet, as if to find exactly the right place to sing from. Behind him, where the sun had gone down behind the mountains, the sky was pale salmon. Higher up, two stars winked between long streaks of charcoal gray. The fire crackled.

Pie Jesu. Henry sang the Latin in a clean, strong tenor. *Dona eis requiem. May they rest in peace.* Behind Lucia, the pines stood black against a royal blue sky. I felt goose bumps. Henry's voice was full of longing. *Pie Jesu, qui tollis peccata mundi, dona eis requiem. Sempiternam.* Grant them peace. Forever. Forever. He let the last notes drift away like an echo. He lowered his dark head for a moment, then raised it, appraising the audience like a seasoned performer.

Lucia nodded. "Thank you," she said quietly.

Henry sat down, settling back onto his log as if he were reoccupying a less adept self.

"Very pretty," Gene said. "Maybe you could have gotten somewhere with your voice." It wasn't a compliment. He sounded shockingly like Cyrus.

"What do *you* do—when you aren't rescuing disturbed children?" I asked.

Adrienne smirked. "She's got you, Gene."

He seemed amused rather than offended. "I used to sail."

"In High Point?"

"In Marblehead, Massachusetts. That's where I live and practice. Unlike my dear sister, I remain a resident of my native state."

I was curious. "You don't sail any more?"

"My wife took the boat in the divorce."

"What kind of boat?"

"It was a Hinckley Bermuda Forty."

A classic boat. The Mercedes-Benz of the sailing industry. "Nice," I said.

"Yeah," he said sourly. "It was."

I took his plate and stacked it on top of mine. The others began stacking and passing theirs to me. I carried them over to the kitchen. Ten years ago, Gene's forty-foot Hinckley might have cost around a hundred and fifty thousand. By the time you added a couple sets of sails, miles of rope, custom-made cushions, and an anchor, it was probably a quarter-million-dollar toy. She gets the boat, and, as Adrienne had pointed out earlier on the trip, half his share of stock in the family mill. He gets to send his twins to Yale which, last time I heard someone complain, cost twenty thou per head, not counting books. Being disinherited had to be more than an inconvenience.

And not only for Gene. Adrienne and Billy had their expenses, a historic old house, a drug-dependent son. Henry had his forthcoming divorce and his new "bimbo," as Adrienne called her.

If financial gain was a motive for murder, any one of Cyrus's children—natural, adopted, or bastard—could be guilty. (How could Cory not see dollar signs when she looked at Cyrus? For one week in the wilderness with his family, he was probably shelling out what she made in six months.) So. Take the need-greed factor, add in several buckets of anger, and the mixture gets explosive.

On the other hand, Lucia was an even handier suspect. She was the one with the expertise in poisonous wildflowers. But why raise a hue and cry about her missing specimens? Why draw attention to the means of murder?

Nonetheless, given the new will, she stood to gain the most by Cyrus's death. She got to play with a $25 million pile for the rest of her life. For a bonus, she got an adoring, silver-haired and golden-tongued lawyer. Not that she seemed thrilled by the latter prospect.

Of course, as it had occurred to me more than once, it could have been Nat. Bump off the client and take the wife and her money.

Or, variation on a theme, they could have been in it together.

156

Pie Jesu, qui tollis peccata mundi, Henry had sung. The melody had been hauntingly sweet. Jesu, who takes away the sins of the world. I didn't want any of them to have done it. I wanted the tea I'd hidden away to be Earl Grey, pure and simple. I wanted to go home. Home to my mother. So what's new in the world?

I poured the cooled, soapy dishwater down the sump hole Cory had dug that morning. Pete checked in. "Make a new pot of coffee," he said. "I told Lucia I'd sit up with her—and Cyrus's body." Clearly, he was reluctant. I wondered how the Salish Indians felt about corpses.

"I'll spell you, if you like," I offered.

He grunted appreciatively.

"Just wake me up. I'd come sit with you, but I think someone ought to stay with the kitchen."

I poured the dregs of the coffee down the sump hole and refilled the pot from our water bag on the tree. Pete fed the stove a few more sticks of wood. I weighed the two-pound bag of Eight O'Clock coffee in my hand and tried to guess how much longer it would last. I gave up, tossed two lavish handfuls in the big enameled pot, and set it on the stove. Then I plonked myself down on the ground. It hadn't gotten any softer, but it was bliss to be off my feet. Pete sat down a little gingerly. I pretended not to notice. The man had been in the saddle for something like sixteen hours out of the last twenty-four. I was trying to figure out how to frame a tactful question about Salish death taboos when Cory burst through the dark. Breathlessly, she stood over us, hands on her narrow hips.

"I went to lay out my bag?" she blurted out. "Down in the meadow there?"

"Yes?" We said it at the same time.

"And someone's been through my gear."

Neither of us said anything for what seemed a long time. I don't know what Pete was thinking. But I was thinking: could she have had Cyrus's new will? It seemed inconceivable that Cyrus would have given it to her for safekeeping. But suppose she had found it in his saddlebag? Suppose she had found it before Henry had come looking?

"Somebody's been through my gear, I'm telling you!" There was a note of fear in her anger.

"Anything missing?" Pete asked calmly.

It was too dark to see her face, but we could feel her retreating into silence.

"Cory," I urged. "Did someone take something?"

She spun on her heels and strode away.

"First Cyrus's cinch gets cut," I recapped aloud. "Then Lucia's flowers mysteriously disappear. Cyrus dies—maybe of said flowers. His heirs spend the afternoon tossing his gear. Then they go after Cory's. Why? What's going on here?"

Pete muttered something that sounded like *Seme*—accent on the first syllable.

"What?"

"*Seme*," he mused. "Salish for bogeyman. Literally, it means not human."

"What the hell are you talking about!"

"Stop screaming," he ordered quietly.

I lowered my voice. "I am *not* screaming," I informed him. "I am simply *extremely* anxious."

"If Cory did have the new will," Pete observed, "that's the end of it. They'll tear it up and get their money."

I felt slightly comforted.

"You'll be all right," Pete insisted, as if reading my mind. "You've got Cyrus's gun, don't you?"

"Yes," I said glumly.

"Well," he said, as if that settled it.

"You want to trade places?" I tried.

He lowered his big head, rubbed the back of his neck.

I tried again. "I mean, how do you feel about dead bodies? You got any kind of traditional tribal taboos?"

His head popped up. I could almost feel his grin before I heard it in his voice. "I grew up Catholic. On both sides. My father was French-Canadian. Not that he was a religious man. But my mother's a full-blooded Flathead. The Jesuits got ahold of them back in the eighteen forties and never let go. The 'old way' among my mother's people is a wake and all three mysteries of the rosary.

That's what Lucia wants. Some one to say Hail Marys with her all night."

"Oh."

He chuckled. "You sound disappointed."

"I guess I was hoping for something more—anthropological."

"You know how to say the rosary?" he asked in a hopeful voice.

"Sorry. I grew up Protestant." I contemplated the prospect of crawling into my bag alone under a skinny pine beside the cook fly. Praying with Lucia over a manty-wrapped body seemed more attractive. "Episcopalian. But not High Church enough for *Aves*. Maybe you could teach me. I've been told I learn quickly."

He laughed. "It wouldn't count."

"Why not?"

"You're not Catholic." In good humor, he lumbered to his feet, poured two cups of coffee, and started off across the campground to join Lucia in her vigil. Then he came back. "I just remembered. Here's something anthropological for you: When a Flathead man died, his wife shaved her head in mourning. They also shaved the mane and tail of his horse. When her hair and the pony's mane and tail grew back, the mourning period was over. You like it?"

"Yeah," I said. "I do."

"I read that for a social studies paper in seventh grade. I got an *A*."

"Be sure and tell Lucia. I'll donate my razor. Don't know why I brought it along. You haven't given me time to even think about my legs, never mind my armpits."

"Your guilty secret is safe with me."

"Get out of here!" I bossed. "No, wait. Tell me what happened when a Flathead *wife* died? Did her man shave *his* head?"

Pete laughed. "That wasn't in the book."

"I'll bet it wasn't," I grumbled

16

That night I slept fitfully under a pine tree every bit as pathetic as Charlie Brown's Christmas tree. Cyrus's six-gun in the toe of my bag kept interfering. Finally, without opening my eyes, I wormed down into the dark nylon warmth and retrieved Cyrus's gun, its belt buckled around its holster. My feet (in rag-wool socks) had kept it toasty. Even the brass cartridges in the belt were body temperature.

I dumped the weapon into my duffle beside me, then quickly drew my arm back into my bag. The night air was very cold. I thought about getting up to pee, but instead I snuggled back down into my bag. I hadn't bothered to get out of my jeans and every time I rolled to the left, the little worry bead of carnelian I kept in my back left pocket dug into my cheek like the famous pea of princess fame.

There was, however, no Prince Charming waiting to kiss away my bruise. The next time I woke up, I heard dull, thudding sounds and small clatterings. It took me a while to locate them. They were not part of a dream. Someone—or something—was moving in the kitchen area. I sat up and listened. The ground was frosty and I could see faint plumes of my breath in dim light from a setting half moon. The tents on the other side of the field were blocks of gray. I wondered if Pete and Lucia were still saying Hail Marys behind them. I strained my eyes at the dark blanket of shadow under the cook fly. A bear? Pete rattling around for more coffee? Or Brett back from Big Prairie and hungry? I heard a muffled clinking of utensils. "Pete?" I called. "Brett?"

There was no answer. *Shit,* I thought. I fished around for my boots and shoved in my feet. The leather was frozen.

Shivering, I clumped over to the cook fly. The contents of the plastic packing crates were strewn across the ground. The edges of cans glinted in the moonlight. I heard a slight sound behind me and wheeled—then whiteout. The right side of my head exploded.

I remember coming to and feeling a patch of bare earth, smooth as icy satin, under my cheek. And I remember vomiting on all fours and crying and shivering, all at the same time. I don't remember Brett finding me. I do remember Cory trying to blind me with a flashlight. ("Her pupils work okay," I heard her telling Pete.)

By the time the sky had lightened to predawn gray, I was sitting cross-legged near the wood stove wearing my sleeping bag over my shoulders and working on keeping down a cup of Cyrus's Earl Grey—from the box. I had a heroic-sized headache for which they wouldn't let me take any aspirin, but they'd swabbed the side of my head with peroxide. It had stung like a swarm of yellow jackets. My hair was still wet and half frozen and I could see blood in the thin tangle of dirty blond ends on my shoulder. "Doesn't look serious," Cory had said. To determine this, she had shaved away what felt like an excessively wide swath of my hair—with the razor I'd jokingly offered to lend Lucia. The joke didn't seem funny anymore, but Pete kept on beating it like a dead horse. "Younger squaw sets the example," he harped.

Cory stood back to admire her handiwork. "Excellent. Now all you need is a safety pin through the nose."

It was just as well they were being crisp about it. Any kind words and I probably would have dissolved. I felt overwhelmed by the unfairness of the attack. Someone had brained me and *I was one of the good guys.* At the behest of a friend, I had volunteered to help out a poor Indian in distress! I was doing my Lady Rescue

161

thing. (Call it shock-induced amnesia: I had no memory of Joey's phone call as the vehicle of my own rescue.)

Pete wouldn't let Cory or Brett clean up the mess around us. "I want them to see this," he said grimly.

"Is the Thermos still there?" I asked. "Cyrus's tea Thermos? He was drinking out of it when he died. I thought it ought to go out with his body on the helicopter. I had it wrapped in a green garbage bag." They searched through the debris of cans, the Tupperware containers, potatoes, plastic ketchup bottles, potholders, picnic-sized cardboard salt cellars, cellophane packages of store-bought cookies, cabbages, oranges, green apples. Some of the eggs were broken, but the flour bags were intact, and Pete allowed Brett and Cory to repack our still half-frozen packages of elk. The Thermos was nowhere to be found.

"You still think he wasn't murdered?" I asked them. The word sounded as rude as my I-told-you-so.

"Murdered?" Brett echoed slowly.

"She thinks he was poisoned," Cory clued him in. Two consecutive nights spent in the saddle had taken a toll. Brett's blue eyes were vague, his tan sallow. Uneven patches of dark blond stubble made smudges along the line of his jaw. Pete hadn't shaven either, but he had only a quarter-sized rash of black hairs on the very center of his chin and maybe five bristles on each corner of his upper lip. He could have plucked out his entire beard, hair by hair, in a leisurely ten minutes.

He sat up, suddenly alert. "Lee. You still have his gun, don't you?"

"Oh God. I put it in my duffle." I started to get up, then groaned.

"Stay there. I'll look." Pete was on his feet.

"I didn't see it when I got your razor," Cory said. "I saw the bullets in your cosmetic bag."

"And I had a box with a few more rattling around inside. Henry gave it to me. It was down at the bottom, but the gun should be right on top."

Pete found the extra ammo, but the gun and its belt full of bullets were gone.

I felt a nauseating wave of guilt and shame. I thought I could

162

handle it. Obviously I couldn't. Pete was standing over me. I didn't look up. "I'm sorry. I should have given it to you. Actually, I was about to." My head pounded.

He sat down. "What makes you think someone couldn't have bashed in my head?" he asked mildly.

I kept my head down. My eyes were tearing up. A fat drop plonked beside my boot. Maybe they didn't notice.

"Okay," Pete said, in his listen-up voice. "We've probably got us a killer dude. And we've definitely got a dude with a gun. They may not be the same dude. Whoever took the gun may just have been looking for the new will."

"If it was just an anxious heir, the Thermos would still be here," I pointed out. "I mean, only the poisoner knew about the Thermos. I didn't tell anyone I'd squirreled it away for the pathologist."

They thought about it. "You were right," Brett said to Cory. "She ain't brain-damaged."

Pete almost smiled.

I blew my nose into my bandanna and felt better. "Suppose the poisoner found the new will in Cory's gear and destroyed it." Cory made a squeak of protest. "Wait," I said. "Say the fortune has been secured and tonight's business was simply a matter of getting rid of the evidence and taking the gun as insurance. Maybe that's the end of it." I turned my head to Cory. *Thump, thump.* "Did someone find the will in your gear? That's all I'm asking, Cory. Did they find it?"

Brett and Pete looked at her with interest.

"No," she said.

"Okay then. The question is, did the poisoner find it along with the Thermos and Cyrus's gun? Seems unlikely to me. I've gotten to know every inch of every food crate. If Cyrus had slipped it into the kitchen, I think I would have found it."

"So?" Pete said.

"So, Cyrus's new, holographic will's still up for grabs. If Lucia has it, she's in danger from her stepchildren. Even if she did Cyrus in with tincture of water hemlock, the children want their money. They're after it. Call them Nemesis."

"Who?" Pete wondered.

I shook my head and regretted it.

"Go on," he said.

I tried. My mind blurred. "Now I'm out of bright ideas. How about calling in the sheriff?"

All three of them snorted their amusement.

"What's wrong with that? At least we'd have a gun on our side. It would make things more even."

"I'm not sure I'd go that far," Brett said.

"What do you mean? You think they'd buy him up?"

Cory laughed. "I hadn't thought of that."

"You don't understand the way it is out here," Brett said.

Pete explained, "Powell County covers a whole lot of mountains but has only about seven thousand people. The sheriff's a former school-bus driver named Boyd Lily. Maybe he finished high school. Once upon a time."

I still didn't get it. Was Pete being an intellectual snob? "So?" I demanded coolly.

"He's just not equipped to deal with a case like this."

Brett offered, "It's like calling in Fred Flintstone. Nice guy, but . . ." He shrugged. "Look, last night I made Big Prairie at eleven-thirty. Turns out they've left the ranger station with a Forest Service volunteer in charge. So I wake the guy up and he doesn't know how to work the radio. But he's not *author-ized* to let anyone else use it either. Then I tell him we've got a body, and he almost jumps out of his longjohns. There he is dancing around in his fancy Everest-weight polypros, but he won't let me touch the radio. Finally he lets me tell him how to get the operator. Turns out the radio can't raise Deer Lodge—that's the county seat. But they've got a repeater up on Jumbo Mountain, right over there"— Brett pointed to the western horizon—"and it boosts the wattage enough to get through to Seeley Lake in Missoula County. They can also get Spotted Bear, but we go for Seeley Lake, and the sheriff's department at Seeley Lake relays the message to Deer Lodge. "We go back and forth like this for over an hour. Seems like Sheriff Lily's out on call. At least that's what his wife says. But the dispatcher thinks he's tucked into his own bed. Finally our operator—and we're getting pretty chummy by this time—persuades Deer Lodge to persuade Mrs. Lily to wake him up. But when the

164

Deer Lodge dispatcher finally gets hold of him, Lily doesn't know what to do. The guy's never had a dead body in the Bob. First he's going to call out the National Guard in Helena. Next we get a message that he thinks he can get a Bell chopper from the Department of State Lands. They've got one there in Deer Lodge, but he's got to locate a pilot. The big problem is, he's supposed to take his grandson fishing in the morning. That's today. We're getting all this through our operator at Big Prairie, you understand. Matty, her name was. You could hear her trying not to chuckle when she talked to them."

"So is he coming?"

"Who knows? Matty said she'd keep trying. I told her we'd stay put today, and if they didn't show, then we'd pack the body out ourselves." He turned to Pete. "I didn't know what else to do. I was getting kind of punchy by that time."

Pete nodded.

Cory said, "The mules won't like it."

I had the feeling it was at least their second time around on the subject. I started to doze, but Cory kept poking me. "You aren't suppose to go to sleep with a head injury," she informed me.

"You said it wasn't serious."

"We're suppose to watch you don't go into a coma."

"Fifteen minutes. You can punch me every fifteen minutes," I pleaded.

"You've got to move out of my way," Pete intervened. "I'm going to start breakfast. We'll get you up when it's ready."

"I don't think I feel like eating."

"I want to talk to them. If you feel up to it, I want you here."

"I'm okay," I said. I stood up and found that, in fact, I was. Despite the pain in my head, I could see straight and walk straight. I'd had worse hangovers; heads that reduced me to blindness and crawling. Cory moved my bag and blue foam mat into the pines behind the kitchen and I lay there, smelling Pete's bacon and coffee on the cold, white morning air. Cory came over once to check on me. I blinked at her. The sky between the pine boughs was turning an angelic shade of blue.

* * *

165

If the mess in the kitchen was exhibit number one, I was exhibit number two. Pete asked me not to pretty myself up. I sat on an overturned packing crate, warming my hands around another cup of tea, and saying nothing as our guests, summoned for seven o'clock breakfast by Brett, stopped short at the edge of the cook fly and exclaimed, "My God, what happened?" Their faces all seemed genuinely dismayed. Lucia clutched Henry's arm. Henry shook his head in concern. Gene and Nat and Billy gaped. Adrienne noticed me. "Lee. What's the matter?" Her eyes widened as she took in my head. "Jesus. Are you all right?"

"What happened here?" Nat demanded in a take-charge voice.

Pete flipped the pancakes on the stove's griddle and turned, spatula in hand. "You all know that Lee had Cyrus's pistol. Last night someone attacked her and took it. One of you has it."

No one moved. Then Billy Caton said, "That's ridiculous."

Pete turned back to his pancakes. He lifted them onto a stack at the back of the stove and poured three new ones on the griddle.

Lucia stepped over a package of pretzels. She looked pale and fragile. She was still in last night's clothes, slim jeans and the oversized tan cardigan. She waved a bewildered hand over the mess. "But why?" she asked Pete. "I don't understand."

He turned to face her. "Maybe someone's looking for your husband's will."

"Oh." She frowned. "The will. But where is it?" she asked Pete.

No one answered. Her stepchildren's faces were carefully blank. They watched her.

"His new will," she repeated. "He had it in his shirt pocket. Henry, have you seen it?"

Henry said, "It wasn't in his shirt."

"You washed it for me."

"Yes." He gave her a smile that managed to be both sympathetic and ironic. "If it had been there, I would have found it."

Her voice rose sharply in distress. "But I must find it! What could he have done with it?"

"He didn't give it to you, then?" Gene inquired gently.

"No, no! You know how he is private in everything he is doing! Where could he have put it?"

She scanned her stepchildren's faces for help. Their expressions were as flat as bricks in a wall. "Oh," she said weakly, as if realizing for the first time what she was up against. She closed her eyes. Her mouth sagged like an old woman's.

"Lucia?" Nat said, his voice alarmed. He stepped forward to her.

She stopped him with a gesture. She studied the younger group bunched together at the edge of the cook fly. "You have been going through our things," she accused her stepchildren.

No one denied it.

"I go to our tent to change my clothes. I can not find my nice navy blue sweater. Something is not right. Everything is a little different, a little odd. I think maybe I am going crazy." She straightened her spine and observed, "You are looking for his will." Her statement was as flat and factual as a declaration of war.

"For pity sake, let's have some coffee," Billy Caton complained.

Pete turned the pancakes. He announced, "We've put in a call for a helicopter. I'm hoping it and the sheriff will arrive sometime this morning. Lucia, if you want to fly out, you can talk to him about it. In any case, they will take Cyrus's body to St. Patrick's in Missoula. After that, we head out. From here to Benchmark, where we pick up our van, it's about twenty-eight miles. If we push, we might be able to do it in one day. I want you to be ready to move out as soon as the chopper's gone. We aren't going to be stopping to smell the flowers. My main concern is to get everyone out of here safely."

Lucia wilted. She pressed the heels of her hands to her forehead. The large diamond on her ring finger flashed a prism on the underside of the cook fly. "Oh," she moaned. "Why did he *do* this to me!"

If she had poisoned Cyrus, it was a *bravura* performance.

"Lucia." Nat's voice was in its courtroom mode, commanding, penetrating.

"Leave me alone," she said crossly.

"The document is safe," he announced.

She looked confused. The rest of the group was acutely attentive. Their ears seemed to give off a communal whir, like a collection of rotating antennae. "What are you saying?" she demanded.

He couldn't resist. He paused, savoring the drama of the moment. He raised his bushy eyebrows slightly, laid a Napoleonic hand atop the belly of his chamois shirt. "Cyrus's new will is safe," he said smugly. He looked as if he had just pulled a prize plum out of a Christmas pie.

Cyrus's children looked ready to kill for it.

"Pick up your plates and forks," Pete said. "Chow's ready."

Obediently, they stooped and, from the flotsam at their feet, fished out scarred plastic floral plates and dime-store stainless. They wiped them on their shirt sleeves and stood in line for pancakes. I tried a couple myself and noted that Pete's hand with the batter was heavier than mine. This made me feel better. For an extra boost, when Cory wasn't watching, I swallowed three Excedrin with a mouthful of Cyrus's Earl Grey. After a few minutes, I could feel their slight burn down the pipe to my stomach. Experimentally, I touched edges of my shaven patch of scalp. The skin felt rose-petal soft. It probably looked like the underbelly of a worm.

Maybe it was the heavy-duty pancakes anchoring my stomach. Or an Earl Grey–Excedrin high zipping around the creases in my brain. Or simply the absolution of daylight: the dome of the morning sky was the exact delicate blue of the Virgin's cloak in an Italianate Assumption. Was there anyplace in the world with a sky as pure? Or was the sky over our campground a special, morning-after effect, the answer to Pete and Lucia's nighttime duet of "Hail Mary"s behind the tents?

Whatever the cause, I felt a fog lift from the swampy turf of my soul. Pete appeared to be back in control. To my mind, Nat had virtually confessed. He had the will. He must have been the one who had bonked me over the head when I interrupted his search for the Thermos. More than anyone, he knew that without physical evidence, without a murder "weapon," the case became weak, purely circumstantial. Had he taken the gun to keep the greedy kiddies at bay? He wasn't a stupid man. Perhaps he had decided to

168

wait until he had Cyrus's sidearm in his pocket before flapping the new will under their disinherited noses.

His announcement struck me as an instinctive male strut, a display prompted by Lucia's show of indifference. He hadn't considered the possibility of her rejection. Why should it occur to him? Look at the lyric surge of his lovemaking, the rose-tinged intensity of his devotion.

He would never tell her what he had done. Never would he admit how, before they had lain in the high meadow under that luminous, fearsome, nuclear-sized cloud, he had stolen her simples, her vegetable drugs.

Cyrus, where are my flowers? she had cried.

Don't be a pain, he had growled. *I'm talking with my friend, my legal adviser, about* your *future.*

I felt a small wave of sorrow for Nat Rosenfeld. I knew he would lose Lucia. I knew it as certainly as a date memorized in childhood, say 1066 for the Battle of Hastings, or 1492, when Columbus sailed the ocean blue.

On the other hand, it seemed likely enough that, for lack of evidence, Nathaniel Rosenfeld, Esquire, would get away with murder. The prospect didn't particularly disturb me. Like Pete, my most immediate concern was the body count. Cyrus was enough. If his children wanted to do battle, let them do it somewhere else.

17

Sheriff Boyd Lily's borrowed helicopter came out of the west, a small dot preceded by an increasing roar. Inside its noise, there was an insistent punching sound, a staccato *whack-whack-whack*. The dot grew into a mechanical insect with a giant, bulbous eye and a skeletal tail of open struts. The whirling rotors were invisible, but their blades tore virginal blue sky with a racket that had horses and mules and us running around in circles. Cory and Brett angrily waved the machine away from the wild-eyed picket horses, then the pilot sidled over to the camp and hovered overhead, nose-heavy, blasting circles in the treetops and billowing the tents in upon themselves. Finally he lifted up over the tops of the pines and set down on the bench above us.

Sheriff Lily climbed out of a door in the bug's eye with a radio and his grandson, a seven-year-old in an extra-large Guns 'n' Roses T-shirt that hung to the knees of his "husky"-sized jeans. Heads low, the sheriff holding on to his straw cowboy hat, the two of them scooted out from under the circumference of the roaring blades. The waiting pilot did not cut the engine. We moved away to the edge of the meadow, but the noise made conventional conversation impossible. Boyd Lily shook hands with Pete and acknowledged Lucia and me with a nod. The others were down at the camp, packing up their gear.

"Where is it?" Lily shouted at Pete's ear.

Pete gestured down the hill.

The sheriff scratched the back of his neck, nudging his hat forward. His grandson watched, then tried his own neck, newly shorn and pale below a bristling summer haircut. "Stretcher?" Lily shouted again.

Pete shook his head.

Lily trotted back to the helicopter for a stretcher. He was a thin man, with a slightly concave chest, as if years behind the wheel of a school bus had given him a permanent, self-protective hunch. He was not wearing tans, but he had buckled on a departmental-looking .38 and had pinned his shield to the right pocket of his mint green, beige-striped shirt. The synthetic fabric, however, was flimsy and Lily's badge of office flopped forward, face toward his boots, like an embarrassed adolescent. In his left pocket, he carried an arsenal of ballpoints. His skin was weathered, so it was hard to tell his age, but I guessed late fifties, somewhere in there. On his left cheekbone there was a large scab—the kind dermatologists leave when they burn off skin cancers.

Down the hill at the campsite, his manner was hail-good-ol'-boy-well-met. It was easy enough to see how he'd gotten himself elected. He didn't flinch at Pete's Indianness. "This your outfit?" he asked. And when Pete said yes, Sheriff Lily met his eyes like a politician and nodded pleasantly, as if he'd expected it all along.

Against the *thud-thud-thud* of the helicopter idling in the meadow above us, he said, "This is Bobby, my grandson." There was an apology in Boyd Lily's voice as he explained Bobby's presence: "The wife's gone to Helena for the day. Her mother's in a nursing home there. Bobby's with us now, so I brought him along for the ride."

Pete radiated disapproval. Just you wait, Henry Higgins, I thought. Just you wait till you're stuck with your own kid on an inconvenient day. But my gloating was premature.

"Bobby," Sheriff Lily instructed, "you just stick with this pretty lady." He gave me a wink. "She'll take good care of you."

Instantly, I hated Sheriff Lily. In the next instant, I hated Pete.

171

"Keep the kid out of our way," Pete ordered me. *Cock-a-doodle-doo*. There was no mistaking it. He was showing off for the sheriff.

I suppose I could have made a stink and gotten the downhill end of the stretcher that bore Cyrus's softening, dead weight uphill to the chopper. No doubt my charge would have been delighted to lend his pudgy seven-year-old shoulder. It probably would have kept him in bubble gum—or worse—all the way through junior high.

But I didn't make a stink. Nor did Bobby. We stood there like two kids who had just been told by the team coach, "Well, you guys can keep score."

Meanwhile, Lucia was busy wrapping Lily around her honeyed pinky. She had a lavender nylon backpack with her. The outline of her camera bulged in the bottom of it and her sketch pad poked out the unzipped top. "But I am ready," she insisted. "I am ready to go out with him right now. Pete will bring out our things."

Boyd Lily raised the pilot on his radio. Bursts of static punctuated their conversation which seemed to have more numbers than words in it. Another male code, I thought angrily. Lily asked Lucia how much she weighed.

"In pounds? Almost hundred and twelve," Lucia said.

"Hundred and twelve," he repeated into the radio.

Lucia smiled at the sheriff. "But this is in the morning without my clothes."

"Make that a hundred and thirty," he amended to his pilot. "You're taking that pack along, ma'am, ain'cha?" he explained courteously.

The chopper, it seemed, was an older model, built to carry only the two passengers plus a litter on the outside. It wasn't capable of flying out Cyrus's body along with Lucia, the sheriff, and his grandson Bobby. After lots of ten-fouring back and forth, it was agreed that the pilot would fly Lucia out with her husband's body, then return for the sheriff and his grandson. Pete looked at his watch. It was already ten o'clock. "We figured on moving out right away," he said to Lily.

"No problem. I've got our fishing gear in the back of the chopper. Bud knows the way back."

172

Pete raised his eyebrows approvingly. "I take it you won't be inconvenienced if Bud takes his time about it?"

Boyd Lily grinned. "No, sir!"

"I can point you in the direction of a couple good holes."

They sounded like they'd been chums for fifty years. I didn't think it particularly becoming to Pete. He was still the thirty-two he had been a week ago when I'd asked Dolores.

Thud-thud-thud, went the chopper. Lucia hiked smartly off into the pines. A quick pit stop before boarding, I figured.

"You going to tell the sheriff about the hemlock?" I asked Pete.

Both men looked at me.

"Our dead client," I told Lily, "might have been poisoned."

Pete looked as if he would have liked to poison me. "She's along as cook," he explained to Lily. "She's worried about accidental ingestion of water hemlock." He turned to me. "If that's what it is, they'll find it in the autopsy."

"Not if they don't test for it," I countered. "Sheriff?" I said, trying not to bat my eyelids too loudly. "Could you ask the pathologist to test for cicutoxin?"

"You're going to have to spell that one out for me, honey!" he chuckled.

"Got a pencil?"

Pete glared at me.

I smiled sweetly. The sheriff unclipped a ballpoint from his shirt pocket, pulled a business card out of his wallet, and flipped it over. C-I-C-U-T-O-X-I-N, I spelled slowly. Carefully, he wrote each letter down. "Okay," he said. "I'll pass it on." He clicked his ballpoint and slid it back into his pocket with the card.

"Where'd you get that?" Pete muttered.

"Out of one of their wildflower books."

"Let's get a move on," Sheriff Lily said to Pete. "That whirlybird ain't for free." They walked off with the stretcher toward the tents.

There was nothing more I could do. I looked at Bobby in his faded black T-shirt. "You into metal?" I asked cheerfully.

His hazel eyes were uncomprehending.

"Your T-shirt. You a Guns 'n' Roses fan?"

He shook his head.

I waited.

"My mom gave it to me before she went away," he said finally. "She got it out of the Goodwill box."

"It's a nice one," I said. "C'mon. You can help me pack up my kitchen."

"Yes, ma'am."

"My name is Lee."

"Yes, ma'am."

"You can call me Lee."

"Yes, ma'am," he mumbled, ducking his head.

I let it drop. I've never been known for my way with kids and dogs.

The helicopter lifted off, making small, violent hurricanes in the tops of the pines. In the litter, Cyrus's manty-wrapped body was suspended like an overweight cocoon—the machine sailed off toward the distant mountains at a tilt. The sky no longer looked so spectacularly promising. Patches of thin clouds were drifting up from the jagged, snow-covered peaks. The noise of the helicopter receded. The silence was almost staggering.

Sheriff Lily and Pete came down from the bench. Lily carried a pair of rods, a tackle box, and olive green waders. His radio was clipped to the back of his gun belt. "You want to do lunch here or what?" I asked Pete.

"Underway," he said.

"Can I make you and Bobby sandwiches?" I offered Lily.

"We brought our own, thank you. But I won't say no to coffee." I poured him and Pete a cup. They seemed in no hurry. But the rest of our group seemed as anxious to be gone as Lucia had been. A pile of their duffles waited for the mules. Henry had started packing up Lucia and Cyrus's things—by this time, he must have known every seam in their underwear. Billy Caton and Gene were striking their tents. Adrienne came over to the cook fly to inspect the sheriff. Pete introduced them.

"What's going to happen now?" she asked Boyd Lily.

Lily tipped his hat back. "I reckon that depends on the coroner's report," he said. He nodded, as if approving what he'd just

174

said. "I'll just need to know where you're staying until we get the all clear."

"You mean we can't go home?"

"Where would that be, ma'am?"

"High Point, No'th Car'line-ah." Suddenly she sounded very southern.

"Ma'am, like I told Miz Strand, it shouldn't take too long to get this straightened out." He removed his hat. Underneath, the top of his head was bald and freckled. "My condolences," he offered.

The gesture appeased her. "Thank you," she said.

"The Holiday Inn in Missoula has a swimming pool," he added helpfully. He ducked his head to put his hat back on, then straightened up and settled it on his head with a little wiggle.

I gave Pete the high sign. It seemed to soar right over his cropped black pate. "I ought to get packing here. . . ." I nudged. The two men took last gulps of coffee. "C'mon, son," Sheriff Lily said to Bobby. Then the sheriff turned to me. "He been behaving himself?"

"He's a good worker." We hadn't spent more than fifteen minutes together, but Bobby had been disconcertingly anxious to please. He had dried the breakfast forks for me like an expert. I gave him a smile. His eyes were worried. I wondered if he got knocked around for "misbehaving."

I felt badly as I saw him go off to the creek with Pete and Lily. He kept a respectful pace behind his grandfather. *You want responsibility?* I asked myself. *You want to take the life of a chubby seven-year-old into your hands?* A vision of my daughter skipped through my mind: her blond hair shining in the sunlight, the fine ends wind-snarled, the little pink plastic clips that she loved and I hated bobbing uselessly around her ears. She would have been thirteen now—a dangerous age for mothers and daughters, I reminded myself. I turned to the business of lunch.

There was only a four-by-five-inch piece of elk steak left over from last night's cookout. It was rare. I sliced it into thin strips and Adrienne and I dipped them in mustard and dropped them into our mouths like college sophomores devouring goldfish back in the days of Debbie Reynolds and Pat Boone.

Thus fortified, we started in on the peanut-butter-and-jellies, tucking pairs of sandwiches into plastic baggies and setting them out with an apple apiece and miniature boxes of raisins. Adrienne washed the knives we'd used. I pulled out Dolores's Tupperware containers of elk chili from the meat locker and repacked them to defrost in the canned goods crate. Adrienne dumped the coffee and I put on Pete's asbestos gloves and started to knock down the stove.

"Lee." Brett's voice sounded peculiar. I had the stovepipe on the ground and was trying to unwedge section A from section B. I looked up over my shoulder. His face was drawn, his blue eyes stunned. I dropped the pipe. "What's the matter?"

"Nat's on the path."

"What?"

"He's lying on the path in woods. He's been shot."

"Oh my God!" Adrienne exclaimed.

Maybe he's not dead, I thought. "Is he dead?"

Brett hesitated.

"Show me!" I demanded. He wheeled and charged off into the pines behind the cook fly. "Get Pete!" I called to Adrienne. I ran after Brett, crashing through the skinny pines, nicking my shoulder on a dead spike. My heart had jumped out of its seat and was knocking away in my throat. This time it wasn't the altitude.

Nat lay in a stand of older lodgepoles off a deer track that led down through the pines behind the campground to the edge of the battlefield where the tack was stored. Through the trees, I could see the green nylon pyramid tent that Brett had set up over the latrine. Nat had been shot in his chest. Twice. But there was very little blood visible. One dark-ringed entry hole through his pale blue T-shirt was obvious. The other I didn't see immediately. It was obscured by the shirt's SAVE THE WHALES logo. His broad chest wasn't moving. I prodded his neck for the carotid artery, but nothing stirred under my fingers. His flesh was soft and still warm, but there was no pink left in his face—even his lips were the color of a manila folder. His brown eyes were open, blank as acorns. His mouth was open, too.

There was no sign of Cyrus's gun, but Nat's plaid outer shirt lay crumpled beside him. The mat of rusty pine needles had been

176

disturbed around him, and there was a pattern of heel marks from his boots that suggested death hadn't come easily. But I saw no footprints. The carpet of pine needles had absorbed everything but the signs of the lawyer's last struggle.

I looked around for Brett. He was further down the path holding a pair of mules by their rope halters. I walked over to them. The mules stood rock still. Except for their suspicious eyes, they might have been stuffed.

"I was bringing up Smokey here, and Miss Peach," Brett said. He gulped down a breath. "I figured we might as well start loading up. Then these ol' mules went and balked on me. They just wouldn't be persuaded. I was getting pretty hot, then something caught my eye up ahead. I thought maybe someone had dropped something coming back from the crapper. So I tied up the mules right where they stood and went and over and . . . "

"You didn't see a gun?"

"No. It was just like you saw it."

"Where's Cory?"

"She was saddling up the horses."

"You better go get her. We aren't going anywhere for a while and the sheriff's going to want a head count."

Miss Peach, a smaller reddish mule, twitched a long, dark-tipped ear. She didn't look stubborn. She looked smart. "Hey, Peachy," Brett rumbled at her. "You win." He rubbed Smokey's white nose. Then he turned them away and led them back toward their pasture. They clopped easily along behind him. I stayed beside Nat's body, scanning the ground. I had no idea what to look for.

Pete and the sheriff crashed through the woods. Behind them trailed our surviving campers.

"Stay right where you are," the sheriff ordered me. He eased the gun belt on his hips. I stayed. "Keep everyone back," he told Pete. He approached Nat as if the dead man might suddenly pop up and start shooting.

"I couldn't find a pulse," I offered.

The sheriff didn't seem inclined to try. "He's shot dead, all right." He looked back at Pete. "How many guns you got along with you?"

"Just one. It belonged to Cyrus—Mr. Strand—but it's been missing since last night. Lee had it. Someone took it off her."

"What was she doing with it?" demanded Sheriff Lily.

Pete paused. Then he said, "She was holding on to it."

Boyd Lily looked skeptical. He hooked his thumb under his gun belt and shifted it again. Then he reached back and unclipped his radio. "Everyone keep back," he commanded again in an official tone. "I'm going to try and raise 'em." He strode off through the woods to open ground.

I moved a couple paces back. Brett and Cory came up from the horses and stood with me as if Nat's body was a crevasse impossible to cross. Pete and the others stood on the other side. I saw Bobby's round face peering between elbows. I caught Gene's eye and rolled my own toward Bobby. Gene got the signal. He stepped around toward Bobby, but Henry had already tuned in. His hand was on the boy's shoulder. Bobby's upturned face was as open and vulnerable as the sky.

Sheriff Boyd Lily came back rejuvenated. He announced that he had contacted Bud, his pilot, and had ordered him to turn around and come back. The relief of it seemed to work for the sheriff like a hit of testosterone: he positively bristled with virility. "All right, let's see what we've got here," he said, his voice half an octave deeper. He swaggered over to Nat, toed the crumpled plaid shirt out of the way, then hunkered down, his eyes scanning the body. He picked up Nat's left arm, then carefully lowered it back into position. I had the distinct feeling that he had no idea what he was doing. Then he frowned. "Pete? Give me a hand here."

Pete, one hand on Nat's shoulder, another on his hip, rolled the side of the body slightly off the ground. Lily reached underneath and pulled out what looked like a three-by-five color snapshot. "Got it," Lily said.

Pete rolled Nat back down and peered over Boyd Lily's shoulder.

The sheriff held the photograph by its edges. With his free hand, he pulled out an ironed square of white handkerchief from his back pocket. He waved it open, draped it across his palm, and lay the photo on it. Like a magician at the end of a trick, he showed the photo to Pete. "Mean anything to you?"

178

Pete looked at it. "That's Cyrus," he recognized with surprise. "It must have been taken a while ago. I don't know who the woman is."

"Let me see!" Adrienne exclaimed.

"That's mine!" Cory burst out, almost simultaneously.

"Hold on, here," said Lily.

"That's my picture!" Cory lunged for it, almost tripping over Nat's legs. Brett and I caught her and pulled her back. She was shaking. "It's mine. He *stole* it off me!"

"Who stole it?" Lily asked sharply.

"He did! He took it!"

There was no question whom she meant. But Nat Rosenfeld's brown eyes made no objection.

"Did you see him take it?" I asked.

"I didn't see anyone. I told you. Someone went through my things last night. But it must of been him. He *knew*," she insisted.

"Knew what, Cory?" Pete asked quietly.

Her face closed. It was as if she had rolled down a window shade on a nosy neighbor.

"What's going on here?" said Lily.

"May we see the picture, Sheriff?" Adrienne requested.

He presented it to her in the handkerchief. She squinted at the snapshot in his hand. The others peered over her shoulder.

"Look at the hairdo, will you?" Adrienne said.

"I remember that Buick," Gene said slowly. "Dad drove up to see me at St. Paul's. It was a 'sixty-six Skylark. He came up for Parents' Day in my sophomore year. Drove all the way from High Point up by himself."

"He looks young," Billy Caton observed.

"Whoever she is, she's got tits," Adrienne cracked.

"She looks familiar," Gene said. "Henry?"

Henry craned his neck. "Of a type, maybe," he sneered.

"She was my mother," Cory spat out at them.

They stared dumbly at her across Nat's corpse. "It's mine," she instructed the sheriff.

He made a wide detour around Nat and confronted her with the snapshot. Brett and I leaned forward. Age had faded the colors. The sky above the couple was greenish and their summer tans had

179

turned creamy. They posed against the black fender of the Skylark. Cyrus, grinning in a short-sleeved, white shirt, held a cord jacket slung over his shoulder. His other arm was around the girl, who was cheesecaking for the camera. She was small-boned and large-breasted, with a mass of teased, streaked hair spilling Bardot-style around her laughing face. One hip, in her denim mini, was cocked against Cyrus's. Her breasts, dished up in an orange halter and thrust toward the camera, seemed a wonderful joke they shared.

Oh, I thought. I felt an old surge, a mix of awe and envy and adolescent longing. I wanted to tell Cory I knew how it felt to be the ungainly daughter of a "beauty." Ann Johnson may not have been "acceptable" to the country-club set. She may not have owned a gold circle-pin or a Peter Pan collar to pin it on. But she *shone.*

"This is yours?" Sheriff Boyd Lily asked Cory.

"Yes and I'd like it back."

He folded the corners of his handkerchief over it, like an acolyte rewrapping a relic. "It's evidence," he told her severely.

"It's a picture of my mother. And my father."

If nothing else, she had the satisfaction of seeing their well-bred jaws bounce off the ground.

For a moment we all stood staring at each other across Nat's body. Then Adrienne's eyes focused on Cory. "Why you little money-grubbing shit!" she accused. "You killed Nat to get the will. Long lost little sister, my ass. Honey, you are *dreaming* if you think we're going to let you get so much as one *cent* of my father's money! We'll fight you every inch of the way!"

"She's going to have to prove it," Henry observed.

Pete stepped forward. "Every one outta here," he ordered.

The sheriff looked grateful. "Right. Clear the area," he echoed.

Adrienne ignored him. She was staring at Pete. "You set us up with her," she said slowly. "You set us up." She turned to the others. "It's a scam. They belong in jail, both of them!"

"Move along now," prodded the Sheriff Lily.

18

Pete was furious. "You knew. You knew all along," he accused.

"Halfway along. I saw it by accident. What would you have done differently if you had known Cyrus was her father?"

He sidestepped. "Lily thinks she did it."

"I know he does. Do you?" I was trying to keep a dark panic at bay, to prevent it from slipping up and seizing my brain. Nonetheless, said brain felt as if it were stuck in first gear and getting nowhere fast. Meanwhile, the Strand family had their heads together in conference and Cory was standing alone, fiddling with a shovel by our campfire, her back to us, her shoulders rigid. "Go talk to her," I urged.

"Why should I believe a thing she says?"

"I suppose you've told her everything about your parents?"

Pete pressed the heels of his hands to his broad forehead. Then slowly, he raked his fingers down his face, as if stretching out a pocked rubber mask. "You think she didn't kill them?" he asked.

"I think she needs a lawyer. Too bad Nat's dead."

Pete's black eyes turned cold. He moved away.

"Shit. Wait. I didn't mean to be flip. What do I think? I think she had the same motive as the rest of them. I don't mean just the money. I mean anger. Cory was abused by her stepfather. Did you know that?"

I stopped to let it sink in. Pete nodded slowly, as if he'd been hunting for that particular piece of the puzzle for some time—a strategic piece lost under the carpet.

I continued, "Whatever happened to her, I know she kept thinking about her real father, how things might have been different. Then she met him. . . ." We stood there, outside the cook fly, looking at the sky. The morning's patchy clouds had gathered themselves into a thin gray blanket.

"They all had the opportunity," I went on. "Nat could have been shot anytime the helicopter was here. The noise would have masked the shot. You and Brett and Sheriff Lily were busy carrying Cyrus up there. You said Lucia was already in the chopper when you got there. I was washing forks with Bobby. Everyone else, including Cory, was coming and going. That's what I think." I paused.

"But if you ask me what I *feel,* I'd say no, she didn't kill Cyrus and she didn't kill Nat." I made a fist and lightly punched my solar plexus. "Here. That's what I feel. Is that reliable? You tell me."

Pete gave me five beats. I was beginning to get used to this, to see it as courtesy rather than an irritating slowness. My speech seemed to have appeased him.

"At least you're honest about it," he said begrudgingly.

"Big help."

Lucia was furious too. Bud, the pilot, insisted he didn't know why the sheriff had called them back but he had refused to let Lucia argue with Lily over the radio. Ten minutes later, they roared back down onto the high meadow, the burden of Cyrus's body still in the litter. She popped out of the helicopter like a hornet, but Boyd Lily had a thick hide. He ignored her as she buzzed angrily around him. He ducked into the chopper, gave instructions to Bud, and then climbed back out with Lucia's lavender backpack. We held our ears as the machine took off. Then Lily broke the news. "There's been another incident, ma'am," was the way he put it.

Preoccupied with the logistics of Cyrus's death, she took

Nat's with little show of emotion. She might have been listening to news of a broken collarbone instead of murder. I wondered if she would have had time to shoot Nat herself before lifting off with Cyrus's body. Certainly she was in a rush to get out. Suppose the lovers had quarrelled. Suppose he had broken down and confessed that for love of her he had poisoned her husband. Then what? Filled with remorse, he turns both the gun and the new will over to his beloved. "Shoot me, my darling saint!" he begs. "I don't deserve to live!" She shoots him.

Yep, maybe Hollywood would buy it. I wondered what kind of royalties soap-writers got.

Of course, the matter of the will had not been mentioned to Sheriff Lily. Rather carefully not mentioned. Lucia changed that. After being told of Nat's death, she asked, "Do you have the will he was keeping for me?"

After half an hour of "ma'am"-ing, Sheriff Boyd Lily had the story (delicately expurgated for official consumption) of how Cyrus had disinherited his heirs.

"So that would leave them short how much, ma'am?"

"My husband had a sizable estate, Sheriff," Lucia said coolly.

"Yes, ma'am. How sizable, ma'am?"

"I couldn't possibly say with any accuracy. You'll have to talk to our accountant."

"Yes ma'am. We appreciate your co-operation. I'm thinking of motive, you see."

She saw.

"Just a ball-park figure, ma'am."

She shrugged, "Perhaps forty million?"

Lily nodded sympathetically. "Sizable, ma'am."

In this way, he managed to extract from her the terms of the original will. Cyrus, before dumping the whole lot into her care, had allotted her half of his estate. Either way, she was in good shape. Mentally, I scratched her off the list of suspects. She had no apparent reason to bump off either her husband or her lover. Boyd Lily seemed to come to the same conclusion.

For Gene, Adrienne, and Henry, however, it was a matter of inheriting, after taxes, a "ball-park" three-million each or zip. Even if you added Cory into the equation as a natural child, the shares diminished to a not-so-measley two-and-a-quarter million—provided the second will was "lost."

Sheriff Lily instigated a search for both it and the gun. The family submitted with a smugness that passed for good grace. It was as if they knew Lily would not find either. Then the sheriff gathered everyone together under the cook fly and asked our names. It seemed to take him a very long time to write them down on his pocket-sized, green-tinted, lined pad. He also announced that he had instructed his pilot to notify the state police in Helena and to request a National Guard chopper and a state homicide investigator. "Reckon it'll take 'em at least a couple hours to get here." He surveyed the sky. "Wind's out of the west," he observed to Pete.

Pete nodded sagely, as if the statement meant something to him. "When they do land," Pete said to the guests, "a couple extra hands to hold the horses would help. We don't want a stampede on top of everything else."

There was a communal murmur of support for Pete and his pack animals. Of course! They'd be glad to help out! Just tell us what to do, Pete, old pal!

"Can I help, too?" Bobby, the sheriff's grandson, piped up. I'd forgotten his presence. If nothing else, he knew how to keep a low profile.

Before Pete or the sheriff could open their mouths, Henry said, "Sure thing, partner! Stick with me." He ran an affectionate hand over the boy's crew cut. Bobby's round face wasn't entirely reassured, but he had certainly latched on to Henry and Henry seemed to enjoy it. I thought of poet Mark Strand's haunting lines:

> My son
> my only son
> the one I never had . . .
>
> Sometimes
> he comes
> and leans his head
> lighter than air
> against my shoulder . . .

184

I wondered what kind of father Henry would be. Enthusiastic, certainly. But beyond that? Tony Flores had died in the mill fire when Henry was nine. What kind of father had he been? Had he shared Cyrus's driving need for control? If only Nat could have invented a will that disinherited the Strand children from their father's hang-ups. Would Henry and Adrienne and Gene then sue for a piece of Cyrus's fear, a share of his anger?

Probably.

Your cynicism is showing, rebuked a singsong voice inside my head.

Tell me about it, I retorted. Besides, I don't have to worry about leaving anything to Rachel, do I?

There was no answer. Only the old emptiness, familiar as a friend.

Riddle me this: Which is worse? The ghost of a child who has lived and died or the ghost of a child never born?

"Now," said the sheriff, frowning over his list of names. "When was the last time anyone saw the deceased, Mr.—er, Mr. Rose—" he studied his pad in vain.

"Rosenfeld," Pete supplied.

Boyd Lily nodded. "When was the last time you saw him alive?" He scanned our faces.

Family eye-contact zipped around like a mercury ball through a plastic toy maze. Their expressions remained politely attentive.

Finally, I threw out, "At breakfast. Around seven. Everyone was there."

"Oh, yes, at breakfast," the group chimed in. "It was at breakfast." They echoed each other eagerly, like a chorus of well-behaved children.

"This is when he told me Cyrus had given him the new will to keep," Lucia reflected. She regarded her stepchildren. "You were all there with me. You heard what he said."

They nodded sympathetically. Their faces were concerned. It was unimaginable that one of them had killed Nat that morning. Suddenly the only possible suspect was Pete's *Seme*—the "not human" who walked through the dark. I felt a shifting sensation

185

in my mind, as though it were about to get up and leave. *I'm going nuts,* I thought.

It was anger that grounded me. As I listened to Boyd Lily questioning Cyrus's middle-aged children, a dark red feeling stirred in my abdomen and rose slowly like a large, maternal animal lumbering to its feet. For what they were doing was weaving a safety net that excluded Cory. They all vouched for each other. They all claimed to have been in sight of each other, in varying combinations, every minute between breakfast and the discovery of Nat's body. No one even admitted going to the latrine alone. There was, according to Adrienne, a line outside the tent. They all had had the same after-breakfast urge. "Must have been something in Lee's coffee," Gene had joked to the sheriff.

Only Cory had no one to corroborate her story. Brett had left her with the stock while he and Pete carried Cyrus's body up the hill to the helicopter. She had been alone with the horses and mules for maybe half an hour. She might have heard a report in the woods while they were gone. No, she wasn't sure. The helicopter was making such a racket.

"But you didn't go look?" Lily asked.

"I told you, I stayed with the stock."

"I see," he said.

The sheriff walked back into the woods toward Nat's body. Maybe he wanted to see if it was still dead. Pete turned to follow. I caught his arm. *"Do something!"* I hissed at him.

"Such as?"

"He's going to arrest her!"

"She may be better off."

"In jail? Great." I let go of his arm in disgust.

"You need a calculator?" he said with quiet sarcasm.

"What do you mean?"

"If Cory can prove she's Cyrus's natural child, their pile gets split four ways instead of three. They each stand to lose about three-quarter of a million to her. Need I remind you that one of them has Cyrus's gun and has already used it?" He trotted after the sheriff.

※ ※ ※

186

The state homicide investigators descended in an enormous, awkward-looking, matte brown helicopter with two rotors. Bud, the pilot of the sheriff's little dragonfly, must have relayed landing information, because they set down on the high meadow without nosing around the camp. The horses and mules were skittish, but Brett and Cory had them all tied to a picket line—a long nylon rope strung like a hitching rail between tree trunks. No one had trouble keeping hold of their assigned halters.

Lily escorted two men with black suitcases into camp. Like the sheriff, they wore jeans and cowboy boots and plain-looking pistols on their hips. The more thickly built man in a red billed cap (COORS, it said) introduced himself as T.J. The other fellow, younger and taller, his eyes shadowed by his brown felt hat, was called Luke. He had a confident jaw and narrow hips. "Luke as in Cool Hand?" I felt like asking. Then I noticed he looked closer in age to Luke Skywalker. Our eyes met for maybe half a second when we shook hands. *Huh,* I thought.

Stop salivating in public, I scolded myself as he walked off into the pines with his suitcase.

Cory looked at me. "What's so funny?" she demanded.

"Nothing."

"This isn't funny, them being here, and everything." She sounded scared. "Look where they found my picture."

Two hours later, after a conference with the state detectives, Sheriff Boyd Lily arrested her as a suspect. The way Lily put it to Pete was that he was taking her out for questioning along with Nat's body. He didn't actually use the word *arrest,* but it was clear she was headed for his jail. He didn't read her rights like they do on TV. I decided not to remind him.

Pete, still as chummy as ever, asked for a piece of paper. The sheriff handed over his pocket-sized note pad.

"You got a pen?" Pete asked amiably.

Lily unclipped a ballpoint.

"Thanks." The ink was green. In large, looping letters, Pete jotted down a name.

Boyd Lily squinted at it, then raised his eyebrows. "Didn't he campaign for senator a couple years back?"

"He's one of my clients," Pete said. He tore off the sheet and handed it to Cory. "He's also her lawyer." He gave the sheriff back his pad and his pen.

"Call him," he said to Cory.

She looked confused. "Pete, I don't—I mean, like no way I can afford a guy like—"

"Call him," Pete said. "We'll work it out."

In the meantime, the two state investigators had "processed" and bagged Nat's body and searched the area for the missing murder weapon. They also conducted a second search of all our gear. They asked us to stand beside our duffles as they went through them. Their hands were quicker and less curious than Lily's.

Billy swayed beside his duffle. "This reminds me of nineteen and sixty-eight at McAllen, Texas," he said. "About six of us, driving back from a spring break in Mexico. We were jammed into this chick's VW and they made us unpack the thing three times." He leaned over T.J.'s back. "You gonna ask us to spread our cheeks?"

No one said anything, not even Adrienne.

"God, it was hot!" Billy exclaimed jovially. "They wouldn't even let us go inside to piss. They had air-conditioned toilets inside and a water fountain—you could see it through this tinted glass they had in the window. But they wouldn't let us in the door. We had to use this hole in the ground 'round the side—just like we were a bunch of niggers."

It wasn't Texas and it wasn't hot—a cool breeze blew under the cloud cover—but Billy was red-faced and sweating.

The state men found neither the gun nor Cyrus's will. Just after three, T.J. took off for Missoula with Nat's body in a green plastic bag. Sheriff Lily, his grandson, and his prisoner, Cory, were the other passengers. And Lucia. With quiet dignity, she had pleaded her case to Sheriff Lily: "I would like to be with my husband."

"I'll see what we can do, ma'am," he'd replied.

The others, of course, also demanded to be flown out, but T.J. refused. "We'd have to make a second trip," he told them. "It's not like there's an emergency anymore."

* * *

188

Thus, Brett and Pete and I were left to tend eight mules, eleven horses, four murder suspects, and one state homicide investigator. Cool Hand was staying behind to escort us out. Pete assigned him Nat's horse. He told Pete his last name was Donner.

At least he was unobtrusive. He didn't have an itch under his gun belt the way the Sheriff Lily had. And when his four charges stood smoldering like molten lumps while we loaded the mules, the man lent his back and shoulder. It wasn't just a matter of willing muscle: he seemed to know what to do with the ropes.

I held Harley, the great black mule, as Pete and Luke Donner hefted and secured the hundred-pound kitchen panniers on either side of his ruler-straight back.

"Where'd you learn to pack?" Pete grunted as he hauled a line through a D-ring.

On the other side, the detective lifted the load, then tugged back. "I spent a summer with the Elsers. Back when I was in high school."

I wondered how long ago that was.

"Smoke Elser?" Pete sounded impressed.

Donner nodded. "Mostly, he used the basket hitch, like you. I kept pestering him to show me how to throw a diamond, but there just never seemed to be the time to fool with it."

"We can work on it tonight," Pete offered.

"I'd appreciate it."

"I hear Elser once mule-packed a piano into backcountry."

"I was there. But it wasn't mules he used. It was an eighteen-hundred-pound Belgian mare he used. What he did was, he cut three lodgepole pines and made this tripod. Then he rigged it with a block-and-tackle, so's we could crank the piano off the mare's back and give her a break."

"C'mon."

"Really. Every half mile or so, we'd set up the tripod, and crank the weight off her back."

Pete chuckled. And there he was again, best friends with a stranger. For all his granite facade, he passed his heart around like a fire-softened marshmallow on the end of a stick. I felt my own heart constrict with anxiety. One day he was going to get burned. One day the marshmallow would suddenly flare up and bloom into

189

an empty black beehive whose ashes would disintegrate with a wave of the stick.

Or was I projecting my own eastern urbanite fear onto Pete? Perhaps in Montana it was safe to trust strangers. Perhaps in Montana you could walk down the street smiling and not worry about getting raped or shot. Of course, the sunny citizens of Montana probably owned more guns per capita than the beleaguered residents of our nation's capital.

I took out the lump of carnelian from my jeans pocket and rubbed it between my fingers. "Good for the heart," Tommy, my mother's masseur, had promised. Did I need carnelian to open up my heart? Or did I simply need a gun to make smiling safe? Of course, I hadn't done so hot with Cyrus's six-shooter.

As for Pete, thanks to me, he didn't have a shooter. The state cop did. *Oh, Pete,* I worried.

I slipped the carnelian back into my pocket. My hand strayed up to the shaven side of my head. It was hard not to keep touching it. I saw Pete's new chum looking at me from under his brown hat. I took my hand away. No doubt I looked like a geek. A forty-year-old geek.

By 4:30 we were underway. Brett led out with the mules in one long string, followed by Pete and the extra horses. Then the dudes and I. There was some question about whether Billy Caton was fit to ride, but Gene and Brett managed to boost him up onto his horse. He dropped the reins a couple times, and they ended up wrapping them around his saddle horn. The horse didn't seem to mind. Detective Donner brought up the rear. I had a scarf wound around my head, à la Ethel Mertz. My slightly more dashing hat rubbed my wound the wrong way.

We went out via the high meadow, and when I looked back through the pines, I felt strangely bereft, as if I were leaving home forever. But there were scarcely any signs that our campsite, now swept by a late afternoon breeze, had ever been "home." Pete and Brett had buried our campfire and artfully strewn pine needles and gray deadwood over its ring. They had similarly disguised our sump hole. I had picked up the confetti of white chips from chopping stovewood and scattered them out in the field. We had all kicked apart the mules' and horses' droppings. (Left in piles, Pete explained, they take years to disintegrate.) Even the flattened patches of grass under the tents had already partially resurrected. It was hard to believe we had been there for three nights. It was even harder to believe two men had died there.

19

It didn't feel particularly great to be back in the saddle again. The trail was one switchback after another winding up to the Continental Divide through pine crosshatches of wind-slanted verticals and dead horizontals. In the flat gray light, the eye-level sea of shade-killed branches was oppressive. The pace was brisker than before. Our saddles creaked and underneath them the horses huffed away like engines. A late afternoon breeze brushed the tops of the pines, but below them it was airless. Rex's tweedy neck and shoulders turned dark with sweat and drew flies. There were no flowers to stop for between the gray boulders along the trail. For visual diversion, I was reduced to observing the new piles of "road apples" dropped by the animals ahead: the clumps were not isolated, but occurred in series, as if defecation was catching—like burps among schoolboys.

I found it hard to yield, as I had on the way in, to the mindless movement of Rex's walk. I found it hard to stay quiet in the saddle. I kept seeing Cory, the sheriff's hand on her elbow, as he steered her toward the big brown chopper. Her shoulders were determined, defiant even, but her prim mouth was uncertain. She had refused to meet my eyes.

"Do I get to take my pack?" she asked the sheriff in a wise-ass tone.

"Pete'll bring it along," Boyd Lily said.

"You gonna lend me your toothbrush?"

"Let's go." He steered her forward.

Cory. I invented dozens of parting instructions for her and swallowed each one like a bitter pill. I imagined reaching out to her, brushing the habitually stray strands of brown hair from her eyes, making it all better for both of us with one enormous, crushing hug and a lick or two on her wounds. Momma Bear.

Get real, I scolded. *There's got to be a way.*

Fallen lodgepoles kept blocking our progress. Sometimes Pete led us off the trail around the barriers and at least those detours added interest: the horses plunged and hesitated on the steep slope as they picked their way over and between barkless gray trunks. But more often the downfall was too thick to penetrate. We would halt and wait, nose-to-tail, while Pete or Brett would unsheathe the ax roped against one of the mule packs and patiently whack away at the deadwood barrier. Chips would fly for fifteen, twenty minutes, then the tree would cave in. They'd strain and push it aside and the rest of us would insert our feet back into our stirrups and we'd move on.

So I rode along on Rex's back, stewing about Cory, but at the same time more than vaguely aware of Luke Donner riding behind me. I felt a lift in my spine, as if my vertebrae had been stretched to let in small cushions of air. I was conscious of the way I held my scarf-wrapped head, the way I slapped at flies on Rex's neck. I rode along as if I were the heroine in an adventure, as if I were playing to an admiring audience.

I'd felt this kind of "staginess" before. When Rachel was in the hospital, I had taken pains with my looks. I had used a cover stick on the dark circles under my eyes and blusher along the ridges of bone. I wore festive, dangling earrings and bright, vegetable cottons: watermelon red and grape and hot pink and leafy green. I waltzed onto the ward like Mrs. Brave and Marvelous. I told myself it was for Rachel. But really, it was for me. And for the nurses who comforted me with diet Cokes from their refrigerator and who knew I was a poet (because I'd told one or two of them).

193

And also, it was for the oncologist, the cancer doctor—a craggy, gruff man with neatly barbered graying sideburns who probably wasn't much older than I am now. He wore Brooks Brothers pinstripes under his white coat. I was attracted to him. How could I not be? The great white doctor, the healing father figure—it was a loaded role he played. Moreover, I could tell that Rachel and I had hooked him. Together we were Circe, luring him into our perilous waters. His pinstripes lost their starch when he talked with me. His eyes would tear in the light from the window. He would stop in at odd hours, lay a surprisingly light hand on her small, stretched brow. In the depths of powerlessness, the fact that we had "caught" him gave me a fierce sexual energy.

Clint was disgusted when I nudged against him. "Our daughter is *dying,*" he said. "How can you . . . ?"

I had no answer for him. He was the psychologist.

Since then, I understand a bit more about the fundamental connection between death and sex. I wonder if they aren't two sides of the same coin—a coin called Surrender. In any case, after Rachel died, my husband accused me of screwing her doctor. "How do you think I felt?" he asked me. "How do you think I felt seeing you dress up like that to go off to the hospital? You got *turned on* by Rachel's death! Did you write a poem about how hot it made you, Lee? Did you?"

Oh, the rest of it doesn't bear repeating. But I had the feeling that he could have forgiven an affair with Rachel's doctor more easily than the poems I wrote about her dying. Of course I wrote about it. And most of what came out was truly awful. But a couple of the better crafted ones I sent around and they were published— if not widely read. On occasion, at readings in suburban libraries, and once in a group reading at the Folger, I'd pull one out and make myself and a small audience blink wetly. Now I've stopped reading them. Now the only one under my skin is just a rough fragment—a private touchstone I have no urge to finish:

> I am trying to love you with no hands
> to let you blow through the corridors of my heart
> my fingers stream in your wind
> I am trying to love you without holding on

Thus we rode up and eastward under a dull evening sky, Cory tying my mind in knots and my daughter's ghost in my heart and a Montana homicide detective perking up my backbone. The woods grew duskier. Then, at some indeterminate point along the way, it clicked. The murky screen of my brain lit up with the obvious: If I wanted to get Cory off the hook for murder, I had to get the real killer on the line. Simple. But what kind of bait to use? Nothing as iffy as a dry fly. I wasn't planning on being sporting about this. What I wanted was a fail-safe lure, the kind that flashes silver in green seawater and trails a large steel hook in its feathers.

I became aware of pressure in my knees. I realized we were clomping downhill. Evidently we had crossed the Continental Divide, but Pete had refrained from pointing it out. For the moment, he had given up playing tour guide.

By this time I had polished up my big fishing plan. I knew what bait to use. The only problem was Pete. I was going to need him to help reel the killer in. But I had the feeling he wasn't going to find my plan attractive. In fact, I was pretty sure he'd veto the whole idea. He didn't behave like a male chauvinist, but I was willing to bet his instincts were too patriarchal to "let" me set myself up.

After almost five hours in the saddle, Pete called a halt near a place called Pearl Basin. The forest opened briefly, allowing a view of distant, dark mountains shouldering a thick, darkening sky. The snowy peaks seemed to give off their own grayish light. Then we turned off the trail and rode down through dense brush into a small hole in the forest, where we set up camp. There was a rushing creek swollen with melt-off, but no grass to speak of. Pete and Brett fed the stock oats from a fifty-pound sack one of the mules had carried. They tied the horses to a picket line for the night, but the mules they left loose. "They won't go anywhere," Pete assured Adrienne. "They get real attached to the horses. Gene's mare is the mother of two of them: Peachy, the little reddish one, and Temper, over there by your tent."

It was a tight site. The two tents—Gene and Henry's and Billy and Adrienne's—were pitched side by side and the cook fly was not ten yards away. We set up the stove but not the outhouse tent. Instead, Pete provided a shovel and a roll of toilet paper in a plastic bag and instructions on digging one-time latrines: a small, ecologically correct hole in the top six inches of soil. It was after ten o'clock by the time I got Dolores's chili heated up. For a salad, I shredded up a head of iceberg. No one could see how anemic it looked in the stainless steel bowl. We ate in the dark brushed by the sounds of the stock. Their stirring, shifting, snorting, surrounded us, as if our campground were a manger dumbly guarded by their breath. But there was no big miraculous star over our heads. Our patch of sky gave no light. We washed up by flashlight. Brett withdrew from the cook fly with his pack. Pete rumbled through the piles of still packed gear and extracted Lucia's sleeping bag for Luke Donner. The dudes moved off to their tents.

Pete and I stood together by the stove. He was finishing up his coffee. I badly wanted a hit of my bourbon. Or a set of strong fingers to work out the cricks in my neck. "Pete?" I said, testing the pitch of my voice.

His head moved sharply. He answered quietly, "I'm right here."

I ignored his cue and kept my voice turned up. "There's something you should know. Cyrus gave it to me."

I listened to the darkness. Then Pete said carefully, "Gave what to you?"

"That will he made." I threw it out to the tents. "He said it was a copy. Just in case. He told me not to tell anyone. I didn't know what to do. I'm sorry. I thought—"

He grabbed my arm.

"Ow. Ouch. I didn't know what to do. How could I say no to him? I was going to give it to Lucia, but there wasn't time— Don't! You're hurting me!"

In fact, he wasn't touching me. He'd dropped my arm like a hot potato. "You're crazy!" he exclaimed.

I latched on to both his forearms. Perhaps he felt some steadiness in my grip. "Help me," I muttered. I took a breath and said to the trees beyond us, "I hid it for him."

I stood there, squeezing down hard on Pete's forearms, listening to the darkness. There was not a sound. Even the mules seemed to have stopped breathing. I loosened my fingers. With deliberate slowness, he twisted his arm and caught my right wrist. His fingers were firm, ready to clamp down on a madwoman. I strained to see his face. I moved my left hand up his arm and placed it solidly on his shoulder, as if he had asked me to dance.

"Where is it?" His voice cracked, but it was loud enough to carry. "Where's the will?" Pete insisted. He brushed my hand off his shoulder, but kept hold of my wrist. "Give it to me!"

Was he acting? "No," I said. I pulled back and stumbled over the basin full of flatware. The knives and forks we'd just washed spilled onto the ground. "He gave it to me," I insisted. "It's safe."

He called me a couple certifiably sexist names. I wondered if he ever used any of them on Dolores. "Let me have it," he ordered.

"Go fuck yourself." I felt a flash of real anger. "Whoever knocked my head in this morning didn't find it. Your chum Lily didn't find it, and neither did those other two cops you were sucking up to. I'm telling you it's safe!"

Pete flung out another hurtful name. I shut up. The dark between us wobbled like a big blister, but neither of us wanted to walk away from it. I felt shaky. I found my whiskey and poured myself a slug. The taste of it was reassuring. It reminded me of living rooms with armchairs and coffee tables, of restaurants with starched white linen and heavy silver. Even without ice, it seemed as civilized as a *New Yorker* ad.

But the lines had gotten blurred in the night, in the wilderness. The fight I'd picked with Pete had gotten nastier than I planned. Moreover, I could almost believe that Cyrus actually had entrusted a copy of his last will and testament to me. I could see it on lined yellow paper. I imagined his handwriting, blue ballpoint letters cramped against each other—a tight, plain hand. It took me some moments to sort fact from fancy. Of course the whiskey didn't help in that regard. But then, maybe life's just a series of trade-offs. Clarity or the blur of Kentucky bond. Both sweet in their own way.

Pete was on his knees, picking his tinny silverware out of the dirt. I put my cup on a crate, and by way of apology, dropped down to help. He was still pissed. "What the hell do you think you're doing?" he whispered.

Quietly, I spelled it out for him. "There's no other way," I concluded. I tossed a stray knife into the basin. "We can do it," I urged with more certainty than I felt.

"Do you have it?"

I didn't answer.

"Jesus, Mary, and Joseph," he swore.

"Shh! I know we can bring it off. Please?"

"I've got a choice? You've got it all worked out."

"Your manly ego's getting in the way."

He was stony.

"What if they decide to prosecute Cory for murder? Think about what that lawyer of yours charges per hour."

He sat back on his haunches. "And what if she did it? What if she was the one who killed them and took the will?"

"And took the gun and opened up my head and then doctored it for me?"

"Yeah," he challenged. He tossed a handful of forks into the steel washbasin.

"Then I'm safe. If Cory did it, she's in jail. I don't have to worry about your dudes coming at me," I argued.

A twig snapped. We froze. "It's me, Luke." His voice was quiet. Pete and I stood. He stepped over to us. In the dark, he was only a long fork of legs and a hat. His voice, however, carried the weight of experience. "I wouldn't count on it," he said softly.

"On what?" Pete's voice was curt.

"On her being safe." His hat indicated me. "Maybe your guests didn't murder their daddy and his lawyer. But they want that will. And they know she has it. I'll bet you could hear her all the way to Pretty Prairie."

Pete deliberated. "We'll take care of it," he said. His meaning was clear: Butt out, pal.

Luke melted back into the shadows. I felt like giving Pete a lecture on teamwork. After all, the man had a weapon and we didn't. But I kept my mouth shut. I didn't want to push too hard.

"Get your bag. You're sleeping with Brett and me," Pete ordered.

I couldn't resist. "Gee, I'm sure you're both terrific, but, well I've got this headache. . . ."

Silence.

"I'm funning you, Pete."

He snorted in disgust. He sounded like one of the mules.

At the edge of the clearing, we lined up our sleeping bags, one, two, three—Papa Bear, Mama Bear, and Baby Bear. I climbed into Mama Bear. " 'Night," I said.

" 'Night," Brett answered.

"How is your head?" Pete asked. He was serious.

"Actually, it aches. But I'm not sure it has anything to do with getting beaned this morning. The cut doesn't feel like it's festering or anything." I inserted a finger under my headscarf and probed the edges of the shaven area. "It's probably just my nerves." I kneaded the back of my neck.

He grunted. "You got some."

"Some what?"

"Nerve. Too bad you don't have any sense to go with it."

I heard a muffled noise from Brett's bag. It didn't sound like a snore. I gave him a poke anyway.

20

That night I learned the secret of how Dolores survived Montana's twenty-below winters in a tin can of a trailer: sleeping next to Pete was like sleeping next to a boiler. The man was not only the size of a furnace, he also threw off enough heat with his snores to keep me from freezing in my dew-dampened down bag.

For our last breakfast I did a double batch of sourdough biscuits and scrambled up the last two dozen eggs with bacon. There were no leftovers. For the lunch bags, along with the usual PB & Js, I made smoked turkey and mustard sandwiches on whole wheat and divided up a bag of dried apricots.

We were off by 8:30. The weather did not look promising. The summer-weight cloud cover of the previous afternoon had bulked up during the night into a somber ceiling. The morning light had a bruised quality and the cold air felt damp enough for snow. We rolled our slickers into sausages and tied them onto the backs of our saddles.

Before mounting up, Pete and I had a brief conference with Detective Luke Donner on the order of our procession toward the mixed boons of civilization: motel ice-machines and hot baths on the one hand; the formalities of homicide law on the other. We argued quietly and hotly. Pete and Luke wanted me to ride between them. "That's going to ruin it!" I told them. "If you want to flush your killer, you can't ride me in like a prisoner. I've got to be accessible." In the end, logic triumphed over chivalry. The idea—it was too casual to be called a strategy—was to separate the dudes and keep Luke, with his gun, at my back.

Thus, Brett led out with a long string of eight mules, Harley in the front setting a dignified pace and the agile, brisk-footed Miss Peach bringing up the rear. Benign and sturdy under their mantied loads, the mules were "pigtailed" together. "Pigtails" are quarter-inch sisal loops used to link a nylon rope extending from one mule's rear saddle-ring to the halter rope of the next mule: a self-tightening nose-to-tail connection.

Brett was not happy taking on all the mules. I gathered that long strings caused more headaches. There were more mules to balk, break a pigtail, and wander up the wrong side of a tree, if not slide down the side of a ravine. But Pete insisted on being unencumbered by mules. He wanted to be able to move quickly, if necessary. Brett could hardly complain.

Behind Miss Peach rode Adrienne. Bundled in a down vest, her head wrapped in a designer scarf beneath her new Stetson, she wore her dark glasses, even though the morning was dark. Pete assigned her the job of leading out Lucia's mare. Behind them, Billy, flapping fringes, also wore sunglasses—gold-rimmed aviator shades à la *Top Gun*. He had moved carefully in them through breakfast, and now, rocking along on his horse, he held his head above the waves of motion like a Victorian lady swimming the breaststroke. So much for the Tom Cruise look.

Then came Pete, his mass reassuring. Then Gene, then Henry, who had volunteered to take Nat's mare in tow, then me. Rex seemed attracted to the mare. I had to keep holding him off her rump. *Great,* I thought. I could see the headlines: COOK PLUNGES TO DEATH ON AMOROUS MOUNT. Then I heard a voice-over: *Squires, the only way your death will make headlines is if your mother sells the story to the* National Enquirer. Okay. Breathe. No, I wasn't edgy. After all, I had Cool Hand at my back. He rode Cyrus's big chestnut.

Going down on the eastern side of the Divide seemed far more

201

precarious than coming up the western side. The upper flanks of the range were exposed, too steep for any trees. The trail snaked down vast, precipitous slides of shale. There was no stopping. The mules sensed it and behaved. Against my left shoulder there was the gravelly bank. Below my right knee was the crumbling drop-off studded with dwarf bushes. The view was stomach-turning. There were no excited cries of "Photo-op!" At one point, if I had spat and missed my right boot, it would have landed directly on Brett's hat a hundred feet below. Seeing him and his string of mules reminded me of riding a cross-country train: on a long curve, you can see the engine from the rear; but our mule train was moving vertically, down the face of the Rockies, not horizontally across the plains. The only way home was straight down.

It began to rain cold, fat drops. They fell through the dense air like single notes from an overture to an opera. The sky was livid enough for Wagnerian gods, but the bulk of music seemed to have stalled behind the curtain of the Divide. The fall we got was slow and insistent. There was no place to stop and put on raincoats. The horses' rumps steamed. Their hooves slipped on wet stones, and all along the edge of the track, shoots of disturbed gravel slid down like small waterfalls. Random pebbles skipped among low shrubs. Pete pointed to yellow clumps of biscuit-root embedded in the shale. "Grizzly food," he announced. "They sniff out the roots in the spring."

I thought of the black grizzly my mother had conjured up for my protection. Mudjekeewis, she had called it.

Adrienne turned back in her saddle. "Grizzlies? Here?"

"Not now. It's summertime."

Gene made a sarcastic noise under a red bandanna tied bandito-style over his nose and mouth. He was holding on to his saddle horn with both hands. If I had to guess from his pallor and his red-rimmed eyes, I'd say his antihistamines hadn't kicked in.

Between switchbacks, the trail leveled out and widened enough to allow a stop. Brett kept going with the mules while we untied raincoats and put them on over our wet jackets. Everyone dismounted for the operation, except Gene. Pete, in a long, olive drab poncho, held Gene's horse while Gene struggled awkwardly into an orange Gore-Tex foul-weather jacket—no doubt flotsam saved from the sloop lost in the storm of his divorce. Billy's raincoat was black like a fireman's, and the rest of us were yellow— Henry being the most resplendent in an ankle-length home-on-the-range slicker that reminded me of Warren Beatty's in *McCabe and Mrs. Miller*.

Luke had no rain gear along with him. The rim of his hat dripped onto the shoulders and sleeves of his darkly wet denim jacket. The long, narrow thighs of his jeans were also soaked. He moved forward to the horses being led and pulled green nylon covers over their saddles. He saw me looking at him.

"There's extra rain gear on the mules," I said. I was thinking of Nat's. "Maybe Brett would know where it is."

"It's okay."

"I could at least get you a garbage bag out of the kitchen pannier. When we catch up to them, we could stop."

"I'm okay," he insisted.

I wasn't about to argue with the man. I probably sounded like his mom.

After half an hour, an hour, we bumped into the mules. I remember thinking seriously about the smoked turkey in my saddlebag, so it must have been close to lunchtime. We had descended into a ragged pine forest. Under the dripping black canopy, the light was purplish. Half of the trees were dead, barkless, and staggering between the upright pink-brown trunks like drunken guests at a party. The drop-off was still precarious in places, but the trail had widened and there was no longer the sensation that the bank against your shoulder might breathe and, in expanding, nudge you and your wretched, wet horse off the edge. Now, among the fir and pine, our uphill side allowed us twenty-, thirty-foot margins strewn with rocks and downfall, both as gray as driftwood. These green shelves seemed as open as beaches. We relaxed.

That was mistake number one. Number two: In our prerecessional tête-à-tête, we had arranged no signals, no codes. (If I start singing "Rain, rain, go away" . . . If I scratch my chin . . .) I had no way to discreetly announce, "Okay, guys, time to call in the cavalry."

So. As I said, we bumped into the stalled tail end of the mule train. Brett and the front mules were out of sight around the corner, but whacking sounds of the ax dubbed Big Mo floated back clearly through the rain. "More downfall," Pete guessed. He dismounted and strode forward to inspect. A minute later he was back. "You might as well eat your lunches. We're going to be here a few minutes. There's a sizable lodgepole blown across the trail and no way 'round. Unless your horse's named Pegasus."

"Can we get down?" Adrienne asked. "I have to pee."

Pete glanced around. There was space enough on our left, though the drop-off on the right was sheer and loose with wet shale. Twenty feet down, the pitch eased up. Scattered live pines, jagged silver stumps, fallen dark trees created an erosion barrier. Low mounds of gravel lay against the treeline like dirty snow melting against a derelict fence.

"You can get down," Pete told the group. "Make sure your horses are secure. If you're going to tie him up, use a short line."

Whack, whack, thumped Brett's ax. Pete tied his horse to a skinny pine, cheek to bark, and moved forward along the line. He rounded Miss Peach's rear and was out of sight. Adrienne gave Billy her reins and began climbing up the "beach" on our left toward a stand of Douglas fir. With a flamboyant flash of yellow, Henry dismounted, took out his water bottle from his saddlebag, and drank. He held the bottle up, measuring its contents against the raining sky, then carefully screwed the top back on and returned it to his saddlebag. I swung down, thinking, *Which first, peanut-butter-and-jelly or turkey?* and there was Henry breathing down my neck. I felt something small and hard poking into my ribs.

He said, "Guess what I found."

I said, "Very funny."

"I want the will." He poked harder.

"Don't," I said. I looked for Luke. He wasn't there. His horse was tied to an uphill branch.

"Give me the will," Henry repeated pleasantly. The situation felt oddly familiar. It seemed as if we were children playing a game and I'd just been caught by someone's older brother. Those games had had their share of pain, their secret cruelties. But this time, it wasn't a cap gun hurting against my ribs. I moved to turn toward him.

204

"No," he said, "Don't turn around. Just keep your hands on your saddle."

"May I cover it?" *Mother, may I?*

He thought about it. "Yes." He leaned into the Colt.

My eyes teared. I pulled the square of green nylon forward and slipped its elastic loop over the horn. "Henry, I don't have it."

"Right."

"Honest to God."

"I heard you last night. We all heard you."

Ah, yes. Like ropes tossed to a skater lying on thin ice, tactics from my childhood floated back. I grabbed the nearest. It was an old favorite, tried, but not always true: *Stall.* I mean, how long can it take an armed detective to use the woods? "I don't have it on me," I told Henry. "It's on the mules. I'll get it for you when we get in."

"Now would be better."

I thought about it. "Okay."

He seemed a little surprised. "Don't get smart, Lee," he warned suspiciously.

I was flattered. As it happened, I was feeling exceedingly dumb. I took a hand away from the saddle horn, slowly, showing him my empty palm, and touched my sopping head rag. "You mean business, right?"

He had the grace to look embarrassed—more, I suspected, by the gangsterdom cliché than the damage done. "All's fair," he intoned. "Shall we?" He stepped back, as if opening a door for me.

Suddenly, I hated him. I dropped Rex's reins. Let the creature run away. I stepped past Henry. He was holding the Colt on me, now making no effort to hide it. Dark eddies of anger propelled me forward along the line of horses. Behind me, I heard Gene's shocked voice, "Henry, what are you doing!"

"Lee's getting us the will," he said.

The rain was now clicking, instead of plonking, on my slicker. It was turning to sleet. We skirted Billy Caton in his black raincoat, holding three horses, his eyes invisible behind his shades. He made no move to interfere. My foot slipped on a rock. "Easy there," Henry said. He might have been soothing his horse.

I can't recall ever having been angry in quite that way. Usu-

205

ally, I "see red," as though a fist of anger had squeezed my heart and sent a blast of blood shooting up behind my eyeballs. Usually, my anger is located between chest and head. But this anger was visceral. It lapped against bowel and womb, tickled bands of smooth, shiny muscle. It was black and instinctive and slow. It encompassed not only Henry and his stolen gun, but Cyrus, and Cory's pain, and perhaps even the loss of my daughter. Certainly there was a fierce, maternal quality about it. I felt as heavy as a five-hundred-pound she-bear. However, unlike a real bear, I could see with heightened clarity. Each icy drop of sleet seemed distinct, each dark, wet strand of Miss Peach's tail, each stem of grass bowing over the eroded edge of the drop-off. I looked back at Henry and his gun. Still no sign of Luke. Maybe he was constipated.

I stopped beside Miss Peach's mantied pack. "It's here."

"Get it. Hurry up."

I studied the maze of ropes looped around the canvas-wrapped packs. Over eighty pounds each, they hung on either side of Miss Peach's back. I fingered a double-looped knot in the center of the uphill pack. It looked important. "This is the release," I bluffed in my schoolteacher voice. "But I need you on the other side to steady the load."

He hesitated.

I jumped in belligerently. "Haven't you watched them unload? One on each side? Look, if you want me to get it for you, you're going to have to hold up the other side while I get it off. Or maybe you want to ask Pete to lend a hand?" I demanded sarcastically.

"Get on with it. But—"

"Yeah," I interrupted. "You already told me. You mean business. Is that what you told Nat? What happened, Henry? He didn't believe you?"

Stung, he moved around Miss Peach's rear to the downhill pack, gun in hand.

I patted Miss Peach's wet neck, then yanked the loop beside me. The pack slid downward, cradled in the hitch, and hung by the ropes, just below the mule's belly. She took a tentative half-step backward, then froze. In unison, we stepped with her. "Got it?" Henry asked anxiously.

"Just a sec. Something's caught. Don't let go!"

He grunted. Had he holstered—or pocketed—the Colt? I stepped up onto the bank, gathered up the bear inside me, and dove against Miss Peach's flank. She jumped and skittered sideways off the trail. Her right hind foot slipped over the edge, then she recovered her footing. I strained against her. But she was entrenched, head lowered, ears flat on either side of her mohawk. Under the suspended mantied pack, I could see Henry's leather-soled boots scrambling on the edge. "Stop!" he bellowed. He was hanging on to the rear of the mule's saddle. I kept on pushing. The little mule's eyes rolled white. She brayed her alarm and the mules in front of her sang back and the din echoed off the cliffs above us. I pushed and strained, my nose squished against the coarse hair of her steaming side. But she held her ground, not heaving Henry over the side as I hoped, but pulling steadily backward.

Then suddenly, there was a loud crack. I thought Henry had shot her. I thought it was the Colt. But it wasn't. Miss Peach had snapped her pigtail. The mule in front of her danced forward. At the same time Miss Peach staggered off balance and tumbled sideways over the precipice. Henry ducked down, dropping onto his knees in the gravel. Miss Peach went over his head. I did a nose plant just below him. The three of us avalanched down the side of the ravine.

Miss Peach slid, trailing the loose pack that was supposed to have Cyrus's will in it, all the way down to a dead pine that shivered with the impact. Henry and I slid about halfway down, I on my face, he (Pete took some satisfaction in telling me later) rather gracefully on his knees, like a skier in deep powder. He hauled me up to my feet by my collar. I felt like a jellyfish. He caught me under my chin with his forearm, pressed his gun into my spine. The vision of a six-thousand-dollar wheelchair rolled through my head.

My hearing kicked in first. I heard Adrienne screaming above us. In my ear, I heard Henry muttering to himself, "Okay. Okay." I heard Miss Peach screaming below us and an answering cacophony of braying and neighing from the ledge above. The sleet stung my face like needles. The side of one cheek felt hot and sticky. In three great downward bounds, Henry dragged me like a limp pillow to the pack Miss Peach had dragged on her way down. He pushed me forward with the gun. "Get it," he said.

The rope around the mantied pack was as indecipherable as runes. Miss Peach kept on screaming. Her legs flailed, gravel flew as she scraped arcs in the dirt. I saw that the pack on her back had anchored her to the ground. The noise she was making had a mechanical sound. It made me wince, like a buzz saw hitting nails, over and over again. I noticed that the inside of her mouth was a surprisingly pale shade of pink and as velvety as a tea rose. Her yellow teeth looked very large.

"Get it!" Henry shoved me forward. Then, in the next moment, he had his arm back around my neck. I gagged. "Stay there!" he yelled.

Pete was riding the gravel slide on his heels.

"Stop!"

Pete held his hands up in air. "Henry. I just want to cut my mule loose." He slipped forward four more feet.

"I said, Stay where you are!"

Pete dug in his heels, then slid another six inches.

Henry lurched closer to the mule, pulling me with him. He removed the Colt from my back, shot Miss Peach twice in the head. I could feel the recoil in his body. The mule's legs jerked, but continued to thrash in a dragging halftime.

Henry poked the long barrel into my right temple. "She's next," he warned Pete. Miss Peach's legs stopped moving. They lay splayed at awkward angles.

"Henry," Adrienne wailed from above.

"Henry," Gene called. "I'm coming down. Just don't do anything stupid." He started down, arms pinwheeling, then lost his balance and fell. His hat rolled down the ravine. Gene slid the rest of the way on the seat of his long, breathable orange sailing jacket. He braked a couple yards above Pete, stood up, and studied Henry and me locked together. "It appears we have a conflict here," he observed.

Shrink to the rescue. Despite the inanity of his words, despite my long-standing hostility toward his profession, I felt slightly relieved. Maybe he knew what he was doing. There was always that hope. For I knew that both my mother and my ex-husband—who was also a psychologist—had in fact helped innumerable people. No doubt Gene as well had his skills, his share of successes.

"We can resolve this," he said kindly. The freezing rain darkened his thinning hair. Drops rolled off his forehead down his nose. He didn't wipe them away. He blinked at us through the rain. His eyes were mild and concerned. "Henry, why don't you move your weapon out of her ear? Find someplace more comfortable for you both?"

To my surprise, Henry lowered the barrel down to my rib cage. Billy and Adrienne slid down, flapping in their raincoats, holding on to their hats and each other. They stopped cautiously just behind Gene, as if the pitch were a staircase and they were five-year-olds anxious for their turn to peek.

"Lee," Gene suggested, "if you will turn over your copy of my father's will to us, Henry will let you go. No harm done."

I thought about it. "Except to the mule."

He acknowledged my statement with a sympathetic nod. "We'll have the means to pay for it, if you cooperate. Plus appropriate—ah, gratuities?"

"And then we shake hands all around?"

He paused. Then, as if my bra strap was showing, he remarked, "You're feeling angry."

"How keen of you. I *am* feeling a bit hostile today, Doctor."

"Lee," Pete said, "For chrissake, let them have it."

Gene nodded at Henry. He shoved me forward. I landed on my knees beside the canvas pack. I looked at them, standing above me, watching expectantly. Henry's long yellow slicker rustled at my back. I latched on to Pete's black eyes. "There's just one problem," I told him.

They all waited.

"Would you like to share it with us?" Gene encouraged.

"How about I just tell you? I don't have it."

"Lee—" Pete burst out.

"I made it up. Cyrus never gave me a copy. I lied."

It took a minute for it to sink in. "I don't have it," I repeated. "I just said I did because I wanted to find out which one of you

209

killed Nat. And now I know. You killed him, didn't you, Henry?" I suddenly felt tired. Curling up on the ground seemed like a nice idea.

Henry let out a bellow. "Bitch!" He grabbed my collar. I twisted around to face him. He put the long barrel of the gun back against my head. I stared up at him from my knees. There were crow's-feet at the corners of his fine eyes and stubble on his sculpted chin. It was the first morning he hadn't shaved. He had white patches in his beard, but no hint of gray in his thick, black curls. I wondered if their raven-wing gloss had come out of a Grecian Formula bottle.

"You set Cory up," I said. "You found her picture while you were looking for the will. You'd already combed through all your father's gear. And Lucia's. And Nat's. You thought maybe Cyrus'd given it to one of us. So you searched Cory's pack and found her snapshot. And you searched my stuff and found Daddy's big six-gun. Was it your own idea, Henry, to go after Nat? Did they help you out at all?"

"Henry," Billy Caton's laconic voice interrupted. "If I were you, I wouldn't respond to *any* of those questions."

"Just keep your mouth shut, Henry," Adrienne echoed.

Again I felt the edge of a bearish, black anger. "Did they stand around and give you advice while you got the will off Nat?" I asked him. "Did they cut you any slack for saving the family fortune? They're using you, Henry. You're doing their dirty work for them. You think you can make it stick on Cory? Guess again."

Gene spoke quietly. "You see what she's trying to do, don't you Henry?" His tone was reassuring, comforting.

"Henry," Adrienne said urgently. "It's okay. There is no copy of the will. Just keep your mouth shut. We'll get you a lawyer."

"The best," Billy chimed in. "Whoever you want. Hang on in there, pal. You're going to be okay."

The family was closing ranks around him. I scanned their faces: Gene's, pale and long and austere as a medieval saint's; Adrienne frowning, her mouth anxious and maternal; her husband, Billy, tense, edgy, in need of a drink. They didn't care about Nat. He was an outsider, a replaceable service. Like Cory. Like Pete and me.

210

I said to Gene: "He killed your father, too. Did you know that?"

One of the mules above us let out a long bray. I looked up and saw Brett looking down at us from the ledge.

"He poisoned your father's tea," I told them. "With one of Lucia's roots."

"Water hemlock," Pete said quietly. "It's extremely toxic. A piece the size of a walnut can kill a cow."

"I've got a rash on my shoulder where your father spilled tea from his cup just before he died," I told them. To Henry, I said conversationally, "Did you make an infusion?"

"I ground it up."

"My God," Adrienne said.

Gene searched Henry's face. "Why?" he asked.

Henry shrugged.

"Was it the money?" Then, in a burst of irritation, Gene peeled off his nonjudgmental white coat. "Shit, you were the one that had it easy. You were Dad's pet. We couldn't touch you! All you had to do was let out one little squeal, and he'd come running."

"He killed my father," Henry said flatly.

"What?" Adrienne said.

"He killed my father."

A long, morbid rumble came from Miss Peach's cooling insides. The sleet was glazing a raised hoof.

"Henry, old boy," drawled Billy Caton, "someone's slipped a funny card in your deck. Your father was killed in a fire at the old mill up in Massachusetts. Cyrus was down in High Point when it happened."

My neck was hurting. I moved my shoulders to ease the stiffness. Henry gave the icy barrel of the Colt a reminding shove against my head. "The fire wasn't an accident. It was arson. I read the insurance company's report."

"When was this?" Gene asked skeptically.

"A while back. I was putting together some material for our ad people. A couple years ago, maybe. I was looking for old photographs of the original mill and I found a file full of pictures the insurance company had taken after the fire. So I dug out the files for 1957. Actually, there were two investigations—the police and the insurance both had their experts in on it. They both agreed that the building had been deliberately torched to collect insurance money."

"But Henry, anyone could have set the place on fire!" Adrienne objected. "There was a lot of bad feeling when Dad decided to make the move down South. There were a lot of disgruntled workers. Even if the fire was deliberate, it doesn't mean Dad killed your father. It was an accident! Your father was drunk! He'd passed out on the floor with the janitor!"

"Night watchman," Henry corrected. "His name was Tommy Monahan. He was a harmless old lush." He smiled bitterly. "I went up there to check, after I found the file. I went up to Massachusetts. It became—like an obsession. I wanted to *know*. I found some of the old-timers. Some of them still hang around the same bars. I talked to one fella in a nursing home. They all remembered Tony Flores and they all remembered the night of the fire. They said my father had come looking for his old pals, and none of them would give him the time of day. They said he was Cyrus's flunky—and worse. They probably called him a faggot. 'It got pretty rough,' was the way this one guy put it. He wouldn't come out and say it. Sure, my father got drunk. . . ."

"It was an accident!" Adrienne cried. "Don't you see? Your father and my father were best friends!"

"I think it was an accident," Henry said reasonably. "But that doesn't change anything. Your father ordered the fire, and my father died in it." He paused. "That's how Nat came into it. Cyrus hired him to clean up. Cyrus needed the insurance money. The mill would have gone down the tubes during the move if he hadn't gotten it. Cyrus was Nat's first big client. Nat got him the money. Cyrus *owed* him. Why do you think your father looked the other way when Nat came sniffing around Lucia?"

Adrienne's eyes narrowed. "You're crazy! That's a disgusting thing to say!"

"Have a look at the books for those years," Henry retorted smugly.

"You have no proof," Gene challenged.

"There was a two-thousand-dollar withdrawal from the company account on May five—ten days before the fire. The check was made out to cash and had Cyrus's signature on it. The police were very interested in it. Your father was in Massachusetts May six, seven, eight. May ninth, a former employee named Johnny Bruno deposited two thousand dollars into his checking account. After the fire, there was another two-thousand-dollar deposit. Bruno hadn't had work since the mill had closed. Then one night, he drove his car off a bridge and drowned."

"You think Nat, ah, engineered *that?*" Gene asked.

Henry shrugged. "There was no evidence, just these mysterious checks. In the end, the insurance company paid off."

"You found this out two, three years ago?" Gene demanded.

"I didn't find out all at once. It took some time. I think Cyrus knew what I was doing. In the last year or so whenever I got short, he'd shell over—no questions."

"Lucky you," Adrienne snapped.

"Henry?" Billy asked. "You *did* get Cyrus's new will off Nat, didn't you?"

"Oh, yes. No problem. I burned it."

"And Lee, you don't have a copy? Is that correct?"

"Yes."

"Well, least we don't have to worry about that anymore," Gene muttered.

Henry's ticket into the club. A wave of relief wafted out of Adrienne and Billy and Gene. Henry seemed to warm himself in it, like a homeless man over a steaming grate in a winter sidewalk.

Adrienne looked at me but wouldn't meet my eyes. Maybe the sight of me kneeling there with the Colt at my ear embarrassed her. "We'll get you someone good," she told Henry. "Lucia will know a good lawyer out here."

"Darlin', she lives in Cody, Wyoming," Billy corrected. "We're in Montana. There is a difference."

They bickered lightly, pick, pick, jab. The noise of it seemed to reassure Henry. I could feel his stance relax under his raincoat. He eased up on the gun. Without moving, I asked him, "I don't get it. If Nat gave you the will, why did you shoot him?"

Henry let the gun in his hand drop slowly to his side. "I'm not sure," he said. "At the time, it seemed the thing to do."

I don't remember being afraid until that moment. The pure banality of his admission paralyzed me. Henry had lowered his gun, but I couldn't shift my weight off the sharp pebble that was piercing my left knee. I couldn't even lift a finger—they all felt like Popsicles, fat and frozen.

"Let the gun drop, Henry," a male voice called behind us. I had forgotten Luke. From the surprise on the dudes' faces, they had forgotten him too.

"Shit," Adrienne said.

"Do it, Henry," Gene ordered wearily.

I heard the Colt fall beside me. I still couldn't move. I was also having a hard time seeing. It ached behind my eye sockets as though my eyes had turned into marbles.

I heard gravel scrambling underfoot. "Put your hands on top of your head." The voice was closer now.

Pete walked sedately over to us and picked up the Colt. He held it on Henry.

"Is this really necessary?" Adrienne demanded haughtily. Pete kept the gun on Henry.

"Henry," she urged, "don't worry. We'll take care of you, I promise."

"You're under arrest," said Luke. "You have the right to remain silent. . . ." We'd heard it on TV for more than ten years, from "Hill Street Blues" to "Law and Order." Nonetheless, there was nothing hackneyed about the words. We listened intently, as if the incantation were new and hid vital clues.

He managed it well, Luke Donner. His manner was low-key and professional. He insisted on handcuffs and would not allow Pete to back him up on the ride out with Cyrus's revolver. It was "evidence," he stated firmly. He wrapped it in plastic and stuffed it in his saddlebag. Henry rode out handcuffed, holding on to the horn. ("This is ridiculous," sputtered Adrienne. "Where do you think he's going to go?")

It was Luke who broke the spell of my immobility. While Pete held the Colt on Henry, Luke hooked me under the arm and pulled me off my knees and out of the way. My slicker crackled coldly and loudly.

"You okay?"

"I think so." I saw his lips were blue. He was shivering under his dripping hat like a skinny kid too long in cold water. But his eyes had warm lights, brown-green, the exact color of a creek bottom in shade, the sort of place a magical speckled trout might hide. I wanted to dive in.

"You sure?" he asked politely.

"Yes. Thank you."

He turned back to attend to Henry. I felt a little sick.

The next thing I remember was Pete saying, "Lee, I need a hand, here." It was curiously comforting to move, to feel muscle dumbly contracting and releasing along bone as if nothing had happened. We untangled rope from Miss Peach. Gene and Billy were cooperative. The three of us worked up a good sweat pushing and pulling the eighty-pound loose pack up the forty-five-degree slide. Brett and Pete cut two lodgepole saplings for levers and lifted the dead mule so Billy and I could haul out the pack she lay on. "God Almighty!" Billy said. Miss Peach's innards made unnerving sounds, but her gases smelled familiar enough. Billy and Brett, with the help of ropes, lugged the second pack up the pitch. I strained against a lodgepole lever while Pete unbuckled and freed her Decker. "Poor mule," I said aloud, as he removed her bridle. "Poor Miss Peach."

Pete gave me a quizzical look. "You pushed her over."

"I'm sorry," I said. "God, I'm sorry, Pete."

"No." He dismissed my apology. "I meant, I'm not sure I could have done it."

"It was an accident. The pigtail snapped and she went over." He gazed at me as if weighing something.

"What?"

"Nothing." The downturned corners of his long-bow mouth straightened into a private smile.

"You're as bad as my mother."

"Oh?" He fingered Miss Peach's halter rope.

"You've both got that same nasty little Mona Lisa smile. Sometimes I think she's a witch."

He grinned. "So that's where you got it from."

"Believe me, we are not alike."

He didn't believe me. He handed me Miss Peach's halter, then

215

made a bundle of her saddle and the fleece pad, winding the cinch and latigos and straps around it. He slung it over his back. "Let's go."

"You just going to leave her like this?" I asked.

"You going to move her somewhere?"

"Oh." I was definitely working in slow gear. "So the animals will get her." There was something satisfying about the idea. The cycles of nature at work. Flesh unto flesh. Mule transmogrified into buzzard, coyote, bear, beetle.

"She's too close to the trail," Pete said. "It's not only the stink. You'll have bear feeding on her all summer long."

"So?"

"The Forest Service likes to keep bear and tourists on separate tracks. Healthier for both parties. We'll have to notify them when we get in. They'll send a couple guys out to dispose of her."

"How?" I wondered.

"Vaporize her."

"What?"

"Blow her up. They use a hundred-foot rope of explosive—the same kind used in forest fires to make a firebreak. Only instead of laying it out in a line, they wrap her up in it and detonate it. There's nothing left bigger than the size of a quarter."

I stared at him.

"A technological advance," he commented ironically. "The old-fashioned way was a couple sticks of dynamite. Messier by some." He ran his eyes over Miss Peach's stripped body. "Four, five summers ago I took this group of Idaho potato farmers camping in the Selway Wilderness area. They packed in a dozen cases of beer and six coolers full of ice, and somehow, they managed to kill one of their horses." His voice was full of contempt.

"They can't get it off the trail, so they keep on going and set up camp downriver. I go out to notify the forest service, the horse gets blasted, and the next day, one of these clowns is out fishing, sucking up his beer, and he thinks he's got this mighty big catch on his line. He reels it in, and what he's got is a rear-end piece of horseflesh—tail hair and all."

"Thanks for sharing that with me, Pete."

He smiled. "They hooted and hollered about it—thought it

was pretty funny—until they got the bill from the forest service." He contemplated the bill. It seemed to give him deep satisfaction.

After we'd climbed back up on the ledge, Pete threw some loops around the saddles of the extra horses and secured Miss Peach's load to their backs. Out of his own pack he produced a red-and-black-checked wool jacket—size enormous. He handed it to Luke, who without protest, stripped off his wet denim jacket and put it on. We started moving. The sleet turned back to rain and eventually stopped. There were more delays due to downfalls. Brett wielded the ax while Pete and Luke sat alert on their horses with Henry, also straight-backed, between them. There were some spectacular views of peaks rising above ranks of black fir that snagged shreds of mist. Lower down, wooden suspension bridges crossed wide, shallow rivers lying under the gray sky like hammered pewter. It took us almost seven hours to get to the Forest Service station at Benchmark. And all the way, I was beset by images of Miss Peach exploding through air in a fine, rosy mist.

21

Off our horses at Benchmark, the world seemed strangely flat and full of wonders. The ground rocked gently underfoot, as though we were seafarers disembarking after a long voyage. The evening air was thicker, warmer, and scented with diesel exhaust. Sheriff Lily met us with deputies, squawking walkie-talkies, and patrol cars spinning blue light out into the twilight. He and Luke arranged transport to Missoula for Adrienne and Billy Caton and Gene Strand. Lucia had reserved rooms for them at the Holiday Inn. Henry went to Deer Lodge in the caged backseat of a patrol car. Cory, with the help of Pete's famous lawyer, had already been sprung and was back at Pete's trailer with Dolores, waiting to help unload.

"Need any help?"

"No. You've done enough already," Pete said.

I felt vaguely disappointed. Pete and I hugged. Brett and I hugged. In the confusion, I missed saying good-bye to Luke Donner.

I thought you'd sworn off falling into men's eyes?

Don't be silly. I just wanted to thank him.

He could have found a minute, if he'd wanted to.

218

True. I felt a small tug of despair.

Driving alone in Pete's speckled egg of a pickup, I flew along for an hour on astonishingly wide gravel roads. Spewing pebbles and waving out the window, I passed Pete and Brett, each driving a monstrously sized trailer full of mules and horses. At a six-street town called Augusta, I hit blacktop and the drive became magically quiet and as smooth as a ribbon. An hour later, I pulled over into a truck stop. The glare of electric light seemed a miracle. Machines spat out cans of exquisitely cold root beer, white porcelain toilets swallowed whirlpools in a single roar. Back out in the dusk, above the store's flat roof, the mountains we had left had a cardboard quality, as if cut from an old black-and-white Roy Rogers movie.

Three hours after leaving Benchmark, I drove into Missoula. I stopped at a McDonald's, then checked in at a budget motel a couple blocks away from the Holiday Inn. My room was brown and beige. A corner of the vinyl wallpaper was peeling. The bedspread reeked of cigarettes. I squirted it with Chanel No. 5. Then I looked in the mirror. My hair was abysmal: stringy, dishwater blond strands with a shaved shield above my ear—a jagged maroon scab rampant on a dead white field. Very enticing. There was also a long scrape down the left side of my face, the effect of my head dive into gravel. It glowed an obscene bright pink. I anointed it with Neosporin. It glowed more thickly. Still, the rest of my face surprised me. Despite all we'd been through, I looked tanned and rested. Gone was my urban pallor, the existential anxiety around my eyes. So how come I felt rotten?

I did the usual number of be-good-to-yourself things: a motel glass full of bourbon and those little ice donuts that you can thread along the length of a pencil; yoga stretches on the shag rug beside the queen-sized bed; a long soak in hot water clouded by toy bars of Ivory soap; a long shower. I emerged with squeaky clean hair and fingers and toes wrinkled white. I sipped my bourbon and turned on the late news. What had happened to Mayor Barry? There was no mention of him on either the local or national news. I thought about calling my mother, telling her a story about a bear and a mule named Miss Peach. I fell asleep.

The next morning, I wrapped a clean scarf around my head and pulled on my cleanest jeans and a knit polo shirt—a deep shade of lapis that (according to my ex-husband) deepened the anemic blue of my eyes. I put Indonesian hammered hoops in my ears and slipped a heavy brass cuff over my wrist and felt armed. (I'd set off the security alarm with it at Dulles.) As arranged the night before, I walked east along a street called Broadway to the Missoula Courthouse, a nineteenth-century Romanesque pile of gray stone with a whimsical clock tower. The courthouse faced an open square of lawn surrounded by the deep shade of maples. I trotted up the steps, passed through granite and marble into the vinyl and wallboard of the Sheriff's Department—an addition tacked on to the back.

I gave my statement to a middle-aged deputy with a deadpan, ruddy face. Sheriff Lily came in and asked some questions I'd already answered. Every time I heard footsteps in the corridor, I felt this peculiar movement in my heart. It reminded me of the first time I felt Rachel turning in my womb—a kind of alien sliding sensation. I would hear footsteps and glance up, hoping to see Luke Donner standing in the doorway, but no one stopped. I saw Adrienne and Billy Caton, but we didn't speak.

Treat it like a twenty-four-hour bug, I told myself. *Take a couple aspirin and go to bed. You don't even know the man.*

I went back to my motel. "Any messages?" I asked the clerk at the front desk. "No, ma'am."

It was one o'clock in the afternoon. My room was dark, the foam-backed curtains drawn. I flicked on the overhead. The maid hadn't been there yet. I picked up a towel, thin and white and wet. I picked up my K Mart "Men's Medium" yellow slicker. There was a lump in the pocket. It was a khaki hat. Cyrus's hat. I pulled it out of the pocket and unrolled it. It made an odd sound. I crunched up the faded canvas next to my ear. There was a distinct crackle. I took it over to the window, drew the curtains, and peered inside the hat. A circle of transparent amber plastic protected the large round label sewn into the crown. The label was loosely stitched to the plastic, and announced HILLHOUSE HABERDASHERS, NEW BOND STREET, LONDON, in gothic letters. I poked it. It crackled again. I slipped a finger under the stitched edge, pried it up, and eased out a folded piece of lined paper.

No, it wasn't lined yellow paper, as I had imagined. Cyrus

had used a steno-sized pad, green with a brown line down the middle. He had torn it loose from the pad, leaving a top edge of tiny teeth. There was writing on both sides of the page. His hand was fluid but precise. He had written in black ink from a fountain pen with a narrow nib and had ignored the center line. His words ran quickly across it. Some were crossed out. *I, C.E.S. III, being of sound mind . . .*

The will covered both sides of the paper. It was dated at the top, but not signed at the bottom. Clearly, it was a first draft, but the corrections (presumably Nat's suggestions) were legible and the intention absolutely clear. As he had stated at breakfast on the day of his death, he wished to leave his estate exclusively in Lucia's hands until her death, at which point the Strand mill fortune would go to the National Wildlife Federation—a prohunting environmental lobby, if memory served. There were several large bequests: directors of both the Wild West Museum in Cody and the public library in his hometown of Emerson, Massachusetts, would dance celebratory jigs. His children were dismissed in one sentence: *For reasons I have discussed with them, my children shall not inherit any part of my estate.*

I sank down onto the side of the bed. Suddenly I felt cold.

No one knows, I coached myself. *You're safe as long as no one knows.*

I took the will to a quick copy shop I found in the Yellow Pages and there paid forty cents for a two-sided copy of the will. I also bought a pack of envelopes—an amenity not provided by my cut-rate motel. Back in my room with a foam cup of coffee, I spent an hour composing a banal one-liner to my mother.

Dear Mom,
In the event of my death, please send the enclosed to the National Wildlife Federation.

Love, Lee.

The problem was, "In the event of my death" had a histrionic ring. After that trumpeting blast, anything but the simplest instruction rang out of tune. I tried variations on "it's been great," including "you've been great," but it sounded too Bogarty to bear.

I put the original draft of Cyrus's will and the note to my mother in an envelope addressed to myself at her house on Capitol Hill. I licked it shut and stuck a stamp on its upper right-hand corner. I tucked the envelope in my purse along with the copy. Then I drained the last sugary swallow of cold coffee and dialed the Holiday Inn. I asked to speak to Mrs. Strand.

She picked up the phone. "Yes?"

"Lucia, this is Lee Squires."

Dead air.

"I was the cook on your trip?" *You expected her to remember your name?*

"Ah, yes," she said politely.

"I hope I'm not disturbing you."

Pause. "No, of course not."

You've woken her up from a nap. "I'd like to see you privately," I blundered on. "Just for a few minutes."

"I am supposed to be at the sheriff's office this afternoon."

"Could I stop by now? I have your husband's hat. . . ."

"Come in half an hour," she decided. "I am in Room one sixteen. I will order tea for us."

"Thank you," I said. "But that's not—"

The line was dead.

I put on my sunglasses. I dropped my letter in the box in the lobby and walked out onto Broadway past a "Motel Inn," a glass installer's shop, a used car lot. Turning south on Pattee Street, I strolled toward a big white *M* inlaid high on the grassy slope of Mount Jumbo. *M* for Montana. It loomed over the campus of the University of Montana like an alphabetic star.

The Holiday Inn overlooked Clark's Fork (of Lewis and Clark fame)—a river that bisected the town from east to west. Lucia's room was done in upscale eighties colors: teal and rose—or maybe it was peach and gray. The draperies were open. Sunlight streamed through white nylon liners onto a round table set with two white coffee cups and a brown plastic pot of tea. Lucia wore loose slacks and a black cashmere shawl over a lemon-colored scoop-necked T-shirt that showed her collarbones. She wore no makeup and her hair was brushed off her face in streaked spikes.

222

Her skin looked fragile and old. Her bearing, however, was youthful, her back flexible, her hands quick.

"Please forgive me for intruding," I said. "It must be a difficult time for you."

"Yes. I imagined I might be a widow." She smiled. "But not yet." She turned her head away. A moment later, she said, "I have talked with Nat's wife. For her also, it is a shock. Poor thing." She waved Nat's wife away and graciously poured me tea. The tag hanging out of the insulated plastic pot said EARL GREY. We sat in a pair of small, upholstered chairs. She seemed serene as a nun in her black shawl, but under the table, her feet shifted impatiently.

I pulled Cyrus's hat out of my bag.

She took it. "Ah. Thank you. I am glad to have it. There is something so—how do you say?—personal?—about a hat."

Then I took out the photocopy of Cyrus's will. Perhaps because it was unsigned, her stepchildren would challenge it in court. Perhaps they'd all go round and round with it, like sinners assigned to a circle in Dante's hell. Although I felt a surface play of sympathy for Lucia, deeper down I didn't really care what happened to any of them. I was looking for a private ending—a kind of justice, perhaps—and I had no qualms about buying it with a piece of paper I'd found by accident.

I gave it to Lucia. From a needlepointed case, she pulled out a pair of reading glasses, and examined the copy. She took her time with it.

"Where is the original?"

I told her the truth.

She nodded. "More tea?"

"No, thanks."

We sat without speaking for several moments. I could almost hear the wheels of her brain turning. When she spoke, her voice was businesslike. Despite the lilt of her accent, her tone reminded me of Cyrus. "What is it you want?"

I explained.

She thought about it. "And for yourself?"

I shook my head.

"Nothing for you?"

I met her gaze. Her eyebrows raised the question elegantly,

then descended. "I see," she said. "You are an idealist. Like Don Quixote."

"I don't think so," I said wryly. "He wouldn't have stooped to blackmail."

She looked puzzled.

"*Il recatto?*" I tried.

"Ah yes. Thank you. I think my mind is leaving me. But you are *italiana?*"

"No, just a groupie. I always wanted to be dark," I confessed.

She made a dismissive noise. "Those are the peasants, the laborers from the south." She pulled up a soft leather bag from beside her chair and plunged her hand into it.

I flew out of my chair onto the floor, diving for cover behind the king-sized bed.

Lucia stood up. "What is it?" she cried. "What is the matter?"

Slowly I raised my head.

Oh, you utter ass!

"Sorry," I apologized. I knelt up. "I thought you were going for a gun." I had imagined a little pearl-handled Derringer—a whore's gun, the sort of thing Cyrus might have got a kick out of giving her. I scrambled to my feet, pulling the bedspread askew in the process. I straighted it out, smoothed the quilted fabric under my hand.

Lucia looked at me as if I were mad. "I have no gun. You see? I was getting my checkbook." She waved a scarred, brown leather oblong at me. Then she sat down and wrote out a check. "Now," she said crisply. "I am going to open this drawer under the TV. There is another checkbook. I do not have enough in this one for both your—requests." There were both irony and annoyance in the way she said it. Clearly she didn't like to have her hand forced.

I watched her write out the second check. She handed both to me with a frown. "These are reasonable settlements," she said. "But if you ask for more . . ." Her unspoken warning was cold and clear.

Irritated, I pushed back: "Well, you still owe Pete for his mule."

"A mule?"

"They didn't tell you? Henry killed Miss Peach, too. He shot

224

her twice in the head. You'll probably get a big fat bill from the Forest Service. They'll have to send in a team to dispose of it." I saw a cloud of pink vapor floating down through black pine boughs.

Lucia's mouth tightened into a severe line. The expense of a dead mule was the last straw. Any shred of pity she might have had for Cyrus's children, any tinge of compassion she might have found in her own grief, hardened into resolve. She studied the paper in her hand as though it were a receipt from an arms dealer. Our transaction may not have been entirely to her liking, but it gave her a big edge going into battle. She straightened her spine. "I am glad to have this. Thank you," she said in dismissal.

"As soon as the checks clear, I'll send you the original. Where will you be?"

She wrote out a Cody address. "I will bring his ashes there. It was our place together."

I moved toward the door, then turned back. "What did the E stand for?"

"Excuse me?"

I indicated the photocopy of Cyrus's will. "C. E. S., the Third."

"Oh. Edward. He was Cyrus Edward Strand." The name and her past tense hung between us. "His mother used to call him Eddie," she said sadly.

Back at my motel, I found my bed made, the shag vacuumed in different directions, the curtains closed again. I left them shut. In the bathroom there was a clean skimpy towel, a clean skimpy washcloth, and a new mini-bar of Ivory in blue and white paper. I turned on the light over my bed, fished a second envelope out of the box, and put Lucia's two checks inside. One was made out to Pete Bonsecours for $200,000 and 0 over 100 cents. Almost half of this amount would come back to her when Pete paid off his debt to Cyrus. The other check was made out to Cory Johnson for a half million. Maybe I could have gotten a full million for her. Maybe not. As it was, Lucia had written the numbers without blinking.

I wrote a note. This one was easier to compose:

225

Dear Pete,
These are from Lucia—in appreciation. You may need to help
Cory manage hers. I need to know when the checks have cleared—
call me.

I gave him two numbers, my mansion's and my mother's, and
signed it "Love." Then I tucked it into the envelope with the two
checks, licked it shut, and filed it in my purse next to my airline
ticket home. Next, I called Pete's trailer. Dolores answered. Pete
was either in Missoula or Deer Lodge, she said. She sounded
pleased to hear from me. We went back and forth, trying to figure
out the best way for me to return Pete's truck. In the end, we
agreed that if Pete and I didn't bump into each other before I flew
out tomorrow, I would leave it in the parking lot at the airport. I
told her I'd leave the keys and an envelope for him at the Delta
desk.

"He liked your cooking," she said.
"Huh," I said. "Well, I liked yours."
We laughed.

It was five o'clock. I smeared more Neosporin on my wounds and
lay down on the brown floral spread. Despite my Chanel treat-
ment, it still reeked. At six, the phone rang. I almost jumped out
of my skin. *It's Pete,* I told myself.
"Hello?" I said.
"Lee?"
"Yes?"
"This is Luke Donner."
"Oh," I said.
"How are you?"
"I'm fine. How are you?" *Brilliant.*
"Oh, I'm fine," he said. "Uh, I wondered if you'd like to have
dinner with me? There's a place here called the Depot that's sup-
posed to be okay."
My raw cheek gleamed in the cheap mirror. *Look at you.*
"What time?" I asked him.
He seemed at a loss.
"Luke? Where are you?"

226

"At the front desk."

I laughed. The needling voice in my head vanished like a soap bubble popping. I felt extraordinarily light. "Don't go away!" I told him. "I'll be right there."

I paused only to pick up the room key off the dresser. And there it was: my small lump of carnelian glowing reddish-brown beside the ashtray. I stared at it for a second. The maid must have found it on the floor, I reasoned. I slipped it into my jeans pocket with the key and fairly flew out the door.